WESTFIELD PUBLIC LIBRARY
333 West Hoover Street

D0648602

ROYAL CAT

ROYAL CAT

GARRISON ALLEN

A "BIG MIKE"
MYSTERY

WESTFIELD PUBLIC LIBRARY
333 West Hoover Street
Westfield, IN 46074

KENSINGTON BOOKS

KENSINGTON BOOKS are published by

Kensington Publishing Corp.
850 Third Avenue
New York, NY 10022

Copyright © 1995 by Garrison Allen

All rights reserved. No part of this book may be reproduced in any form or by any means without the prior written consent of the Publisher, excepting brief quotes used in reviews.

Kensington and the K logo Reg. U.S. Pat. & TM Off.

LIBRARY OF CONGRESS CARD CATALOG NUMBER: 94-074557
ISBN 0-8217-4957-9

First Printing: June, 1995

Printed in the United States of America

For Ann LaFarge,
Editor and Friend,
With Love and Affection Always,
From Garrison and Big Mike

THE PLAYERS
More or Less in Order of Appearance

The Empty Creek Authentic Elizabethan Spring Faire. A celebration of spring held in winter to avoid the searing desert temperatures when even the lizards carry stilts to cool their little feet. Authentic is sometimes a misnomer.

Carolyn Lewis aka Old Hatchet Face. The Queen of England at the Faire who, contrary to the reputation of the real Elizabeth I, is not much loved by her subjects.

Penelope Warren. Owner of Mycroft & Company, a small mystery bookstore in Empty Creek, Arizona. Penelope is also an amateur detective of considerable skill.

Mycroft aka Big Mike, Mikey. An Abyssinian alley cat from Abyssinia and friend of Penelope's. He possesses formidable detecting skills as well as an uncontrollable appetite—nay, passion—for lima beans.

Empty Creek, Arizona. A desert backwater to the north of Phoenix, populated by a curious collection of rather free spirits. Penelope and Big Mike are right at home there.

Harris Anderson III. Penelope's main squeeze, a gangly Ichabod Crane look-alike and editor of the *Empty Creek News Journal*. He is about to play Sir Walter Raleigh at the Faire.

Cassandra Warren aka Storm Williams. Penelope's sister, a frequent visitor to Empty Creek. She is an actress worthy of roles better than Princess Leogfrith in *Amazon Princess and the Sword of Doom* and the comely astronaut of *Space Vampires*.

John "Dutch" Fowler. Chief of the Empty Creek Police Department. He is ga-ga over Stormy. Fortunately, Stormy is equally ga-ga over Dutch, who acquired his nickname when he was with the Los Angeles Police Department and arrested a man with a shoe fetish who happened to be carrying a pair of wooden shoes down the street at the time.

Mistress Kathleen Allan. A former serving wench—a politically correct term in 1595—at the Faire who has risen to the gentry and, by virtue of her position as an assistant at Mycroft & Company, is much in favor at the Faire.

Timothy Scott. A skillful juggler, demented poet, and devoted roommate of Mistress Allan's. He writes heartfelt, if rather lurid, verse, about two particular portions of his roommate's anatomy, termed her "luscious alabaster mounds of pleasure."

The Pillory. That ancient wooden frame with holes in which to lock a miscreant's head and wrists. Oft used during the reign of Old Hatchet Face. Many a fair maid and robust young lad has been clapped in its embrace to do penance for some offense, real or imagined.

Lawrence Burke and Willie Stoner, aka Tweedledee and Tweedledum. They are the ace homicide detectives for the Empty Creek Police Department. "Ace" does not begin to describe their abilities.

Nora Pryor. Author of *Empty Creek: A History and Guide.* Slight in stature, large of smile, great of heart, and quick to blush, Nora does not actually appear in this tale, but she should. She is possessed of the most wondrous strawberry-blond hair and the sexiest voice north of Nogales.

Christopher Marlowe. Playwright and spy in the service of Her Royal Majesty, Queen Elizabeth I. He surfaces some years after his apparent death in a tavern brawl, apparently the beneficiary of an Elizabethan witness protection program.

William Shakespeare. An upstart playwright and pretender to Marlowe's position as the preeminent author of Elizabeth's England.

Sharon O'Bannon. A sprightly Irish lass with blond hair and an impish sense of humor; an actress of considerable talent. She plays Rosalind in *As You Like It,* much to Marlowe's dismay.

Alyce Smith. Empty Creek's resident astrologer and psychic who has a booth at the Faire, where she regales the snowbirds with their fortunes. Unfortunately for Alyce, she is unable to predict her own future with any degree of accuracy, a lacking that has gotten her into trouble in the past.

Elaine Henders aka Laney. Best friend to Penelope and an author of erotic romance novels set in old Arizona. She has a roommate who is an enthusiastic participant in her research.

Wally. Laney's roommate, an unemployed cowboy who possesses an uncanny ability to crinkle his eyes laconically. He has some other talents as well.

Alexander. A cheery little Yorkshire terrier with a penchant for yapping ferociously; Mycroft's best friend. They frequently go horseback riding together. Alex lives with Laney and Wally.

Chardonnay. The third member of Penelope's household. She is a sweet-tempered Arabian filly and doesn't mind at all when Big Mike and Alex want a ride through the desert.

Leigh Kent. If there were a Sexy Librarian Pageant, Leigh would win it hands down, hands up, or hands any which way. Her smoldering eyes have reduced most of Empty Creek's male population to lovesick puppies at one time or another.

Burton Maxwell, aka Ben Jonson. Leigh's intended. He won the fair maiden's heart by whispering the love poems of his namesake in her lovely ear.

Samantha Dale. A financial wizard and president of the Empty Creek National Bank.

Blaine Edwards. An ironmonger and a purveyor of chastity belts and other fine wear by appointment to Her Majesty the Queen.

Justin Beamish. A private detective who comes to the Faire as Robin Hood, blissfully unaware that Robin lived in an earlier era, if at all.

Ralph and Russell. Twin brothers in the employ of Beamish. Loyal to Beamish, they come to the Faire as twin Little Johns equally unaware—and uncaring—that they are some four centuries out-of-date. They also operate a mail drop and an adult bookstore with a goodly supply of marital aids. Laney constantly urges Ralph (or Russell) to compile a mail order catalogue of some of the more interesting items.

Lola LaPola. A breathless—"This is Lola LaPola reporting from the scene of the tragedynowbacktothestation"—reporter for a Phoenix television station.

Sir Francis Bacon, Sir Francis Drake, Sir Walter Raleigh, Sir Philip Sydney, et al. Members of the royal court.

And the bawdy Elizabethans. To wit—various noblemen, noblewomen, peasants, gentry, jesters, yeomen, mongers, sea dogs, fools, pirates, lusty wenches, players, musicians, alchemists, astrologers, witches, cuckolds, papists, Puritans, cutpurses, jugglers, rakes, clowns, and gulls.

ROYAL CAT

A PROLOGUE

The Spring Faire was off to an inauspicious beginning. The royal procession, in which Her Majesty Queen Elizabeth I greets her loyal subjects and visitors to the Faire, began late. This started the royal temper to fuming.

So when the royal progress finally began wending its way through the village, Her Majesty punctuated her regal waves with smiles through grimly clenched teeth.

Following behind the Queen, Lady Kathleen Allan was in a much better humor. She beamed, delighted to be at court. In Faires past, the Lady Kathleen had been only a lowly serving wench. Now, after months of study and preparation for her new role, she was a member of the nobility. The Queen's bad mood could not infect Kathy's happiness and she practically leapt out of her stays as she waved at a comely juggler.

Once under way, the procession went well as the Queen and her court—trusted advisers, ladies-in-waiting, and various officials—followed the Lord High Mayor past the archery range, the craftsmen's shops, the astrologers and soothsayers, the Globe and the Bear Garden, the ironmonger, the maypole, the blacksmith.

At each of the various public houses, the Queen was greeted enthusiastically.

"Huzzah!"

"Long live the Queen!"

The cheers restored the Queen's good frame of mind.

Unfortunately, the Lord High Mayor, who appeared to be drunk, took a wrong turn at the fencing green and the royal procession wound up in a confused melee at the ducking stool, across the small artificial lake, quite opposite from the Royal Pavilion, where the procession was supposed to be greeted with the flourishes of a hundred trumpets.

That put the Queen, fondly known among her loyal subjects as Old Hatchet Face and That *Virgin* (or on occasion *That* Virgin), in a foul mood once more.

When the royal procession finally entered the Pavilion for its triumphant turn around the arena, the Queen almost immediately stepped in a pile of horse puckey. This misstep was followed by a discordant blast of the massed trumpets which set her ears to ringing.

The Queen was having a most wretched day. Those experienced at court recognized the signs of Royal distemper and shrank away from the royal presence as the tournament began.

The Lady Kathleen, who was not yet practiced in the many nuances of court matters, took a seat at the rear of the Royal Pavilion. She had barely settled her skirts about her, when a hand grasped her ankle. The hand was followed by the head of a juggler.

"Timmy," the Lady Kathleen whispered, "what are you doing here?"

A finger to his lips silenced her, except for a little giggling as he tickled her foot.

The Royal jousting went badly for the Queen's champions. One after another was unhorsed by the Black Knight, whom the Queen loathed for his arrogance.

Then one of the Queen's knights, in attempting to mount a spirited steed, was thrown to the ground and wound up chasing the horse through the arena in full sight of God and everyone else. The pursuit came to an inglorious end when Sir Knight, who used to be one of the Queen's favorites, slipped on another pile of horse dung and wound up on his armored backside, unable to rise. Attendants pulled him from the ring to the hoots of the rather considerable audience gathered on this, the first day of the annual festival.

The Queen might have survived all that, even regained her good mood once again, if Sir Robert Dudley, her trusted confidant, adviser, and rumored lover (there was considerable speculation among Her Majesty's subjects as to Her Majesty's storied virginity), had taken his usual place at her side.

But when Her Majesty sent the Sheriff's men in search of the missing nobleman, Sir Robert was found backstage at the Globe, making moon eyes at a pretty young Irish actress, currently appearing in *As You Like It.*

As the Authentic Elizabethan Spring Faire wound its glorious course through its allotted time each February and March in Empty Creek, Arizona, the participants, good Elizabethans all, were supposed to remain in character for those ancient times and the personae they chose to assume.

But when news of Sir Robert's whereabouts and apparent new affection reached the Queen, she flew into a most unelizabethan rage. In short, gentle reader, the Queen was pissed!

Thus, the time was certainly out of joint when the Queen turned angrily and discovered one Lady Kathleen Allan, perched on the lap of a juggler who was wearing a three-pointed fool's cap with bells dangling his presence from each point.

"Arrest them!" the Queen cried.

The Sheriff's men, recently returned from their mission to the Globe, scurried to do her bidding.

The juggler, who had no business in the Royal Pavilion, rose suddenly, plopping Lady Kathleen most unceremoniously to the floor, and fled.

Lady Kathleen attempted to gather her skirts and her composure, all the while staring at the back of the rapidly disappearing juggler who, in real life, was her roommate and lover. "Timothy, you cad!" Lady Kathleen shouted, "Take me with you."

Two of the Sheriff's men hauled Lady Kathleen to her feet and took her to face the wrath of her Queen.

"Good morrow, Your Majesty," Lady Kathleen said, perhaps hoping to brazen it out.

"Good morrow, my big toe," the Queen mumbled through clenched teeth. "I'll give you good morrow, you brazen little hussy."

"But, Your Majesty . . ."

"I was wrong about you. You're nothing but a serving wench, and that's what you'll be again on the morrow."

"But . . ."

"The time, Master Sheriff?"

"The hour grows late, Your Majesty."

"Good. The pillory," the Queen cried.

Lady Kathleen's protestations of innocence and wronged virtue went unheeded.

"The pillory!" the crowd shouted as the Sheriff's men marched the former Lady Kathleen at a brisk pace through the rabble to her fate.

When this not-so-royal procession reached the village green, a grateful young milkmaid was released from the pillory. She fled across the green, hotly pursued by three young suitors who had grown enamored of her charms.

The Lord High Sheriff himself read from a royal proclamation that he had quickly composed while admiring the sway of the prisoner's rather attractive backside on her way to the pillory.

"Hear ye, hear ye, Lady Kathleen Allan has been declared a wanton, demoted to serving wench, and sentenced by royal prerogative to suitable penance in the pillory. Such punishment to commence immediately and last until Her Majesty's justice is satisfied."

The Lord High Sheriff looked around, pleased with himself for getting the proclamation out in such a steadfast manner for, if the truth be known, he had been tippling most of the long afternoon with the Lord High Mayor.

"Do your duty," the Lord High Sheriff ordered. The command was followed by a mighty burp. The ale served at the Royal Pavilion was of excellent quality.

Kathy struggled in the grasp of her captors.

Timmy, I'll get you for this, she thought as the crossbar of the pillory was raised and the Sheriff's men forced her to bend and place a slender neck and two delicate wrists in the half-circles cut into the smooth wood.

One of the Sheriff's men gathered Kathy's long blond hair and arranged it to fall about her face. The other copped a feel before lowering the crossbar and snapping the lock closed with a grim click of finality.

"Jerk," Kathy cried, swiping at him with a daintily shod foot.

From her stooped position, Kathy looked out at the rabble who loudly mocked her. Her fingers fluttered helplessly. *Just you wait, Timothy Scott.*

The licentious assistant sheriff who had taken such unfair advantage of the vulnerable young woman now hung the placard about her neck declaring her a WANTON.

Kathy watched as he went to purchase an overripe tomato from the little rascal who did a thriving business before the pillory.

"Ripe tomatoes," the boy cried. "Penny, ha'penny. Pelt the wench with a ripe tomato."

Wench pelting was quite the sport, as was wench dunking, and wenching in general. Puritan pelting was also popular on those occasions when one of the holier-than-thou fanatics was sent to the stocks, but there was nothing quite like a pretty young wench for titillating the groundlings.

The assistant sheriff leered before winding up and throwing the tomato at poor Kathleen. She closed her eyes.

Splat!

Fortunately for pretty young Kathy, the assistant sheriff had a lousy aim.

Oh, Timothy, just wait until I get you alone.

———

The subject of the former Lady Kathleen's ire, disguised as a wandering minstrel, was standing in the rear of the crowd behind the pillory, where his poetic muse inspired him to compose yet another ode to his beloved's breasts, the twin subjects of his collected works. He struck a chord on his lyre.

Splat!

Unable, then, to bear the sight of his beloved Kathy suffering the cruel jibes and taunts of the rabble, the wandering minstrel wandered off. He would return after darkness fell and the rubes had been hustled from the Fairegrounds to offer comfort and provide a few sips of beer for Kathy. If he didn't, Timmy knew she would damn near kill him.

Exhausted from a most trying day, the Queen retired to her royal chambers, where, once divested of her royal gown and that hideous cramping bodice, she lay upon the camp cot and plotted a most Machiavellian revenge against Sir Robert. Even sending that poor chit of a girl to the pillory had failed to overcome the black bile of her humors.

Betrayed.

At the hands of an Irishwoman.

I'll get you, Dudley. Just you wait.

The Queen nodded off to sleep, for she needed her rest. There was yet a hard night's work ahead of her.

And that, gentle reader, is how the Queen, still out of sorts with the world, later came to be wandering through the shadows of the village in search of miscreants.

It was one thing to preside over the rites of spring as presented annually at the Elizabethan Spring Faire during the weekend days, when the village was crowded with tourists and snowbirds and assorted carousers. Then, her unruly subjects at least remained in character, if at times bawdy character, to the shock of the Faire's patrons. But it was quite another thing to keep her lusty subjects in check after the gates closed and there were none but Elizabethans of all rank left and they continued in what they believed was the proper role of all good Elizabethans, the unbridled quest for pleasures, chiefly those dealing with the flesh.

The nightly party at the Queen's Own Men Public House was already growing rowdy. At the Peasants' Guild it was probably time for the very popular, if highly unelizabethan pastime—a wet T-shirt contest. There would be many a bleary eye to greet Fairegoers with a hearty, if feigned, "good morrow," when the gates opened Sunday morning.

Throughout the Elizabethan village, many a pretty maid fled (but not very fast) from the advances of her suitor.

Old Hatchet Face sighed. A Queen's work was never done. There!

At the pillory on the village green, a shadowy figure offered refreshment to the penitent locked in the stocks. It was a blatant violation of the royal decree.

"Varlet!" Old Hatchet Face cried as she emerged from the darkness and rushed across the cool grass. Thank God, she had changed from that awful royal gown. It was much easier to pursue rogues and scoundrels while wearing jeans, tennies, and a sweatshirt that proclaimed simply THE FAIRE.

Too late; the villain had fled across the wooden footbridge.

The Queen puffed to a stop before the imprisoned penitent. The placard hanging around Kathy's neck was askew. The Queen straightened it. Old Hatchet Face was a freak for neatness among her subjects.

"And what do you have to say for yourself now, Kathleen Allan?" the Queen asked sternly.

The penitent giggled as she peered up at her Queen. Apparently, she had received earlier ministrations to ease her hardship.

The evidence was obvious.

Kathy's lips were flecked with the foam of strong ale.

"First, the spectacle of this afternoon, and now this."

"But, Your Majesty, I was only sitting on his lap."

"A juggler's lap, and in the Royal Pavilion too." The Queen remained horrified at such uncourtly behavior.

"I don't care," Kathy replied. The strong brew had obviously addled her senses.

The Queen said, "An additional hour."

"But, Your Majesty, the parties will all be over by then."

"I should certainly hope so. I shall return at ten o'clock and release you. By then I hope you will have learned your lesson."

Quite haughtily the Queen continued on her nightly patrol.

When she was quite sure that the Queen was out of earshot, Kathy whispered, "You old poop! Who wants to be in your court anyway?"

Kathy sighed and waited for Timmy's return.

The Queen crossed the bridge and was gone from sight.

"You again!"

"Aye, Your Majesty."

"But you're supposed to be in Italy. I've told you that."

"I tired of sunny climes."

"But that's not playing fairly. You can be someone else. Anyone."

"Nay, I desire my own persona."

"It cannot be. Your place is taken by another."

"It will be. Else you die." He drew a dagger from his belt.

"I'll call the Sheriff's men."

"Those fools lie abed drunk."

Elizabeth Regina turned, intending to summon help.

Too late.

He struck, plunging the dagger deep into the Queen's back.

"Assassin!" The Queen thought she had screamed loud enough for the Tower warders in distant London Town to come to her rescue, but in reality her cry was naught but a whispered croak before she died.

The killer looked down at his victim for a moment before he walked away, whistling a jaunty little tune.

The young poet practically tripped over the Queen's body.

"Oh, shit," Tim said, before rushing to raise the alarm.

And that, gentle reader, is how a lowly juggler in the guise of a wandering minstrel who loved a gentle woman of quality came to discover the death of a queen.

The Queen was dead.

Long live the Queen.

CHAPTER
ONE

On the Tuesday afternoon following the demise of the Queen, a delegation from a not so merrye olde England descended upon Mycroft & Company. Since Kathy Allan, the disgraced noblewoman, worked at the small mystery bookstore when she was not doing time in the petite version of the Elizabethan slammer, she was already present when Sir Francis Bacon, Sir Francis Drake, and William Shakespeare arrived.

Befitting his status as the preeminent poet of his day, Shakespeare spoke for all when he said, "Penelope, we want you to be our new Queen." He peered owlishly at Penelope Warren over a pair of incongruous spectacles. Then he turned his attention to Mycroft, the bookstore's namesake, a twenty-five-pound Abyssinian alley cat from Abyssinia.

Big Mike returned the Bard's gaze with interest. After all, Shakespeare was his favorite playwright. The complete works had long served as a convenient, sturdy, and enduring scratching post.

For her part, Penelope didn't think Shakespeare—the real Bard of Avon—wore glasses. But then, she had often thought the Faire should be called the Empty Creek Almost Authentic Elizabethan Spring Faire.

"And find the assassin," Sir Francis Bacon said. "You've become quite adept at catching murderers. You exposed poor Mrs. Fletcher's killer."

"Don't forget Santa Claus," Shakespeare said. "She discovered Santa's killer too."

"The police are, as they say, stymied," Sir Francis Drake contributed.

"Besides, we're going to party like it's 1599," Shakespeare added.

"It's only 1595, of course," Sir Francis Bacon said, "but we always party like it's 1599."

"I don't know," Penelope said. She enjoyed a party as much as the next woman, but as Queen?

"Just like we always celebrate the defeat of the Spanish Armada," Sir Francis Drake said, puffing his chest out. "It's traditional."

Both Shakespeare and Bacon scowled. They were sick of hearing about Drake's 1588 triumph. Jesus, one little battle. Big deal.

"Come on, my lady, I mean, Your Majesty," Kathy said. With the resilience of youth, she had quite recovered from her ordeal in the pillory and the discovery of the royal body. "It'll be fun. You're going to be the best Queen Elizabeth ever, much better than Old Hatchet Face."

"Don't speak ill of the dead, child," Penelope said.

"I'm sorry, Your Majesty, but she was an old hatchet face."

"True, but still . . ."

"The show must go on," Will Shakespeare pleaded. "In this case, the Empty Creek Authentic Elizabethan Spring Faire."

"Well . . ." The Elizabethans—the real ones, of course—*had* desired nothing so much as an orderly succession to the throne upon the death of their beloved Queen, fearing intrigue, religious strife, bloody civil war, and foreign interference. Penelope *would* be performing a great public service in accepting the throne, for at least this Faire season. "Who took over for poor Carolyn on Sunday?" Penelope asked.

Drake snorted. "That lout of a Lord High Mayor. He was drunk again."

"Be a trouper," Bacon said. "Please."

"I don't know," Penelope repeated, fearing she was about to add another bizarre entry to her already rather eclectic résumé. In addition to her service in the United States Marine Corps and the Peace Corps, three degrees in English literature, a sometime position as an assistant professor of English, and sole proprietress of Mycroft & Company (along with Big Mike, of course), Penelope seemed about to become Queen of England. It was a good thing she didn't want or need a real job.

Of course, it might be dangerous. One Queen of England had already been assassinated, and, as Drake said, the police were baffled. The two homicide detectives of Empty Creek's finest were always baffled, and *someone* had to find Carolyn Lewis's murderer.

Well, Penelope and Big Mike weren't honorary members of the Empty Creek Police Department for nothing.

"I've got your costume, Your Majesty," Mistress Allan said.

"I worked on it all of yesterday. You'll be positively scrumptious."

"You're in on this scheme."

"Well . . . I did suggest you."

"I thought so."

"Just try it on," Kathy pleaded. "It's in the back."

"What do you think, Mycroft?"

Big Mike meowed. He meowed twice, in fact. Probably he was already envisioning his royal coat of arms. The Spanish Armada better not get in *his* way. An already regal Abyssinian from Abyssinia would, of course, be delighted to be Penelope's royal consort. Boy, just wait'll Murphy Brown hears about this. Murphy was the cute calico who lived down the road from the small ranch Mycroft shared with Penelope and Chardonnay, and mother of two of Big Mike's litters of cuddly kittens.

"Well . . . I'll just try the costume on," Penelope said, "but I'm making no promises. And *if* I do it, Kathy, you must be a lady-in-waiting."

Hot damn. From Lady Kathleen to serving wench and back to royal lady-in-waiting, all in less than a week.

Sir Francis and Sir Francis browsed among the mystery novels while waiting impatiently to greet their new Queen. Will Shakespeare filled the time by inspecting the wall display of miniature movie posters dedicated to Penelope's sister, Cassandra, an actress who had starred under her screen name of Storm Williams in such epics as *Biker Chick*, *Space Vampires*, and *Amazon Princess and the Sword of Doom*. Stormy's latest release seemed to be entitled *Return of the Amazon Princess*, although it was difficult to ascertain because the scantily clad princess dominated the movie poster, relegating the title to very fine print. Will decided to go next door to the video store and rent the film after this Queen business was finished.

In the back room of the bookshop, however, it took some considerable time to transform Penelope Warren into Queen Elizabeth I. She grumped and complained the whole time her lady-in-waiting assisted her into the royal dress. Mycroft's willing assistance in the process did not speed things along.

"My God, it's heavy with all these petticoats and stuff."

"You get used to it, my lady, I mean, Your Majesty," Kathy said. After practicing her Elizabethan English on Penelope for so many months, it was going to take some doing to change her title from gentility to royalty.

"My God, it's positively indecent," Penelope cried when she looked in the mirror and saw how the bodice plumped and exposed a goodly portion of her attractive bosom.

"You get used to it, my . . . Your Majesty."

"Easy for you to say with that deranged poet continually writing odes to *your* breasts. I'll have to get sun screen."

Kathy stood back and admired her handiwork. "We'll have to do something about your hair, of course. Queen Elizabeth probably didn't wear a ponytail."

"And I'm positive that William Shakespeare didn't wear spectacles either."

"Oh, he wears contacts during the Faire."

"Humph."

"You look splendid. Don't you think so, Mikey?"

Meow.

"You see, Your Majesty."

Penelope looked in the mirror again and had to admit she did look rather resplendent—except for the breasts peeping coyly above the bodice. Coyly, hell. They were positively bulging.

"Her Majesty, Elizabeth the First, Queen of All England," Kathy announced.

The Queen of All England had to turn sideways to get through the door.

William Shakespeare bowed low. His glasses clattered to the floor, breaking the solemnity of the occasion somewhat, but he was followed in the sweeping courtly gesture by Sir Francis Bacon and Sir Francis Drake.

"Your Majesty," they chorused. Shakespeare fumbled for his glasses.

Mycroft knocked the glasses across the floor. They came to rest against a bookshelf, just below a neat row of Tony Hillerman paperbacks.

"Off with their heads," Penelope replied. It was the only queenly pronouncement she could think of on such short notice.

The door to Mycroft & Company opened with a clanging of the attached bell.

"What in the world are you doing, Penelope?" Harris Anderson III asked mildly. "Can it be Halloween already?"

"I am Queen of England," Penelope announced grandly. "All England," she added.

"Of course you are, dearest," Andy replied.

"And Mycroft is the Royal Cat."

"Where *is* Mycroft?" Kathy asked.

The Queen giggled. "He's underneath my gown, tickling my legs."

"Mycroft, you get out of there," Kathy said.

Big Mike, it seemed, had discovered an excellent hiding

place. It was dark and warm and had lots of weird things to explore while waiting for the perfect moment to launch a surprise attack on whatever rogue or peasant slave happened by—of course, the Bard had not written that particular line yet; it was only 1595. But there were always those dastardly Spaniards.

After the Royal Cat was enticed from beneath the gown with a liberal helping of lima beans—Mycroft had somehow, inexplicably developed a passion for lima beans in kittenhood—the delegation to the new Queen of England departed. Once freed of the royal gown, Penelope and Kathy quickly closed Mycroft & Company and accompanied Andy across the street to the Double B Western Saloon and Steakhouse, the gathering place for Empty Creek's elite.

Big Mike immediately bellied up to the bar, leaping easily to his accustomed stool, to wait for Pete the bartender to pour his double shot of nonalcoholic beer.

The others took a table away from the clatter of the nonstop game at the pool table.

"Hi, guys," Debbie D said. "The usual?"

"White wine all around," Andy said.

"Be right back," Debbie said. On her way to the bar, the pretty cocktail waitress skittered away from a table of cowboys, who were engrossed with two of her more ample features. Debbie D had acquired her nickname honestly—it referred to what was believed to be the cup size of her brassiere—for she possessed what a wag had once termed national treasures. Red the Rat, who had also acquired his nickname honestly simply because he *was* an old desert rat, once declared that Debbie should "register them things as deadly weapons."

"Now," Penelope said, "that I am Queen, tell me what happened Saturday night."

"I've already told you," Kathy said. "Twice."

"Tell me again."

"Well, I was in the pillory . . ."

"And what were you doing in the pillory?"

"Timmy snuck under the tent at the Royal Pavilion and I was sitting on his lap. . . ."

"There'll be none of that hanky-panky in *my* court, young lady."

"Of course not, Your Majesty."

"But I thought the Elizabethans went in for hanky-panky on a rather large scale," Andy said. "In fact, I was looking forward to participating in the royal shenanigans."

"All in due course, Andy. We'll speak to Laney. I'm sure she'll be able to come up with a suitable game to play in the royal bedchambers."

"But, Your Majesty," Kathy protested, "you're the Virgin Queen."

"Hah!" Penelope replied, much to Andy's relief. "We're certainly not playing that role."

"Talk about *my* hanky-panky."

"What *were* you doing while sitting on Timmy's lap, providing inspiration for another of his ubiquitous odes?"

"That came later, while I was in the pillory."

"Recite all."

"Must I, Your Majesty?"

"Andy, don't listen to this part."

Kathy blushed prettily as she leaned over and whispered, " 'Ah, yon soft dangling fruits of enticing passion, Patience,

WESTFIELD PUBLIC LIBRARY
333 West Hoover Street
WESTFIELD IN 46074

untended fruits so ripe for the harvest, await your lover's soft pluck.' That part's not finished yet."

"It's up to his usual standards, I see."

"I think it's quite good, Your Majesty."

"Of course you do." Penelope smiled. She was quite fond of Timmy, but she was constantly amazed at the number and infinite variety of metaphors the Bard of Breasts found to describe Kathy's bosom. Kathy's chest had launched more ornate lines than Helen's face launched ships.

Kathy was relieved when wine arrived. "I hear you're the new Queen of the Faire," Debbie said as she distributed coasters and glasses of chardonnay.

"Now, how do you know that? I didn't know myself until an hour ago."

"Shakespeare, Bacon, and Drake were in for lunch. They said you were perfect for the role. And you are."

"And what if I had refused?"

"Oh, they knew you would want to track down the killer," Debbie replied. "I bet them they would have a new Queen within ten minutes of their arrival."

"Am I so transparent to my friends?"

"I knew that you couldn't resist a good mystery. Was I right?"

"Guilty as charged," Penelope said. "What did you win?"

"A pair of passes to the Royal Pavilion. I've never been in the Royal Pavilion."

"Nor have I," Penelope said, "come to think of it."

"So, who do you suspect?" Debbie asked.

Penelope thought for a moment. Carolyn Lewis had not been universally liked by her subjects. "Everyone except

Kathy," Penelope said. "She was incarcerated in the pillory at the time Carolyn was murdered."

Debbie looked at Kathy incredulously. "Again?"

Kathy nodded forlornly.

"You seem to spend a lot of time locked up in that thing."

"I was framed."

"You certainly were." Debbie wandered back to the cowboys at the pool table, who were clamoring for another beer.

"While you were in the pillory, did you see anyone or anything?" Penelope asked.

"Alyce Smith brought me some beer."

"That was nice of her."

"She stayed for a while, protecting me from the rabble until Timmy came. You know what *they* can be like, always trying to kiss you. And if you don't kiss them, they start with those awful tomatoes. Drake's sea dogs are the worst. They act just like real sailors."

"Yes, I can just imagine. What did you and Alyce talk about?"

"Oh, this and that. It's kind of hard to have a civilized conversation when you're all stooped over and people have been pelting you with rotten tomatoes all afternoon. She gave me a back rub."

"And then Timmy came and you don't need to tell me what he did."

"And then the Queen chased him away and sentenced me to another hour for giggling. I was kind of tipsy by then. She said she'd be back at ten o'clock, only—"

"She never arrived."

"And it took forever before Timmy could convince anyone to get the key off the Queen's body. The police wouldn't let anyone touch it until the medical examiner had been there. And so it was midnight before they let me out. I think that Detective Burke liked seeing me in the pillory."

"Isn't that just like a man?" Penelope glared at Andy, who happened to be the only male handy. "I suppose you'd like to see me locked up in that contraption."

"Well . . ."

Penelope turned back to Kathy. "You see. Men!"

"But . . ."

"Well, Andy, since you are to be the Royal Consort . . ."

"I am?"

"Of course. And you must *be* someone."

"I must?"

"How about Thomas Dekker? I've always admired Dekker. I got an A in minor Elizabethan drama, you know."

"How about Prince Philip?" Andy said. "I've always admired *him.*"

"Someone Elizabethan, silly."

"I think Andy would make an excellent Puritan," Kathy said.

"Not in my reign, he won't, although you're probably right." Andy, who was tall and lanky and always reminded Penelope of Ichabod Crane, could be easily transformed into a Puritan, snorting fire-and-brimstone sermons. But Penelope planned a starring role for him in the royal shenanigans, one that was ill suited to Puritanism. "Well, it's only Tuesday and we have until Saturday. I shall research the question tomorrow."

"How about Sir Walter Raleigh?" Kathy asked. "Our old Raleigh moved to Dallas."

"Perfect!" Penelope cried. "Although why anyone would move to Dallas is beyond me."

"Raleigh?" Andy questioned. "Wasn't he executed?"

"Not by me," Penelope said. "That was later. James the First did that. Raleigh was one of my favorites. Mostly."

"Oh, well, in that case . . ."

"Now, as for Mycroft . . ."

While Penelope and Kathy designed suitable raiment for the Royal Cat, an unsuspecting Big Mike lounged on his barstool, listening to Red the Rat ramble about the murder of Carolyn Lewis. "She was a fine figger of a woman, Big Mike." That was hardly a news flash. All women were possessed of fine figgers in Red's view of the world, and the death of any one of them diminished the field of play, although the one time Red came dangerously close to acquiring a fine figger of a woman—a predecessor of Debbie's—he fled to the sanctuary of the desert until the news reached him that she had run off with a purveyor of Australian saddles and now lived in a mobile home park near Prescott. "Yes sirree, Big Mike, ol' Red almost got catched that time."

By the time Penelope and Kathy—both fine figgers of women—descended upon Big Mike with a tape measure borrowed from Debbie, Red the Rat was staring mournfully into his drink, probably contemplating the vagaries of life in a Prescott mobile home park.

"Stand up, Mycroft."

Why?

"Howdy-do, Penelope, Kathy," Red the Rat said.

"Hey, Red."

"Mycroft, please."

"Whatcha doing, Penelope?"

"Measuring Mycroft for his royal vestments," Penelope said, although there was very little measuring going on. Mycroft whacked the yellow tape measure, but without a great deal of enthusiasm. His dollop of nonalcoholic beer always mellowed the big cat to such an extent that he really wanted only a short nap. That was the nice thing about a conversation with Red the Rat. You didn't have to do anything but listen and the old prospector took no offense if you nodded off.

"Oh, never mind," Penelope said, turning to Kathy, "we'll just take the measurements off one of his other coats." On game days Mycroft wore the red and black of the San Diego State football team (to which Penelope was passionately devoted) and, of course, he had a scarlet and gold coat emblazoned with the Marine Corps emblem for the birthday ball every November tenth.

"So, you gonna catch the murderer again, Penelope?"

"Yes, indeed, Red."

"That's good. She was a fine figger of a woman."

Elaine Henders—self-appointed chairwoman of the celebration committee—was waiting impatiently when Penelope, Mycroft, and Andy arrived at the little ranch. Laney's entourage consisted of Wally (he of the laconic crinkling eyes) and Big Mike's best friend, Alexander, a lovable Yorkshire terrier with a perpetual grin.

The entourages converged, mingled. Greetings were exchanged. Eyes crinkled. Yip. Slobber. Meow.

"Laney, what are you doing?"

"I'm opening the bubbly, silly."

"I can see that. But why? Have you finished another novel?"

"Of course not. This is for your elevation to the throne of England."

Penelope knew better than to ask how Laney had found out so quickly. Laney knew everything. Penelope often wondered how Laney found the time to write her highly erotic romance novels set in old Arizona when she spent so much time on the telephone, polling her extensive network of gossips.

After several toasts to the new Queen and to Sir Walter Raleigh, Andy and Wally were dispatched to start the barbecue, Big Mike and Alex were admonished to play nicely and not destroy anything in the process, while Laney marched Penelope into the kitchen.

"We're having my nuclear-meltdown hot dogs," Laney declared. "It's the best I could do on such short notice. Really, Penelope, you should have told me sooner. I could have planned."

"I didn't know."

"Well, you should have," Laney said, tossing her thick mane of flaming red hair indignantly. "Who else could they ask?"

Laney's recipe for nuclear-meltdown hot dogs was simple and greatly resembled Penelope's own recipe for boom-boom hot dogs. It should. Penelope had shamelessly stolen the recipe and renamed it. Take one jar of hot dog relish. Add chopped onions and tomatoes. Mix in Tabasco sauce to taste (Laney's taste was for hot hot hot and hence the name). This concoction was prepared in advance of charring turkey dogs (low in fat) on the barbecue. The buns were smeared with fat-free cream cheese. All in all, it provided a simple, and delicious, repast.

"How *is* the writing going?" Penelope asked as she chopped the onions.

"I left poor Rebecca panting and heaving her lovely bosom in the clutches of the one-eyed savage," Laney replied. "I think the little minx wants to seduce him. She doesn't seem able to resist that eye patch."

Laney gave a heave to her own lovely bosom. "I can see the attraction," she continued. "Wally looks quite dashing in his eye patch when we play Colonel's Beautiful Daughter in Captivity." Laney prided herself on the careful research she did to make her novels authentic, particularly the frequent scenes where the heroines were ravished. As ravishing as any of her heroines, Laney's own bodice had been ripped more often than Rebecca's.

"And what about the handsome Lieutenant Kit Christopher, late of West Point?"

"Oh, he's riding furiously at the head of his gallant troop to Rebecca's rescue."

"And does he arrive in time to save her honor?"

"I'm not sure. Poor Rebecca may get staked out on an ant-hill all covered with honey."

"Yuk."

"Oh, it's not so bad." Laney smiled. "Except all that honey made poor Wally quite sick."

It was certainly interesting having Laney for a best friend.

"What *are* you doing, Penelope?" Andy asked after the celebrants had gone home.

Penelope was on her hands and knees before the bookcase next to the fireplace, where Mycroft was stretched out, luxuriating in the warmth. "I'm searching for some of Sir Walter's poetry. I'm sure he must have written something romantic." She discarded one anthology after another. She sat back in disgust. "Nothing. I'll have to research it tomorrow. And I was looking forward to a good game of the Queen and Her Courtier."

"Now where are you going, Penelope?"

"To the refrigerator. I think I have some honey."

"Honey? Mycroft, do you know what she's talking about?"

Mycroft stirred at the mention of his name, perking his ears up a little.

"Aha!" Penelope cried from the kitchen. She returned to the living room triumphantly, bearing a small jar of honey.

"What is that for?"

Penelope smiled wickedly. While she wasn't able to crinkle her eyes laconically like Wally, despite hours of practice before the mirror, Penelope did possess a most seductive smile. "You'll find out. You don't happen to have an eye patch with you? No, I suppose not. We'll just have to make do with the Two-Eyed Savage."

"Savage?"

"That's you. And the Colonel's Beautiful Daughter. That's me. I'm your helpless captive, but we'll have to do without the ants. You can play their roles."

"Ants? You've been talking to Laney again."

"Isn't she wonderful? Such a creative and inventive mind. I don't know what we'd do without her. Come, dear, sweet, wonderful savage."

Andy complied.

Mycroft padded along behind but, as usual, the bedroom door was rudely closed in his face. Ever since an unfortunate incident with a previous lover, Mycroft had been excluded from the bedroom when passion loomed.

Big Mike growled and complained loudly, but finally settled down to listen—he was quite the voyeur—and wait for his eventual admittance.

He waited a very long time.

CHAPTER
TWO

The Two-Eyed Savage had departed long before, leaving Penelope and Mycroft to their untroubled slumber. Mycroft, at least, dreaming of giant lima beans and mewing softly in his sleep, was untroubled. Penelope, however, was plagued by a question that penetrated even her championship-caliber ability to sleep.

Who killed the Queen of All England?

It was unseasonably warm for late February, and the mid-morning sun flooded the bedroom, bathing woman and cat in a lustrous glow. It was not unusual for Penelope and Mycroft to lie abed till noon. Upon her discharge from the United States Marine Corps, Penelope had vowed never to greet another dawn unless, of course, she happened to be coming home at that hour, having danced the night away in the arms of her beloved. While Mycroft did not dance—except when the electric can opener whirred—he matched Penelope wink for wink and then some.

Penelope turned over.

Mycroft, who was sleeping on her legs, growled softly, protesting the disturbance.

Who killed the Queen?

Penelope clenched her eyes against the morning.

Why?

She turned over again.

Big Mike growled, louder this time.

Damn.

Penelope gave it up. The questions were forcing her to action. "Reveille, Mikey."

Reveille, my big tail.

Mikey was having none of it, although Penelope knew he wasn't asleep. She tried to ease her legs free of the charcoal-gray cat with black stripes, but twenty-five pounds of determined cat is not easily dislodged. Mycroft tensed, ready to defend his constitutional right to sleep, but Penelope surrendered. She could think in bed quite well, even without coffee.

There were two important things to do before going to Mycroft & Company, perhaps three, but she couldn't remember the third item just now because her legs were going to sleep. Damned cat. First, she must run by the Empty Creek Police Department and get all of the reports on the Queen's assassination.

In the normal course of Empty Creek Police Department meanderings, those crime reports would already have been in Penelope's hands. But since John "Dutch" Fowler was off on vacation visiting her sister, Penelope would be forced to deal with Detectives Larry Burke and Willie Stoner—the Tweedledee and Tweedledum of what was referred to with a straight face as the Homicide/Robbery Bureau.

Although Penelope loved her younger sister dearly, Cassandra's passionate romance with the chief of police was irritating at times, especially when there was a murder to be solved and she was forced to deal with the groundlings of the E.C.P.D. Still, principal photography on Cassie's latest film was scheduled to wrap at the end of the week and the two of them would be back in their hideaway high atop the northern slope of Crying Woman Mountain. Until then she could put up with Tweedledee and Tweedledum.

Penelope wiggled her goes in a vain attempt to restore feeling to her legs. They were definitely asleep, even if the rest of her wasn't. And now she could smell coffee, a rich and tantalizing aroma that wafted through the house to the bedroom although she hadn't brewed it yet. She wanted to, but . . .

Damned cat.

Penelope also wanted to visit the Empty Creek Library after the police station. Sir Walter had to have written some suitable verses of love for Andy to use in tender and endearing moments at the Faire. And the Faire's program had to be changed. Although Sir Walter's name was oft spelled R-a-l-e-i-g-h in the popular press (and the program of the Almost Authentic festival), all the best anthologies—even Bartlett's—used the traditional spelling of R-a-l-e-g-h. And so would Andy. Attention to detail was important.

So was coffee.

Penelope readied her move, grasping the covers tightly. She was poised to fling Big Mike in the air and escape his clutches, when he suddenly stretched, one lazy paw after another, looking up at her as if to say, Let's get going. Things to do. Places to go. Lima beans to eat. Crimes to solve. All that with but one quizzical glance before he ambled off to the kitchen.

As Penelope and Mycroft entered the police station they were greeted by Peggy Norton, who was working the desk. Mycroft leapt to the top of the high desk to say howdy.

"Mikey," Peggy squealed, "my favorite person." She scratched Big Mike's chin. He immediately raised his head for more. "Hi, Penelope. We've been wondering when we'd see you."

"Am I that transparent?"

"It's just that you can't resist a murder. You should have been a cop."

"Why, thank you," Penelope said, pleased at the compliment.

"Even Burke and Stoner were getting worried. They were afraid you might be sick."

"Are they here?"

"Go on back. They'll be delighted to see you."

"I'll bet."

When Penelope tapped on the door of the tiny cubicle that housed the Homicide Bureau, Detectives Larry Burke and Willie Stoner were eating jelly doughnuts on opposite sides of the two desks that had been pushed together.

"Gumgumph," Tweedledee, whose mouth was full, mumbled by way of greeting. He immediately rolled his chair away as Big Mike leapt to the desktop. Tweedledum rolled *his* chair away in the opposite direction, leaving the field to Mycroft, who didn't really like jelly doughnuts. Besides, they were all gone. Nothing remained but a greasy, red-stained bag.

"Gumgumph," Tweedledee repeated, although Penelope doubted he was greeting Mycroft with fondness. The matched set of dueling scars Big Mike had once given the burly detective were faint but unmistakably visible on his cheek.

"You're going to spoil your lunch," Penelope said, "and dinner."

"Tisumughgumph," Tweedledee said.

Penelope translated that curious phrase as, This is our lunch. She picked up a file folder with the name Carolyn Lewis on it. "Is this for me?" she asked sweetly.

Tweedledee swallowed and nodded. "Yes," he said.

"Ah, intelligible conversation." Penelope opened the file and quickly scanned the contents. There were advantages to being the future sister-in-law of the police chief. There was little in the file, however, that Penelope had not already learned from Kathy and the gossip around town. Carolyn Lewis had been murdered by a person or persons unknown. Left to the investigative skills of Tweedledee and Tweedledum, the chances were excellent that the person or persons would remain unknown for all time.

"They're crazy," Tweedledee said.

"Who is crazy?"

"Them people out there at the Faire. They dress funny. They talk funny. They act funny."

"It's living history," Penelope explained. "They are re-creating a most interesting period of the past. Their dress and their speech are as accurate as they can make them."

"Gotta give 'em credit for one thing."

"And what is that?"

"Them bodkins the women wear. Sure are revealing. Lots of tor—"

Penelope, who had once severely chastised Burke for referring to Debbie's national treasures as torpedoes, interrupted. "Bodices," she said.

"Huh?"

"They are called bodices," Penelope said. "A bodkin is a small dagger."

"Whatever. Lots of boo—"

Penelope waggled a warning finger. "If you must refer to those portions of the female anatomy," she said, "call them breasts. Repeat after me, breasts."

"Aw, Penelope, I don't mean nothing by it. I just call a boob a boob."

"So do I," Penelope said.

"You see?"

What a dullard, Penelope thought, giving up. It was impossible to turn a boob's ear into a silk purse in the space of a few moments. With Burke, it was a lifelong project.

Mycroft, meanwhile, was not about to relent. He scavenged and burrowed through the papers on the two desks, scattering files hither and yon. There had to be some real food somewhere. What kind of way was this to run a police station?

"What's he doing?" Tweedledum asked as if to prove he, too, possessed the power of human speech.

"Looking for clues," Penelope replied, although she knew Big Mike's true purpose, "which is what you should be doing. What about motive?"

"Nobody seemed to like her much. She really thought she was the Queen. She was bossy."

"Queens have that tendency, I suppose. I shall be a most benevolent queen, of course."

"You!" Both detectives chorused the accusation.

"I am now Elizabeth Regina, Queen of All England."

Burke groaned. Having Penelope and Big Mike as honorary members of the Empty Creek Police Department was bad enough. Her position as future sister-in-law to the chief was even worse. But Queen of All England . . . "I ain't gonna curtsy," he said.

"Oh, but you must," Penelope said. "It's the rules." Being queen might be fun after all.

Burke groaned again.

"What about opportunity?" Penelope asked, ignoring his displeasure.

"Anybody who slipped away from the parties could have done it," Stoner said. "Anybody who snuck into the Fairegrounds could have done it just as easily. Somebody could have hid after closing." He shook his head. "Random attack. Hardest crime to solve. Probably never find him."

"Some bum after her money," Burke offered. "She resisted. Bad idea."

"Nonsense. There's no mention of a purse. Where are on earth was she going to carry money? She was wearing jeans and a sweatshirt. Why would she carry money anyway? Everything was closed."

"Probably had it between her alabaster mounds of pleasure," Tweedledee said with a smirk.

Penelope wanted to sic Big Mike on him, but restrained herself. "Someone must have heard something. Seen something."

"Like I said, there was a big party going on at the time."

"Wet T-shirt contest."

"Is that historical?"

Penelope sighed. "So that's it?" she said. "That is the some total of your investigation?"

" 'Course not, but there ain't much hope."

"Not unless we catch him in the act."

Penelope was tempted to deliver a lecture on the Elizabethan need for order in their tumultuous times, but since Mycroft was the only one present who would understand, she again restrained herself. Besides, Big Mike had already heard her views on the topic and, doubtless, agreed, having a high need for order in his universe as well. Of all the creatures on God's brown earth, cats were most Elizabethan in their fondness for intrigue, occasional violence, and food.

Instead, Penelope said, "Let's go, Mycroft. We'll just have to restore order ourselves."

Big Mike withdrew from the in basket he had been energetically exploring, knocking a stack of files to the floor in the process.

"It ain't enough to be queen. You're gonna go out there and try to solve this crime," Tweedledee accused, "just like them other times."

"I certainly am." Penelope waited, expecting the standard don't-interfere-in-the-course-of-justice speech, but Burke surprised her.

"You be careful out there," he said softly.

Penelope, who firmly believed that Larry Burke had accumulated his knowledge of investigation and police procedure from reruns of *Hill Street Blues*, *Dragnet*, and *Perry Mason*, was touched. Tweedledee was actually blushing.

"Mycroft," Penelope said, "give the nice detective a kiss."

"I'd rather eat worms," Burke said.

Big Mike seemed to share the sentiment.

The Empty Creek Public Library was a most excellent depository of knowledge in most respects, thanks largely to Leigh Kent, the new—by Empty Creek standards—librarian who had taken up her post several years before and immediately set to improving and expanding the collection. A by-product of her presence was an immediate increase in circulation statistics, not because of a sudden and inexplicable thirst for knowledge among the denizens, but rather because Our Leigh—as she had come to be known among a possessive citizenry—was, quite simply, the sexiest librarian in all Christendom, and her smile had cut a wide swath through the majority of the local male population, young and old alike. Her recent betrothal, duly recorded in the *Empty Creek News Journal*, to Burton Maxwell, an instructor of English literature at the community college, had broken many a heart.

Leigh, who was seated behind the reference desk when Penelope and Mycroft entered, rose quickly and performed a most credible curtsy. "Your Majesty," she said. "I'm honored by your visit."

Penelope giggled.

"You really must work on your royal presence, Penelope. Elizabeth Regina does *not* giggle girlishly."

"I was thinking of the esteemed Detective Burke, who told me less than twenty minutes ago that he was not going to curtsy. I did not explain the difference between a curtsy and a bow."

"Well, that's all right, then. I think you're going to make a wonderful queen."

"I have some doubts, especially under the circumstances."

"It was horrible," Leigh said, returning to her place behind the desk. Mycroft, who knew that Our Leigh was not a cat person, immediately followed, settling into her lap to demonstrate once again what a fine furry feline fellow he was. "Mikey, you're the only cat I like, you know."

"He admires such single-minded devotion," Penelope said. "What can you tell me about poor Carolyn's death?"

"Nothing that you don't already know," Leigh, who now played Celia to Burton's Ben Jonson at the Faire, replied. "We didn't stay overnight, so we didn't even hear about it until the next day. What does Dutch have to say about it?"

"He's out of town. Burke and Stoner think it was a random attack."

"What do they know?"

"Exactly," Penelope said. "Mikey, you keep Leigh out of trouble while I look up Sir Walter."

"I thought he moved to Dallas."

"He did. Andy is taking his place. I'm having nothing to do with that Sir Robert Dudley."

"Andy will be a good Sir Walter. I hope he has a cape handy for your every step."

"He'd better. I'll be right back."

Despite Our Leigh's efforts at enlarging the collection, there was little to be found of Sir Walter Ralegh's poetry and such as there was dealt chiefly with such gloomy topics as death rather than the lyrical references to love that Penelope had hoped to find. Penelope wanted nothing to do with death, what with one queen already assassinated and another ready to ascend the throne.

Penelope wandered out of the stacks and said, "Fie on it. We'll just write our own."

"Write our own what, Penelope?"

"Love poetry, of course."

"Of course."

" 'Drink to me only with thine eyes,' " Penelope recited, " 'And I will pledge with mine; / Or leave a kiss but in the cup / And I'll not look for wine.' "

Leigh immediately responded, " 'Come, my Celia, let us prove, / While we can, the sports of love; / Time will not be ours forever; / He at length our good will sever. / Spend not his gifts in vain.' " Leigh sighed. "Who could resist such lines?" she asked. "The first time Burton whispered them in my ear . . ."

"And here I am stuck with the depressing Sir Walter."

Things were hopping when Penelope and Mycroft finally arrived at Mycroft & Company.

"Praise God that you're here, Your Majesty," Kathy cried when Penelope pushed her way through a knot of curious onlookers gathered around the door. "Everyone wants to see you."

"What on earth for?"

"A delegation of the soothsayers was here. They'll be back. The Picts and the Celts came to pledge their fealty. They want Stormy to be in your court—or theirs. I'm not quite sure. They were quite taken with her role as the Amazon princess. The Lord High Sheriff came—he's tired of being jeered because he's the tax collector—and the Lord Mayor thinks he should have his own parade. And the fools . . . I've forgotten what the fools wanted. Something important to fools, I suppose."

"My goodness," Penelope said when Kathy paused to catch her breath, "one would think that I was the real Queen."

"But, Your Majesty, you are."

The silence provoked by Kathy's earnest pronouncement was broken by a birdlike chirp. "Well, Penelope Warren, what do you have to say for yourself now?"

"Oh, yes," Kathy said, snapping her fingers, "and Mrs. Burnham is here."

"Mrs. Burnham is, indeed, here," said Mrs. Eleanor Burnham, appearing from behind a high display of Laney's romance novels.

"Eleanor, how good to see you."

"Fiddlesticks, Penelope. Fools and soothsayers and you're to be Queen of the May, I suppose. You must tell all."

Penelope bristled. Mycroft began his stalk. Mrs. Burnham, Empty Creek's very own town crier, affected them in that way. Eleanor irritated Penelope, and the constant chirp, chirp, chirp, of her voice always brought out Mycroft's hunter instincts. "There's nothing to tell," Penelope said. "I'm to take the place of Carolyn Lewis as Queen of the Faire."

"That's not what I meant, and you know it. Whom do you suspect?"

Penelope was tempted to deliver a flip answer but knew that anything she said would be all over town by nightfall, something on the order of And I'm not supposed to repeat this, so don't tell a soul, but Penelope believes the postmaster did it. Instead, Penelope said, "Someone with a dagger."

"Exactly!" Mrs. Burnham cried. She turned abruptly and

marched out of the bookstore to the great disappointment of Mycroft, who had barely reached the ears-flattened-and-tail-swishing portion of the stalk. And those brown sensible shoes had been such a tempting target.

"Talk about fools . . ."

The rest of the afternoon was spent delivering royal pronouncements to one delegation or another. To each, Penelope explained the Elizabethan need for orderly transition as justification for making no changes whatsoever. That seemed to satisfy everyone but the fools. But, fools being fools, Penelope never did quite figure out what it was they wanted.

Still, business was brisk and that was good for the local economy, to say nothing of the Royal Exchequer of the second Queen Elizabeth I. But the steady stream of delegations, the curious, some well-wishers, and even a few legitimate customers, prevented Penelope from looking at the Carolyn Lewis file until after dinner.

Since Wednesday evening was Andy's deadline, and he was busy attending to the last details for the Thursday edition of the *Empty Creek News Journal*, Penelope and Mycroft were alone when they finally went through the file, page by grim page, and found nothing.

Absolutely nothing.

Thus, the day ended as it had begun. Penelope was in bed. Mycroft was asleep on her legs, which were also rapidly going to sleep, leaving her mind behind, alert and still pondering *the* question.

Who killed the Queen?

CHAPTER
THREE

B ecause the *Empty Creek News Journal* was published only on Thursdays and Saturdays, the little community newspaper had been scooped on the story of Carolyn Lewis's demise. Andy hated being scooped by the larger newspapers, but if he were to transform the *News Journal* into a daily, he would be forced to print every news release that came across his desk—publicists across the nation massacred whole forests to promote one silly thing or another—in order to fill the newspaper and, quite likely, would go broke in the process. Empty Creek simply did not produce enough news or advertising in a week to fill seven papers. As Andy was quick to point out, it barely produced enough material to fill two modest editions each week.

Usually.

But if Carolyn Lewis's murder was old news for the larger newspapers now, it was still *the* news in Empty Creek and Andy had to satisfy his voracious and curious readers. And the long gap between event and publication allowed Andy to seek other angles, to pursue topics in greater depth, to allow for thoughtful reflection.

So, as Penelope carried her third cup of coffee outside to retrieve the *Empty Creek News Journal,* she looked forward to reading Andy's account of the murder, knowing that he would have given human dimension to the tragedy. While still horrible, Andy's story would be better than reading the grim and impersonal crime file which was devoid of all emotion.

It was a banner headline, of course, spread across all six columns. There were photographs of Carolyn, one in her role as Elizabeth Regina, and another, probably taken from *The Gila Monster,* the yearbook of the Empty Creek High School, where Carolyn had taught history.

With Mycroft beside her, staring placidly out at the desert landscape that was his fiefdom, Penelope sat in the pale morning sunlight and read.

"The first revels of the annual Empty Creek Authentic Elizabethan Spring Faire turned tragic late Saturday night when an unknown assassin's dagger took the life of Carolyn Lewis, who for many years had played the role of Queen Elizabeth I to perfection. Beloved by her loyal subjects . . ."

Penelope quickly scanned the lead story. It recounted all the known facts of the case. There were quotes from Timmy and Kathy and others from among the royal court, as well as Burke speaking for the police department. That part ended with the usual meaningless sentence: "The investigation is continuing."

While Penelope turned to the sidebar, Mycroft continued to stare out over the bleak yet still-beautiful desert landscape, pondering questions and answers beyond human comprehension, the very mysterious delicacies of life itself—the existence of God, the sound of one hand clapping, lima beans. . . .

The sidebar dealt with Carolyn Lewis's teaching career and her background. There were tearful quotes from students who professed undying love for their beloved history teacher. Twice she had been named teacher of the year. Four years ago *The Gila Monster* had been dedicated to Carolyn Lewis. A collection was being taken up for a permanent memorial in the main foyer next to the athletic trophy case. There was certainly ample room for a memorial, Penelope thought, since the Empty Creek Gila Monsters hadn't won a football game for two years and the other sports were little better.

But as she read on, Andy's story didn't ring true. Penelope knew for a fact that Old Hatchet Face was not beloved by her subjects at the Faire and doubted that was the case with her students. Penelope hadn't liked many of her high school teachers—that cute Mr. Wilson who taught American literature was a notable exception—seeing them as a torture inflicted on an inquiring mind. And yet here was Judith Setzer, described by Andy as a distraught junior in Mrs. Lewis's American history course, saying "she was the best teacher anyone could ever have."

Penelope shook her head. "I suppose she could have been a Dr. Jekyll and Mrs. Hyde," she told Mycroft. "What do you think, Mikey?"

Since the imponderable questions had Mikey nodding off to slumber land again, there was no reply. Penelope finished reading the story. There wasn't much left.

Carolyn was divorced (no children) and no one knew where her former husband now lived. He had disappeared years before, probably eliminating him as a suspect. That was too bad. Close relatives and friends always made good suspects.

Having finished the paper, Penelope now finished her coffee, stood, stretched, and said, "I think we need to visit dear old Empty Creek High, Mikey."

Big Mike, a self-educated cat despite spending his formative years on the small Ethiopian college campus where Penelope had taught English as a Peace Corps volunteer, yawned. It wasn't that he had anything against formal education. He didn't. In point of fact, Big Mike loved books, especially the neat rows of books on a shelf—whether at home or at Mycroft & Company—that provided such wonderful and dark hidey-holes for sleeping and from which to peer out at the world while remaining unobserved. One could learn a great deal in such a fashion. After all, detailed observation was an integral portion of the scientific method. But Mycroft was a cat of the world and a devotee of action, not the classroom. In another way of looking at it, the world was Big Mike's litter box.

When Penelope and Mycroft arrived at the bookstore, they found a sign in the window. In an ornate Old English style of lettering the sign proclaimed:

HEAR YE, HEAR YE, HEAR YE.

TEMPORARY NEW HOURS FOR MYCROFT & COMPANY ARE:

MONDAY–FRIDAY FROM 10 A.M.–5 P.M.

CLOSED ON WEEKENDS TO CELEBRATE SPRINGETYME.

BY ORDER OF HER ROYAL MAJESTY, QUEEN ELIZABETH I.

E.R.

"Well, thank you for that," Penelope told Kathy upon entering the shop. "I had completely forgotten we would have to change hours to accommodate the Faire." Normally, Mycroft and Company closed on Sundays and Mondays.

"That's what a lady-in-waiting is for, My Lady, I mean, Your Majesty," Kathy said. "I wanted to put your seal on it in red wax, but you don't have a seal."

"Or red wax, I daresay."

"I'll find some," Kathy said. "You must have a seal."

"Don't bother. I'm going to be queen for only this one Faire."

"Oh, no," Kathy protested. "Your Majesty will have a long and fruitful reign."

"I'm abdicating," Penelope said firmly. "On the evening of the last day of the Faire, this queen will be history."

If the telephone had not rung at that moment, Kathy might have continued the discussion. Instead, she went to the counter and answered it brightly. "Ye Olde Mycroft and Company, by Appointment to Her Majesty the Queen." After a moment Kathy covered the telephone and whispered, "It's Dutch. He sounds upset."

Penelope frowned. What does Dutch have to be upset about, she wondered, off gallivanting with Cassie in California. She took the telephone from Kathy and said in her very best English accent, which was quite good indeed, "British Museum Reading Room."

Kathy giggled.

"Pen-e-lo-pe," Dutch said.

When Dutch dragged her name out like that, Penelope knew she was in trouble.

"What is this nonsense I hear?" he asked.

"If it's nonsense, you must have been talking to your detectives again."

"Is it true?"

"Is what true?"

"Is it true that you're going to be Queen of the Faire?"

"Why, yes. The most distinguished delegation asked me. Sir Francis Bacon, Sir Francis Drake, Master William Shakespeare. How could I refuse?"

"By saying no. N-o. No!"

"Why on earth would I say no?"

"Because it might be dangerous. It didn't occur to you that there's some nut out there killing women who pretend to be the Queen of England?"

"Someone killed Carolyn Lewis, *not* Elizabeth the First. It could have been one of her students. . . ."

Penelope would have expanded the theory to include colleagues, administrators, friends, a spurned admirer, et cetera, had Cassie not grabbed the phone away from her betrothed and squealed, "I think it's wonderful, Penelope. It's such a terrific part. You can be just like Bette Davis in *The Virgin Queen.*"

In the background Penelope heard Dutch muttering, "How did I ever get mixed up with the Warren sisters?" It was the tone of voice that conveyed profound disgust. He might have been saying How did I ever get mixed up with toads?

"Who can I be?" Cassie continued. "Oh, never mind. I'll think of someone. I'll go to costumes and get the best outfit I can find. I'll get something for Dutch too. He can be a wizard, perhaps. Don't you think he'd make a perfect wizard—"

"I think he'd be the perfect court jester," Penelope interrupted.

"Oh, don't be angry at Dutch. He's just worried about you. But we'll be there to take care of you."

When Penelope and Mycroft arrived at the principal's office, Big Mike immediately leapt to the counter separating school administrators from the student rabble. Penelope, for her part, immediately remembered another reason she hadn't liked her own high school days.

"No animals allowed on campus," a woman with a very distinct mustache announced through thin, pinched lips. Penelope made it a rule never to like a mustachioed woman or a man with a weak chin.

Penelope read the nameplate on her desk. Miss Sophie Wheeler. "He's not an animal," Penelope said, "he's a very well-mannered cat."

"No cats, no dogs, no animals," Miss Sophie Wheeler said with determination.

"No horse, no wife, no mustache," Penelope said with her own determination.

"Pardon me?"

"That's what they used to tell the cadets at West Point," Penelope explained. "Perhaps they still do. No horse, no wife, no mustache. It was a silly rule. Just like yours."

"I shall have to call the authorities if you do not remove that beast this instant."

"We *are* the authorities," Penelope said, whipping out her leather case and badge that identified her as an honorary member of the Empty Creek Police Department, "and we are here to see Mr. Vander Costen."

Miss Sophie Wheeler now had her eyes warily on Big Mike, who had his eyes not so warily measuring the distance between the counter and Miss Wheeler's desk. "He's at baseball practice," she said hastily. "Now, take your . . . cat . . . and go."

"Come on, Mycroft, let's go shag some flies."

In his youth Big Mike had been quite adept at shagging flies of the winged variety, but once at the baseball field he was instantly distracted by a ground ball hit foul through the first base coaching box. He tore off in pursuit, bringing it to bay near the right-field foul line, where, lacking the wherewithal or the inclination to toss it back, he settled down to await developments.

Van was throwing batting practice, and when he saw Penelope, waved and hollered, "Come to try out?"

Penelope glanced out at right field, where Big Mike and a diminutive outfielder were apparently involved in a discussion over who owned the ball now nestled between Big Mike's paws. "Why not?"

"Grab a bat."

Penelope grabbed three bats in fact, and swung them slowly as she approached the plate. Arnie Wilson, the baseball coach who had been hitting fungos to the outfield, stopped to watch.

The bulky catcher, who resembled Cecil Fielder *after* a Big Mac frenzy, grinned up at her through his mask with an expression that proclaimed, This oughta be good.

Penelope discarded two of the bats and stepped into the box, digging imaginary spikes into the dirt.

"No batter, no batter, no batter," the second baseman hummed in the eternal singsong cry of baseball and youth.

"Stick it in her ear," the third baseman shouted.

"Nice butt," the catcher said.

Penelope didn't take her eyes off the ball in Van's hand as she said, "Nice way to talk, but thanks anyway."

"You're welcome."

The third baseman crept in until he was midway between the base and the plate. "Knock her down," he cried.

Van wound up and delivered a fastball down the middle of the plate.

Penelope pulled it, undressing the third baseman with a line drive that screamed past his ear and wound up in the left-field corner. Easy double, Penelope thought.

"I told you to knock her down," the third baseman shouted as he hastily retreated to play deep behind the bag.

"Awesome," the catcher said with respect in his voice.

Line drive to center. Line drive to right. Back to left. All clean singles. Perfect bunt down the third-base line. Another down the first-base line.

"Time," the catcher shouted. He trotted out to the mound for a brief conference with the principal.

"Okay, this is for real," he said when he returned to the plate. He spit into the dirt before pulling the mask on again. "Bases loaded. Bottom of the ninth. Two out. Down by three."

Penelope stepped back and looked out at the diamond. There were runners at all the bags now. The chatter came up from the infielders. The outfield was shading her to left. Penelope stepped back into the box and spat before waggling the bat and her butt.

"Here's the windup . . . she steps out of the box. . . ."

Startled by the booming announcement, Penelope did step out of the box and looked up to where the student announcer sat in the ramshackle wooden booth.

She rubbed a little dirt on her hands before stepping back in.

"The batter's ready . . . the windup . . . the pitch."

Crack.

Actually the crack of the bat was more of a ping because, despite the best traditions of baseball, aluminum bats were all the rage.

"It's a long fly ball to deep left center. . . ."

Penelope did not look at the ball as she raced for first, making the turn as the first-base coach waved her on. She was halfway to second when she looked up and saw the ball disappear over the fence. She slowed into her home-run trot.

"Home run," the loudspeakers boomed. "The Monsters win! The Monsters win! The Monsters win!"

As Penelope rounded third base, Arnie Wilson (who had quickly pushed a player from the coaching box) shook her hand and patted her backside.

Penelope touched the plate and gave Mycroft a low-five and the catcher a high-five.

"I'm in love," the catcher said. "Will you marry me?"

"Where'd you learn to do that?" Van Costen asked as they climbed into the bleachers. Mycroft stayed in the dugout, where he had taken up residence in the empty ball bag, peering keenly out at the action.

"I played a little ball," Penelope replied. "I could have done better with a wood bat. Biff . . . Biff's my father . . .

didn't believe in aluminum bats. I grew up with his old Louisville Sluggers. My favorite was an Al Kaline model, much to Biff's dismay. He was a Red Sox fan, of course."

"I'm a Cubs fan," Van said with the tinge of sadness in his voice common to all Cubs fans.

"Better than the Padres."

"Just barely."

"What are the Monsters' chances this year?"

"About the same as last year."

"That bad?"

"Afraid so."

They sat quietly for a moment, watching the ageless routines of infield practice. Sitting in the warm sunshine was almost enough to distract Penelope from her purpose.

Almost.

"What can you tell me about Carolyn Lewis?"

Van Costen sighed. "She was an excellent teacher. Very patient and understanding with her students. She made history come alive for them. We're going to miss her. Students, faculty, and administration."

"Really?"

"Yes, really. Carolyn Lewis was a wonderful human being. No one could have a reason for wanting to kill her."

"Someone did."

"No one at Empty Creek High School."

"Mrs. Hyde," Penelope said quietly.

"What?"

"Oh, nothing. Thanks for your help, Van."

"Anytime you want to come back . . . we could use a hard-hitting outfielder. . . ."

Big Mike was stretched out on the Oxford English Dictionary, not the full nineteen-volume set—he wasn't *that* big—but the two-volume, boxed compact edition that came with a magnifying glass for reading the fine print. Since Penelope kept the O.E.D. on top of a three-shelf bookcase, it was a fine perch from which to survey proceedings and, incidentally, avoid the creepy-crawlies that abounded in the vast desert and sometimes slipped through the door left carelessly ajar.

In the kitchen Penelope dropped a few peppermint candies in the pocket of her Windbreaker and then filled a plastic Baggie with carrot stubs and lettuce. Looking in on Big Mike in the living room, Penelope asked, "How about a little walk, Mikey?"

Big Mike joined Penelope for the stroll down the dirt road to the stables, where Chardonnay, the sweet-tempered six-year-old Arabian filly, lived on the banks of the nearly always empty Empty Creek.

Chardonnay whinnied, snorted, and pawed the earth by way of greeting their arrival. Penelope switched on the stable light, and while Mycroft went to greet the bunnies who had already gathered for their nightly handout, she unwrapped the candies that served as Chardonnay's hors d'oeuvres and fed them one by one to the filly, who took each daintily. With Chardonnay now distracted, happily munching the last peppermint, Penelope distributed lettuce and carrots to the small rabbits waiting patiently in a circle around the edge of the light. Big Mike was stretched out on the patch of grass—the only grass on the twelve-acre spread—ears flattened and tail swishing in the beginning stage of his stalk. It was a game that both he and the rabbits found amusing. Big Mike would suddenly rush his intended victim. The victim would leap straight in the air, easily avoiding the charge, and come down to continue feasting placidly while Big Mike washed a paw nonchalantly, telling one and all, Good thing I wasn't serious.

Penelope left Big Mike and the rabbits—too numerous to name, although she had tried—to the pleasures of their evening and went to mix the healthy concoction for Char's supper. She had just hung the pail on the rail, when a car turned in at her driveway and stopped. That will be Andy, she thought. She turned and waited, knowing that he would be down as soon as he found the house empty. A moment later, when his gangling, awkward figure loped through the late-evening shadows, Penelope walked to the edge of Empty Creek to watch the last rays of the sunset fade beyond distant mountains.

His hands closed over her eyes from behind. "Guess who?"

"J. D. Salinger," she replied promptly.

"You peeked."

"Did not."

"Did so."

She snuggled in his arms, ending that discussion.

Standing there in the arms of her lover, basking in the fading light and the quiet solitude of the desert with her animal friends near at hand, it was easy for Penelope to believe that all was well with the world. But the desert, like life, lulled the unwary into a security that could be taken away in an instant. Prowling the sanctity of her make-believe realm, Carolyn Lewis had no doubt believed herself in the midst of tranquility.

How wrong, Penelope thought, how very wrong.

CHAPTER
FOUR

The morning dawned bright, clear—and clueless. If Penelope had hoped for inspiration from her dreams—often quite lurid and colorful—she had to grump herself awake in disappointment. Beside her, the men in her life slept on, blissfully unaware of Penelope's mood. But then, being a night person, Penelope was always somewhat cross in the morning. Perhaps that was the reason Andy always feigned sleep until Penelope had had a cup of coffee.

Big Mike—once granted admittance to the royal bedchamber—had wormed his way between Penelope and Andy as usual, an always-forceful reminder of their respective status in matters concerning the Queen. But if the Olympics had a sleeping competition, Mycroft would win the gold every time, and so he only twitched his ears when Penelope stroked his thick gray fur before crawling from the bed.

As for Andy . . . well, he had a very nice butt that Penelope was fond of patting. Being the first to arise did have its compensations, she thought as she slipped into her robe and made her way to the kitchen, rubbing sleep from her eyes, ricocheting off a wall or two in the process.

Penelope was quite adept at making coffee while sleepwalking. She had done it most mornings of her adult life. Since the current coffeemaker—a present from her mother—was too damned slow, Penelope alternated between holding her cup and the pot under the hissing, spluttering contraption. When her cup had an inch or so of life-restoring liquid, the pot was placed under the spout while she sipped and sighed. Then, the pot was removed and the cup was inserted for another infusion. In this fashion Penelope gradually acquired nearly a full cup of coffee, enough at least to get through the interminable process.

Sitting at the kitchen table, Penelope slowly awakened but found little inspiration for crime solving in the steam arising from her coffee cup. By the third cup of coffee, however, she was almost ready to confront the world, when she heard Mycroft coming down the hall, complaining all the way.

Meow. Raow. Raow. Meow!

As Mycroft rubbed sleepily against her legs, Penelope leaned down and scratched his ears, translating his various grievances as Why are we up so early? Why aren't you in bed keeping a cat warm? Why did you leave without saying goodbye? Where are my liver crunchies?

Penelope poured the dry food into his bowl and, while he tucked in for a little something to get the heart started, refilled her coffee cup and prepared one for Andy. Taking them to the bedroom, she announced with a great deal more cheer than she actually felt, "Another day, another deadline, precious sweetheart of mine."

Andy groaned, pretending a deep sleep.

"Is that any way to greet your devoted love slave who, incidentally, brings you coffee?"

"Oh, well, why didn't you say so?" He popped up in bed like bread from a toaster. "I missed you," he said, taking the coffee.

"You could have come into the kitchen and offered succor in my moment of need. Mycroft did. He rubbed against my legs."

"I would look positively foolish on all fours, rubbing your legs and purring."

"I don't know about that. I might like it."

Penelope snuggled into his waiting embrace. "I like this," she said happily, purring just a little bit herself. Waking up wasn't so bad after all.

"What are your plans for the day?" Andy asked.

"I suppose I'll assist the police with their inquiries, as they say on the telly."

Andy took the reporter's notebook he always kept on the nightstand for writing down any great thoughts that might occur during the night. It was nearly empty. But once he had written, "Bananas are good with peaches and cream."

Now, pen poised, Andy asked, "What avenues do you intend to pursue?"

"On the record?"

"Of course. Everything is on the record."

"Even last night?"

"Well, perhaps not everything."

"On the record, then, I don't know what I'll do. Something will occur to me."

"That's not much. Famed sleuth Penelope Warren said

today that something will occur to her." Andy put pen and notebook back on the table. "Off the record, then," he said.

"I thought everything was on the record."

"There are exceptions."

"Well, then, off the record. I still don't know what I'm going to do. I *hope* something will occur to me."

Inspiration occurred when the Bard of Avon arrived at Mycroft & Company behind the wheel of a compact recreational vehicle. Entering the bookstore, Will Shakespeare gestured grandly and asked, "Do you like it, Your Majesty?"

"I suppose so," Penelope answered dubiously, "but what is it for?"

Shakespeare, who in real life made quite a good living renting RVs and campers to tourists for their excursions to the Grand Canyon, the Mogollon Rim, the Superstition Mountains, Old Tombstone, and other Arizona points of interest, seemed perplexed. "Why, it's the royal living quarters, of course. Poor Carolyn preferred her tent, but somehow I don't think you're the tent type."

Admiring the Bard's alliteration, Penelope smiled and said, "Quite right." After serving in the United States Marine Corps and as a Peace Corps volunteer in Ethiopia, Penelope's concept of roughing it was to walk barefoot across the living room rug, although she could be enticed into the wilderness when duty demanded. "But I had no idea there were such royal perks. I expected to commute."

Shakespeare was aghast. "And miss the parties?"

Kathy was equally astonished. "Oh, you can't do that, Your Majesty."

Shakespeare's glasses clattered to the floor as he stooped to give a curious Mycroft a scratch under the chin. Retrieving them, he said, "Let me give you the royal tour."

The royal living quarters were actually quite spacious. Penelope noted the double bed above the cab of the truck with approval. Approaching the door, she had feared that Elizabeth Regina, Sir Walter, and the Royal Cat might be crowded.

Big Mike immediately bounded up the wooden steps leading to the royal bed and perched there as Master Shakespeare showed Penelope and Kathy the conveniences—a dining table seating four, two-burner stove, refrigerator, cabinets, a closet, shower, bathroom.

"It's quite nice," Penelope said. "Thank you."

"It's the least I could do for our new Queen. I'll drive it out and set it up right now."

Penelope snapped her fingers. "Is the old Queen's tent still there?"

Shakespeare's face darkened. "I'm afraid so. The police said it couldn't be taken down until the investigation was further along. It's very depressing."

Burke and Stoner had searched the tent. It was right there in the report, but they had found nothing to indicate the identity of the assassin. Ditto with their search of Carolyn Lewis's condominium. "Hmm," Penelope said. It wouldn't hurt to retrace their steps . . . perhaps a fresh eye . . . and a cold nose . . . it wouldn't be the first time Big Mike had happened upon an important clue. Decision made, Penelope said, "I'll follow you out there and just take a look through Carolyn's tent."

"But what about the police?" Shakespeare asked. "They might not allow—"

"Fiddlesticks. Of course, they want our help."

———

That wasn't quite true, but after a bit of grumbling and quite a number of admonishments not to destroy evidence, Burke and Stoner relented, even giving Penelope a key to Carolyn Lewis's condo. As she pulled away from the police department sans Big Mike, who had refused to budge from the RV's bed, Penelope's sense of futility lessened. At least I'm doing something, she thought.

Penelope had been to the Faire any number of times over the years, but never when the Elizabethan village had been deserted. The silence was eerie. Even in the bright sunshine of an Arizona afternoon, ghostly shades hovered, spectral presences from a dim past, watching Penelope with a grim and brooding silence.

Penelope looked over her shoulders frequently as she hurried through the village, past shuttered food stalls, gaming areas, an archery range, the juggling school, several pubs, the dunking tank for wenches, the military encampment and its parade ground.

She paused at the village green to examine the pillory. The lock was snapped shut through one hasp only, allowing Penelope to lift the crossbar. It was heavier than she expected. Although the frame had been cleaned, there were still dried tomato seeds adhering to the wood, evidence of near misses for the poor wenches imprisoned there. Penelope wondered if these were the very tomatoes hurled at Kathy as she dropped the crosspiece. A thud of finality broke the silence.

Crossing Kissing Bridge, Penelope thought, I'll have to bring Sir Walter here one fine evening. Then she stopped. On the far side of the bridge four wooden stakes marked with yellow crime scene tape formed a square. She approached cautiously and stared down at the spot where Carolyn Lewis had died.

Looking back, Penelope could just see the top of the pillory.

Hmm.

Retracing her steps, Penelope put her purse on the ground, lifted the crosspiece again, and placed her neck and wrists in the half-circles cut into the wood. The position was stooped, but by straining, imagining the hold of the pillory if it had been locked in place, she could just see the murder scene. But, of course, it had been dark and there were doubtless sounds of revelry. Even had Kathy been expecting something to happen, she probably would have seen or heard nothing.

Oh, well.

Engrossed in her experiment, Penelope did not hear the man who approached from behind on tiptoe. Her first warning was the creak of the hinge as he quickly lowered the bar over her neck and wrists. By then it was too late.

Oh, oh!

"And what do we have here?" a cheery voice exclaimed.

Penelope decided not to panic, although her heart was rattling around her throat at the moment. She pushed against the heavy plank to no avail. He—whoever *he* was—held it down tightly.

Damn. Double damn!

"Let me go," Penelope said, immediately ranking her statement as one of the dumbest things she could say under the circumstances, rather like people who fainted and awakened to say, Where am I?

"Not until you give me your phone number."

Penelope craned her neck and looked up to find a handsome young face smiling down at her. She thought it odd that his blondish hair was closely cropped. "Certainly not. Who are you?"

"Just a poor struggling actor bewitched by your charms."

"Oh, *donnez-moi un* break," Penelope said disgustedly, but added politely, *"s'il vous plaît."*

"Huh?"

"I said give me a break. In French. Bewitched, indeed."

"I studied German."

That would explain the hair. "What are you acting in?"

"Oh, just some scenes here at the Faire. I'll let you go if you give me a kiss."

"Ha!"

"We've reached an impasse, I'm afraid."

"I'm going to scream."

"There's no one to hear you," he said reasonably.

That was probably true. Will Shakespeare and Big Mike were all the way across the grounds. Mycroft was probably still asleep. Big help he was. "I'll do it anyway."

"Will you go out with me?"

Penelope had been approached by suitors in a variety of ways since reaching adolescence. Andy had babbled idiotically, blushing and stammering, until Penelope had consented to go out with him as a life-saving act of mercy, fearing he would die of acute embarrassment otherwise. But no one had ever asked her for a date while holding her locked in a pillory, when a gigantic itch was building in the tip of her nose.

It started in the sole of her left foot, traveled like a raging wildfire through her body, and settled at the very end of her nose. She twitched her nose to no avail. By crossing her eyes she could just bring the offending part of her body into a fuzzy focus. Penelope really was going to scream if . . .

"Would you scratch my nose, please?"

"I'd be delighted."

Penelope sighed. How did Kathy stand being locked up so long? Of course, she had Timmy to happen by and scratch her nose—and anything else that might itch. "Thank you."

"You're welcome. Now, how about that date?"

"I never date actors. My sister is an actress. You're all unstable." Although Penelope loved Cassie dearly, her sister was . . . well . . . given to artistic quirks.

"You're Penelope Warren. Storm Williams's sister."

"How did you know that?"

"I have to go now." He retreated hastily, turned, ran.

Penelope freed herself in time to see the back of her would-be suitor disappearing between the ironmonger's establishment and the candlemaker's shop.

Now, what was that all about?

Penelope arrived at the campgrounds to find Master Shakespeare pacing nervously in front of the RV. An awning was unfurled from the roof, creating a small shaded patio area. Red pennants fluttered gaily from the struts. Mycroft emerged from the door, stretching and yawning.

"There you are. I was getting worried. I thought you were lost."

"I decided to walk through the Fairegrounds. I bumped into someone." Penelope described her Lothario, leaving out the details of their encounter.

"There's no one at the Faire by that description," Shakespeare said.

"But he said he was an actor at the Faire."

"I know all the actors and actresses, even those in Marlowe's upstart company, and there's no one like that."

"That's strange."

"Yes, indeed. He's an impostor. Do you think . . . ?"

A sudden chill made Penelope's flesh crawl. But he was so handsome with a nice smile and a strong voice. How could he be a killer? Still, that's what they had said about Ted Bundy. How could he . . . ?

"I don't know," Penelope said. "I should have asked for *his* phone number."

Refreshed from his nap, Big Mike burrowed eagerly beneath the flaps of Carolyn's royal enclosure while Penelope and Master Shakespeare raised and fastened the side flaps to allow in light.

Penelope paused to survey the interior. The crime lab technicians had dusted for prints. The thin residue was on everything that might conceivably yield a usable print.

On a small wooden crate beside the spartan camp cot where Carolyn Lewis apparently slept there was a framed photograph—most unelizabethan, Penelope thought—of Carolyn as the Queen with Sir Robert Dudley, both resplendent in their finery, smiling happily for the camera. Penelope blew at the dust and unfastened the backing and looked behind the photograph. Nothing.

As she replaced it, Master Shakespeare said, "There was quite a scandal brewing before . . . before Carolyn was killed. Sir Robert was caught with an Irish actress. Carolyn was quite angry about it."

"I will speak to Sir Robert about that on the morrow," Penelope said, looking around the tent. It was quite large and spacious, big enough to hold an armoire, two ice chests, camp cook stoves, a small bookcase filled with books about Elizabethan England, and a boom box.

Idly, Penelope turned the radio on. An awful squall of heavy metal blasted through the tent. She hastily reduced the volume and pressed another button. It was preset to a classical music station. The haunting melody of Tchaikovsky's *Swan Lake* now drifted soothingly through the tent, making Penelope's heart ache with its beauty as it always did.

Once started with the boom box, Penelope continued through the other preset stations. Radio stations, like books, were revealing of an individual. Rush Limbaugh nattered on about liberals. Ugh! Surely, Carolyn wasn't a Rush devotee. Next came soft rock. Then easy listening, oldies but goodies, country-western.

No heavy metal. That was strange, Penelope thought, someone other than Carolyn had been listening to that station. She went back to *Swan Lake.* "Sorry, Mikey," she said, turning to the armoire, "no Jimmy."

Jimmy Buffett was Mycroft's favorite singer. But as Penelope was fond of telling everyone, "Of course he's going to like anyone named for a cat food." A devoted Parrot Head, Big Mike would even, on occasion when the mood struck him, wear the shark's fin Penelope had made for him.

Penelope flung the doors of the armoire open, and sifted through the royal gowns and bodices hanging there. Mycroft decided to explore the lower levels and rummaged through the royal slippers carelessly tossed aside.

When he emerged, Penelope asked, "Find anything, Mikey?" Taking his silence as a reply in the negative, Penel-

ope turned to find Master Will staring at them with bemuse-
ment. "He's quite good, really," she explained. "He has
found important clues on other occasions."

Master Will only nodded.

"Really," Penelope persisted.

"I better close up the RV," Will said. "We can leave the
tent open. It needs a good airing." He didn't need to add that
he thought the royal brain could use a good airing as well.

Although Mycroft sniffed dutifully about the tent—somewhat lackadaisically, Penelope thought—his nose failed to
turn up anything of interest unless you counted the lizard that
scurried from beneath the cot to climb the wall of the tent, a
retreat from harm's way.

After dropping Will Shakespeare at his place of business, Penelope and Big Mike repeated the process at Carolyn's condominium. Small, pleasant, and light, the condominium was
exactly what Penelope expected. The bookcases were filled
with various historical works. Carolyn had set up a small office, where she doubtless corrected student papers, planned
classes, and attended to personal business.

No heavy metal. The CDs tended to the classics, as did the
radio stations. In fact, the stations were preset to the same stations as the boom box in her tent, including Rush Limbaugh.

Double ugh!

There were no secret compartments hidden away, no fantasy apparel tucked away at the back of closets, no diary to
yield a suspect—Burke and Stoner were working through
Carolyn's address book—nothing taped beneath the lid of the
toilet or the dresser drawers.

The yearbook dedicated to Carolyn was in a place of honor

on the coffee table. While Mycroft, worn out from the afternoon's exertions, curled up beside her on the couch, Penelope leafed through the yearbook, reading the inscriptions from Carolyn's former students. The sentiments were of the gushy sort, proclaiming what a wonderful teacher Mrs. Lewis was, how much they had learned, how they would never forget her.

Penelope closed the yearbook finally and looked about the condominium again. It was all disgustingly normal. So much for assisting the police with their inquiries.

What a wasted day.

"Come on, Mikey, let's get back to the shop. Maybe we can sell a book or two at least. Contribute to the pursuit of literature in some small way."

When Penelope saw the long white stretch limousine parked in front of Mycroft & Company, she knew that literature would be on hold for a time.

Storm Williams, Empty Creek's favorite B-movie queen, had returned from her latest triumph in Tinsel Town. Her stage name had been acquired over lunch in the Polo Lounge with her agent. It was a tribute to his fondness for various burlesque queens in his youth.

There was a great deal of squealing, giggling, and mewing—Mycroft adored Stormy, his auntie Cassie in real life—as Penelope and Big Mike exchanged greetings with Stormy and her entourage of Dutch Fowler and John the chauffeur.

"We decided to skip the wrap party," Cassie said when calm was restored. "Dutch was worried about you and I didn't want to miss your royal debut."

"I'm perfectly capable of taking care of myself, Dutch."

"Just like Christmas?"

"We had the drop on him."

"He had the drop on you."

"Whatever. I would have come up with something."

"Not again," John groaned. "Death follows Penelope Warren."

"Don't you start in on me, John."

"I worry about you too, sweetie."

"Well, what have you been up to since we talked?" Dutch asked. He couldn't stay mad at his future sister-in-law for long. And, he had to admit, Penelope and Big Mike did make pretty damned good detectives.

"Well . . ." Penelope quickly outlined the day's nonevents for the police chief, saving her brief imprisonment in the pillory for last.

"Describe him," Dutch demanded. His face darkened as he listened.

"Do you know him?"

"No," Dutch replied. "It didn't occur to you that he might have been the killer?"

"Of course it did," Penelope said, "but as it turned out, he just wanted a date."

"Why did he run, then?" Dutch asked.

That very thought had been in and out of Penelope's mind all afternoon.

Why *did* he run?

"Fear of rejection?" Penelope replied lamely.

CHAPTER
FIVE

The little community of Empty Creek, Arizona is more than a trifle whimsical in its odd collection of personalities, various free spirits, old desert rats, snowbirds, aging refugees from the 1960s, and a variety of fiercely independent individuals.

The varying strata of Empty Creek society is also sharply divided in loyalties to various pastimes and activities.

In addition to all of the more normal groups found in any community—the chamber-of-commerce set, the civic-minded crowd, the do-gooders—there's the horsey set—men, women, and children who live, and sometimes die, in the pursuit of all things equestrian, especially those in the Arabian community. Their activities culminate each year with the Empty Creek Arabian Horse Show, a respected preliminary to the Great Arabian Show of Scottsdale.

The cowboy-and-cowgirl faction are equally devoted to the Old Western Days celebration when, for a glorious long Labor Day weekend the small city is given over to gunslingers who enthusiastically recreate Empty Creek's own lesser-known and vastly overrated 1892 version of the Gunfight at the O.K. Corral. It was actually a shootout at Miller's Feed Store in which, despite the copious amounts of ammunition expended, the only casualty was to Bad Bart Brown when he rolled off the roof into a horse trough, managing to break his leg in the process. Most eyewitnesses agreed that Bad Bart was drunk at the time and no threat to society. And, as Nora Pryor, the well-known local historian pointed out in her excellent little book *Empty Creek: A History and Guide*, the trough had served a public need because Bad Bart was certainly badly in need of a bath.

They hung him anyway with a two-by-four strapped to his leg as a makeshift cast and a festive day was enjoyed by all, including Bad Bart, drunk again, who went to the gallows singing a bawdy version of "The Girl I Left Behind Me." They were going to hang her too—the girl he was leaving behind, at least momentarily—just for good riddance, but the sheriff took a shine to Milly and ended up marrying the little trollop who, after bearing ten children in holy matrimony, founded a church choir. Milly Street, Milly Lane, and Milly Park remain as permanent testimonies to the strength of her conversion.

At least the horse show and the Western Days celebration bear some slight resemblance to Empty Creek's frontier heritage. Not so with the Springe Faire and those who passionately spend the greatest part of their year devoted to all things Elizabethan and to planning the rites of spring in Merrie Olde England in a bleak, if beautiful, desert setting where the mock English village is surrounded by forests of stately saguaro cactus.

Now, that, as Tweedledee had pointed out, is a crazy group.

Penelope found driving into the Faire for the first time as Queen rather incongruous. For one thing, it was too damned early in the morning. Here she was at seven o'clock, practically the middle of the damned night, on her way to the Faire.

For another, the trappings of the twentieth century were all too visible. Contrails from an airliner streaked across the blue sky. In the distance, a train huffed its way across the desert.

For yet another, Penelope's Jeep was hardly the conveyance for Elizabeth Regina. God save the Queen. Hip, hip, huzzah. Hip, hip, huzzah. Hip, hip, barf.

Besides all that, the damned bodice was too tight.

"How did we get into this, Mikey?"

Mycroft, on the other hand, despite the early hour and the indignity of wearing a rabato around his royal neck and the royal cloak, seemed eager to get started. Probably he had heard about the roasted turkey legs to be had for the asking.

The road was marked by signs at intervals.

1995

Of course it's 1995. What else could it be?

1895

Really.

1795

Penelope pulled to the side of the road and stopped. The desert hardly provided the proper atmosphere for an Elizabethan village nestled in the green fields of Merrie Olde England. Saguaro cactus stood their lonely vigils, arms outstretched to the heavens. Penelope shook her head and drove on.

1695

Again Penelope stopped. She closed her eyes and willed the twentieth century to go away. The distant train whistled and destroyed the mood. Penelope squinched her eyes tight. I am the Queen. I am the Queen.

Once again Penelope drove down the dirt road, curving around a bend to approach the last sign. She had arrived.

1595

The green fields of Olde England!

Huzzah!

My God! I do feel like Elizabeth Regina.

Panic set in, however, when Penelope parked the Jeep near the RV and stared from the twentieth century across the fence into the sixteenth. She sighed and climbed out of the Jeep. Accompanied by the Royal Cat, armed with a number-fifteen sun screen, and more than just a little daunted, Penelope hiked her voluminous skirts and started across the footbridge. Big Mike, who was rarely daunted by anything, raced ahead to peer down into the placid man-made stream at several big fat fish swimming in the clear water. Despite an aversion to water, Mycroft's tail twitched eagerly and he seemed determined to find a method for fishing without getting his paws wet. The Royal Cat left the fish behind and followed the Queen only after much urging.

The same delegation that had persuaded Penelope to ascend the throne of England now waited at the Faire's gate. "Your Majesty," Sir Francis Drake, Sir Francis Bacon, and Master Will Shakespeare chorused, doffing their hats. A bright-eyed—and far too cheery—Lady Kathleen Allan curtsied deeply.

"Oh, get up," Penelope said.

"We can't, Your Majesty."

"Not until you say, 'Good morrow.' "

Penelope smiled graciously, inclined her head in a most regal manner, and said, "Good morrow."

"Oh, perfect, Your Majesty," Lady Kathleen said, rising.

"Yes, I rather thought so myself."

"Now, for the business at hand," Bacon said.

"There's a great deal to do," Drake said. "You must meet everyone and then there's the royal procession at ten and the jousts at two, several civil matters pending that must be decided, various affairs of court. . . ."

The next hour passed in a flurry of activity. The new Queen met a succession of personages, courtiers, ladies-in-waiting, the Lord High Mayor, the Lord High Sheriff, Sir Phillip Sydney, and Sir Robert Dudley.

"Your Majesty," Sir Robert said, bowing low and taking Penelope's hand, kissing and holding it a great deal longer than propriety dictated. "It will be such a pleasure to serve you. I shall be your constant companion."

"But what of Rosalind, Sir Robert?" Lady Kathleen asked sweetly.

"A mere trifle, Your Majesty. I shall be at *your* side now. After all," Sir Robert said, leering at Penelope's sun-screened breasts, "Sir Robert and Elizabeth Regina *were* lovers." He smiled, bowed, backed away, and tripped over the Royal Cat, who squalled loudly, more for effect and to get the rules straight from the beginning than out of pain.

"Goddammit," Sir Robert cried as he fell to his backside.

Sir Francis Drake guffawed loudly. Bacon and Shakespeare were more circumspect in their display of amusement.

Her Majesty held up a warning finger. "Sir Robert," she said sternly. "There will be no strong language at court."

"Of course, Your Majesty," he said, scrambling to his feet, attempting to regain his dignity.

Penelope giggled and dismissed him airily. "What was that all about?" she asked when Sir Robert had fled.

"Well," Kathy said, "Sir Robert, his real name is—"

"Never mind his real name. I'll have enough trouble remembering all the Faire names. This place is a schizophrenic's delight."

"Anyway, Sir Robert is an old lech," Kathy said. "He's from Scottsdale," she added, as though that explained everything.

"I know all that. Shakespeare told me. And now he thinks he'll resume his affair with the Queen just because it's historically accurate. I think I'll banish him to the Americas. He can go off and discover yams or something."

"But, Your Majesty, this *is* the Americas."

"So it is. Well, he can just keep out of this Queen's way. I shall pick my lover for the Faire."

"Where is Sir Walter anyway?"

"Oh, he'll be along later. At any rate, Sir Walter is in and Sir Robert is out."

Strolling through the Faire before the gates opened, greeting her subjects, Penelope was reminded of the opening of Laurence Olivier's magnificent film *Henry V*, where the actors of the Globe scurried about frantically offstage, getting into costume, applying makeup, rehearsing difficult lines, nervously waiting for the play to begin. Then the chorus spoke the opening lines, and the Globe, scarcely noticed by the viewer, was transformed from a stage to the vast fields of England and France.

So it was with the Faire. All about the royal entourage, the players of the day's drama prepared for their roles. Jugglers juggled, fools fooled, archers arched, wenches wenched, singers sang, fiddlers fiddled, criers cried, trumpeters trumpeted—all in nervous discordant bedlam.

Some few of her subjects, Penelope was pleased to see, were more engrossed with opening their eyes, drinking coffee, and eating hot cross buns cheerfully dispensed by a young serving wench singing "Alive, alive-o," as she stroked Big Mike, who was on the counter, probably trying to decide whether or not he wanted a hot cross bun or if he should wait for a roasted turkey leg. Drake, Bacon, and Shakespeare excused themselves to join the Royal Cat.

A company of pikemen drilled on the village green, marching and wheeling about rather raggedly. Penelope thought she might get out there one day and shape them up. Any boot platoon at Parris Island could march better after a day or two of screams and curses from impatient drill instructors.

Drake's mariners were busily engaged in putting the Golden Hind, a rather unseaworthy replica, to sea in the shallow lake.

Penelope stopped abruptly when the shutters on Master Edwards's shop, Ironmonger by Appointment to Her Royal Majesty, flew open with a clatter. Apparently, ironmongering covered quite a wide range of wares, as well as instruments for guarding the moral turpitude of the Queen's subjects. There on display in the bright morning sunshine were good English broadswords, lances, foils, daggers, and knives of all descriptions, various shackles, manacles, lengths of chain—and chastity belts.

Lady Kathleen, who had been following her Queen at a discreet three paces to the rear, was momentarily distracted by the juggler of her dreams and nearly rammed the royal personage.

"Be careful, child," Penelope said mildly.

"Sorry, Your Majesty, I was—"

"I know. You were making goo-goo eyes at Timmy," Penelope said. "Again. Don't you two ever think of anything but the S word?"

The Lady Kathleen blushed. "Sometimes we—"

"Oh, never mind." Penelope turned her attention to Master Edwards, a burly individual with a graying full beard. Bare-chested, he wore breeches and a leather apron.

"Welcome to our humble Faire, Your Majesty."

"Good morrow," the Queen replied. "I see you have an interesting array of weaponry."

"The very finest in the land, Majesty."

"Do you sell to my loyal subjects as well as Fairegoers?" Penelope asked.

"My best customers, Majesty. Why, only last week Sir Robert Dudley purchased a new dagger. He's quite the collector, you know."

"Isn't that interesting? Do you keep records?"

Master Edwards nodded. "Ever since I started at Faire, Your Majesty. Ten years now, it is."

"Who else has made purchases of late?"

"Oh, too many to count, Majesty. Several members of Captain Sneddon's Companie of Foote were here last weekend to equip themselves. There was"—Master Edwards enumerated a great many loyal subjects and members of court—"and then if we count the rubes—"

"Rubes?" Penelope questioned.

"That's what we call the Fairegoers. Rubes."

"How uncharitable."

"They can be rather impossible on occasion," Lady Kathleen offered helpfully. "Sort of like Mrs. Burnham."

"I see," Penelope mused, fingering a dagger.

"Something in a royal stiletto, Majesty?"

"No, I think not." Penelope turned to Kathy and smiled rather ominously. "I was thinking more of a chastity belt."

"Should I wrap it or will Your Majesty wear it?"

Lady Kathleen giggled.

Her Majesty said, "Don't be impertinent. Do you deliver?"

"For Your Majesty, anything. . . ."

"Good. Send it to my . . . my . . ." Penelope was stuck. Asking for a chastity belt to be delivered to a recreational vehicle hardly seemed appropriate under the circumstances. Then she snapped her fingers most unroyally. "Send it to Windsor. I shall be in residence there. You do take credit cards?"

"Of course, Majesty."

"Good. And since you'll be in the neighborhood, you might as well send along copies of your records for the last five years."

Master Edwards groaned. "But, Majesty . . ."

"Five years, Master Edwards." Penelope glanced at the Lord High Sheriff. "Otherwise, well, a word to the Royal Tax Collector might be in order."

"As you wish, Majesty," Master Edwards said with a heavy sigh.

"Come, Lady Kathleen, we must collect the Royal Cat and be off."

A subdued Kathy waited until they were away from the ironmonger before asking, "You're not going to make me wear that horrid thing, are you?"

"It's a thought," Penelope said, smiling gently, "but, no, I was thinking it would be a nice gag gift for our friend, the Ravishing Redhead."

A cannon boomed and there was a flourish of trumpets from the main gate.

"We must hurry, Your Majesty," Sir Francis Bacon said. "The Faire is open and we have to get ready for the royal procession. The stage manager doesn't like us to be late. He was always threatening to kill . . ." Bacon nearly choked on his words.

"Do go on, Sir Francis," Penelope said. "Kill whom?"

Sir Francis Bacon swallowed before replying, "Carolyn. She was always late."

"Really? We shall have to speak to the stage manager about that."

If Penelope had thoughts of questioning the stage manager before the royal procession began, they vanished with the onset of a severe case of stage fright. Big Mike, resplendent in his royal accoutrements, seemed to revel in the chaotic activities. Perched on the gate of an enclosure open only to Faire participants, he looked on with interest as the stage manager scurried about frenetically in an effort to organize his charges in the proper order.

Her Majesty, however, closed her eyes and forced herself to think of lemons, hoping that the sour taste thus imagined would drive the dizziness away. It did. But then her hands began to tremble and her knees shook. Oh, how did I ever get into this?

A pike clattered to the ground.

You'll sleep with that pike tonight, Penelope thought automatically, despite the queasiness in her stomach—the memories of Parris Island and boot camp never faded. Your pike is your best friend. Your pike will save your life. You must take care of your pike. A marine dropped her rifle only once. The ensuing lesson was never forgotten.

The stage manager—wearing the brightly colored regalia of the court jester and the floppy three-pointed fool's cap with bells attached—tinkled as he ran to and fro, alternately shouting commands at the members of the royal procession and whispering into the walkie-talkie hidden in the cardboard baton he carried.

"Form up!" the stage manager cried. "The rubes are waiting. The rubes are waiting."

"Who is he whispering to?" Penelope asked.

"The security guards," Kathy replied. "They keep him informed."

Penelope groaned.

"Your Majesty, are you all right?"

"In the words of the immortal Sheridan Whiteside," Elizabeth Regina replied, 'I may vomit.' "

Despite her stage fright, Penelope managed to plant a smile, if a frozen and ghastly one, on her face as she climbed into the sedan chair, arranged her skirts about her, and took the Royal Cat from Lady Kathleen.

Two muscular pages hoisted the sedan chair to their shoulders. "The damn cat's too fat," one grumbled.

If Big Mike heard the remark, he decided to grant mercy and allow the offending page to live.

The trumpets blasted a flourish and the royal procession set out on its tour of the Faire.

A page stepped out smartly, carrying the Queen's banner with the intertwined initials ER.

A crier was next. "Hear ye, hear ye, Her Gracious Majesty, Queen Elizabeth, Ruler of All England, Keeper of the Faith, et cetera, et cetera."

The trumpeters punctuated each announcement of the royal presence with flourishes.

The Lord High Mayor and the Lord High Sheriff were next.

"Keep your distance," the stage manager hissed as the Queen and the Royal Cat passed through the gate.

The court followed at a respectful distance.

The company of pikemen brought up the rear.

"Huzzah!" the cheer went up from loyal subjects and rubes alike. "Huzzah!"

Penelope paled. My God, she thought. All of Empty Creek is here.

"Huzzah!"

Penelope was beginning to relax and enjoy her new role when trouble loomed. Smiling, naturally now, inclining her head, waving most regally, Elizabeth Regina greeted her subjects.

Debbie and Sam Connors waved to her. Alyce Smith curtsied deeply. Alyce wore a gown decorated with the signs of the zodiac. I shall make her the Royal Astrologer, Penelope thought as she acknowledged Alyce's curtsy.

All along the Queen's passage, men and women, boys and girls, bowed and curtsied and cheered.

Stormy wore an elegant brocaded gown in blue. She waved and jumped up and down, curtsied, and bounced some more. A dour Dutch Fowler, wearing cowboy boots and hat, jeans and a western shirt, stood beside Stormy. Apparently, the wizard costume had met with little enthusiasm.

Penelope did something that Elizabeth Regina would never do. She stuck her tongue out at Dutch and made him laugh. That's better, she thought.

The Royal Cat traveled back and forth over the Queen's lap to greet his admirers—and there were many who sent up a cheer for Big Mike.

Wally grinned and waved shyly. Beside her constant companion, Laney held Alexander up to see his friend. Alex barked excitedly. Alexander was tiny, but the same could not be said for his heart and bark.

And therein lay the rub.

A peasant dog in the form of a German shepherd took up the cry. He was quickly joined by a collie, two shih tzus, and a pug.

The sedan chair swayed precariously as the excited dogs barked and yapped and jumped and generally got underfoot.

Big Mike, never one to shy away from a good fight, raised the hair on his back, flattened his ears, hissed loudly, and then issued a challenge of his own, sending up a heart-stopping howl.

For a brief instant Penelope was tempted to grab Mycroft, but sanity instantly intervened. She had once come between

Big Mike and another tomcat during a less-than-friendly discussion about Murphy Brown, Mike's sleek—if sometimes
fickle—paramour. Big Mike let Penelope know immediately
that a cat's gotta do what a cat's gotta do. After sending the
intruding tom in hasty flight, Mycroft apologized, of course,
as Penelope attempted to staunch the flow of blood from her
cheek. She looked on it now as her own dueling scar but had
no intention of getting another to match. The dogs were on
their own.

Big Mike squalled and emitted another ferocious howl and
then apparently decided to hell with it. A little exercise—
nothing to excess—was a good thing.

Big Mike picked his target and leapt, landing on the German shepherd's back, digging in with all four paws. The
shepherd's mother had apparently neglected to instruct her
litter to beware of Abyssinian alley cats from Abyssinia wearing rabatos, an oversight Mycroft was busily correcting until
the big dog managed to dislodge the cat, sending him flying
and skidding through the dirt. A whimpering shepherd fled
the battlefield to lick his wounds behind a Porta Potti.

"Put me down!" the Queen cried over the bedlam.

The pages nearly dumped Elizabeth Regina right into the
melee, but somehow managed to right the sedan chair and
lower it to the ground.

Despite Laney's efforts, Alexander squirmed free and
joined the fray, racing to his friend's rescue.

More dust flew as Big Mike dropped the pug with a right
cross. The pug howled as streaks of bright red blood appeared
on its nose.

The shih tzus were high-tailing it out of Dodge with Alexander in furious pursuit. Laney shrieked and took off after them.

The collie growled and stood its ground.

Penelope had to admire the collie's courage, if not his brain, as Big Mike went into his bear imitation, rearing high on his hind legs, squalling loudly, skittering sideways toward the lone dog, who was trying desperately to uphold canine honor.

Courage failed the collie, however. He turned and ran, leaving Big Mike in sole possession of the field of honor.

"Stand back," Penelope cried. "Give him room."

Big Mike lowered himself to the ground, sat, and began to wash a paw. His rabato was askew, hanging by a thread, but he didn't seem to mind. It was a little too frilly for his taste anyway.

When Mycroft was calmed and order was restored, Penelope briefly considered issuing a royal proclamation that all dogs must remain on a leash, at least in Mycroft's presence, but she didn't believe that dogs should be restrained. They deserved their freedom, but they would just have to take their chances with Big Mike.

"Goddamnedest cat I ever saw," a man said.

It was a comment Penelope had heard quite often over the years. Shaking her head sadly, Penelope thought, so much for my first royal procession.

Then she saw Lothario lurking at the back of the crowd.

CHAPTER
SIX

"Forsooth, what a cat, Your Majesty."

"Those who'll play with cats must expect to be scratched," Penelope replied.

"How very wise, Your Majesty."

"Cervantes wrote it," Penelope said. "He was, indeed, wise."

"Oh, but *Don Quixote* hasn't been written yet."

"More's the pity."

Other sentiments regarding cats, dogs, and the human condition buzzed through the crowd, but Her Majesty was distracted. It was definitely her Lothario of the afternoon before. He was in costume now, wearing a doublet and a long, dark-haired wig. Still, Penelope was positive of the identification. She ignored the stage manager and his attempts to reorganize the procession and turned to the Lord High Sheriff.

"Arrest him!" Penelope commanded, pointing to the crowd.

"Who, Your Majesty?" The Lord High Sheriff was willing

to arrest anyone the Queen wanted in custody. After all, he had told the Lord High Mayor just before the caterwauling started how cute he found the new Queen, and he was eager to make a good impression. But confronted with a milling crowd of performers and patrons alike, he wasn't at all sure which *him* the Queen referred to.

"Quick! He's getting away!" Penelope cried as Lothario ducked from sight.

"Get him!" the Sheriff ordered his assistants, who were equally baffled.

"Oh, never mind," Penelope said. "He's gone now."

Not wanting to disappoint the Queen any more than he already had, the Lord High Sheriff asked, "Is there anyone else you would like arrested, Your Majesty?"

As a matter of fact . . .

The royal eyes fastened upon the stage manager. Penelope had grown rather tired of his running about, hissing like a demented lizard, pushing and pulling people into line. He was quite out of line for a lowly court jester or a fool or whatever he was. Still, he might have been granted the benefit of the royal doubt had the Queen not heard him mutter, "Stupid damned cat."

"Arrest *him*. Toss him in the royal hoosegow."

"Happily, Your Majesty," the Lord High Sheriff said.

After the stage manager had been hustled away to the loud cheers of the court, the royal procession resumed without further incident. Apparently, the word had quickly spread throughout the canine community not to mess with the Royal Cat, just as the word was rapidly communicated through the Faire community not to mess with the new Queen.

The procession even managed to make it to the Royal Pavilion at the appointed hour of eleven o'clock, where Queen Elizabeth I took her throne to the cheers of the assembled multitudes sitting in the stands around the lists. Big Mike— sans rabato and cloak—nestled in her lap and promptly fell asleep while a series of proclamations were read, declaring the Faire open for various amusements, urging one and all to eat, drink, and be merrye for the duration of the springe fest.

Captain Sneddon's Companie of Foote marched in and raised a cheer for Her Gracious Majesty.

"Hip, hip, huzzah!"

After Captain Sneddon and his troops retired, armored knights clattered in on horseback to pledge fidelity and spirited combat during the afternoon jousts.

The Spanish ambassador presented his credentials.

Through it all, the Queen smiled and nodded patiently, pronouncing her royal blessing on each of the proceedings, blissfully unaware that behind her the royal court seethed with Machiavellian intrigue as members of the court plotted to gain favor with the new Queen, bring old scores to a reckoning, and settle new ones with a vengeance.

To say nothing of the special guests in the Royal Pavilion.

Andy, in the guise of Sir Walter Raleigh—Penelope had pleaded to no avail to have the programs changed to the correct spelling of his name—hurried into the Royal Pavilion and stopped abruptly, blinking with amazement at the assembly of characters standing about with flagons of ale singing "God Save the Queen."

When the rendition was over, he approached the Queen and bowed awkwardly, doffing and dropping his cap and cloak in the process. The members of court withdrew politely to allow the Queen and her consort a moment of privacy, taking the opportunity to belly up to the bar and refill their flagons.

Sir Walter kissed the proffered royal hand before rising. "I'm sorry to be so late, but I was doing the laundry and my underwear was too hot when it came out of the dryer and so I put it in the freezer to cool for a bit."

Penelope stared at him.

"Thirty minutes was too long," he added solemnly.

"My God," Penelope said, "I have a boyfriend who freezes his underwear. Wait until I tell Laney."

"You wouldn't!"

"I would! At the earliest opportunity. I hope nothing important caught a chill."

"I don't think so. It seemed like a good idea at the time."

They were interrupted by the Lord High Mayor, who handed each of them a flagon.

"Thank you," Penelope and Andy said.

"Ruling the world is a thirsty business, Your Majesty," the Lord High Mayor said. "And remember, there is justice to dispense later."

"Oh, very well," Penelope said. "What must I do?"

"The cases will be presented to you for arbitration. Your decision is based on the facts and the merits of each. It's all ad lib and your subjects will try to make you break character. It can be quite amusing. At least, it was in the old days. Carolyn was such a prude. No sense of humor."

"I shall do my best," Penelope promised. If the rest of her reign was like the first morning, Penelope decided, she would have no sense of humor left either.

Her friends crowded around.

Stormy gave her a sisterly kiss on the cheek. "You were wonderful," she said proudly. "I couldn't have done better myself."

"Not bad," Dutch said. High praise.

"Wasn't Alexander brave?" Laney said. "Jumping right in to help Mikey like that? He chased those shih tzus all the way to Scotland. I think you should make him a privy councilor or something."

The laconic Wally crinkled his eyes in approval.

"Pretty good, Penelope, pretty good," Debbie said.

"Sure was," Sam Connors said.

"Thank you all," Penelope said. "Dutch, could I see you a moment, please?"

Big Mike, befitting a cat of his royal rank, intelligence, curiosity, size, and appetite, explored the Royal Pavilion, beginning with the plates of hors d'oeuvres set out at one end of the long bar where members of the court clustered, enthusiastically slaking their thirst. Mycroft sniffed disdainfully at the fruit plate, various cheeses and crackers, and the bowls of mixed nuts. Someone was going to have to speak to the Royal Caterer. There wasn't a chicken liver or a mixed grill to be found in all England apparently.

Fortunately, however, the lusty wench behind the bar quickly realized the Royal Pavilion was severely lacking in feline delicacies and filched the roasted turkey leg that had just been delivered for the bartender's lunch.

"Hey, that's mine," he protested, quite out of character for the Elizabethan publican he portrayed.

"Send for another," she replied, taking a knife to the turkey leg and chopping the dark meat into cat-sized bites, thereby making a friend for life if temporarily putting the landlord of the Royal Pavilion out of sorts.

Big Mike tucked into the repast with considerable gusto, demonstrating his gastronomic pleasure with soft growls, eating with a single-minded dedication until the last speck of meat was lapped up and the empty dish gleamed. He looked up at the barmaid then with placid sparkling eyes and purred loudly in gratitude before settling back on his haunches to wash his face.

Thus, finished with his ablutions and resting comfortably on the bar, Big Mike had an excellent view of what would come to be known as the Day the Spanish Ambassador Got His.

"I saw him again," Penelope said. "He was lurking at the back of the crowd just after Mikey was attacked by the dogs."

"I thought it was the other way around," Dutch said. "Big Mike attacked the dogs."

"He was provoked. Be that as it may, I saw him."

"Who?"

"Lothario."

"Who?" Dutch repeated.

"Really, Dutch, if you're going to be a member of our family, you must follow conversations better than this," Penelope said with a degree of exasperation. "Lothario. The man who wouldn't let me out of the pillory until I gave him my phone number. He was disguised, but I know it was him. The Sheriff was going to arrest him, but he got away."

"I really wouldn't worry about him, Penelope."

"Not worry!" Penelope cried. "You were the one who told me he might be the killer."

"That was the other day." Dutch shrugged.

"Aren't you going to sic those two beagles of yours on the trail?"

"I don't think it's worth the trouble."

"Well, then, I'll just find him myself."

"You'd better not," Dutch muttered.

Penelope didn't hear these last words because she had turned away, steaming at Dutch's nonchalant attitude, just in time to see Sir Robert Dudley haul off and pop the Spanish ambassador in the jaw.

Now what?

Sir Robert danced from the pavilion hurriedly, rubbing and flexing his right hand, muttering, "Ow, ow, ow." In his wake, the Spanish ambassador sat in a dazed lump on the sawdust, rubbing his face and said most undiplomatically, "The son-of-a-bitch sucker punched me."

"Why?" Penelope asked.

"I don't know."

"You must have said or done something."

"All I said was that heavy metal was an affront to the human ear."

Penelope agreed. It was little more than din disguised as music, but it seemed to have some dubious role in the murder of the Queen. "I . . . I mean, we . . . will speak to Sir Robert. In the meantime, please extend our apologies to España and have a beer on the House of Tudor." She smiled graciously and helped the Spanish ambassador to his feet.

Now, where in the hell was Sir Robert? After all, there was that business with Amy Robsart.

During the short procession from the Royal Pavilion, the Queen took pity on the stage manager and ordered his early release from the pillory.

"I'll get you for this," the stage manager said as he wiped the residue of several well-aimed tomatoes from his face and hands. His fool's cap was askew.

"Just like you got Carolyn Lewis?" Penelope asked.

The stage manager paled. "I had nothing to do with that."

"I'm told you threatened to kill her on more than one occasion."

"A figure of speech. No more. She was always late. I try to do a good job, but no one cares, always running about, drinking, men chasing after women, the women more interested in parties than the performance. I get no cooperation whatsoever. I'm surprised we ever get the show started."

"Perhaps, if you were less demanding . . ." Penelope straightened his cap.

"Thank you."

"You're welcome."

"Without me nothing would ever get done."

As she watched the stage manager shuffle off, Penelope regretted her impetuous order. Lord Acton was indeed correct. "Power tends to corrupt and absolute power corrupts absolutely."

Justice was dispensed in the shade of a scrubby oak tree. A thronelike chair was provided for the Queen. Sir Walter Raleigh stood on one side; the Lord High Mayor took his place on the other side.

"Sheriff, do your duty."

A peasant was pulled from the crowd. He fell to his knees before the queen and clasped his loosely manacled hands beseechingly. "Mercy, Your Majesty," he cried.

"What is the complaint?" the Lord High Mayor asked.

"Charged with coveting Her Majesty's royal melons," the Sheriff announced loudly.

The rubes snickered.

Penelope felt a warm flush spreading through what she considered the royal melons. Another application of sun screen was definitely in order.

"But they were just there for the taking, all round and big and plump and warm from the sun. I couldn't help myself, Your Majesty. They were just so beautiful and succulent. Fairly ripe for the plucking."

Succulent, indeed. What kind of peasant was this?

Penelope's question was answered by the sly grin on the peasant's face. The handsome young rogue knew he had embarrassed his Queen.

"Poaching the royal melons is a most serious charge," Penelope began, eager to be finished with the case of the peasant and the royal melons.

The crowd guffawed.

The Queen blushed furiously and started anew. "You must keep your hands off the royal melons. . . ."

The crowd roared.

The Queen surrendered. "Oh, take him away and put him in the pillory."

"Bring Mistress Lockwood forth."

The Lord High Mayor leaned over and whispered to the

Queen. "Mistress Lockwood is well known for a variety of misdeeds and a sharp tongue. She's quite spirited."

"Aye, and keep your hands to yourself," a shrill voice cried. A handsome woman of about forty emerged from the crowd at the urging of the Sheriff's assistants. She was restrained in the shrew's fiddle, a wooden device with three rings, one locked about the woman's neck. The other two rings at the end of a wooden rod imprisoned her wrists before her.

Penelope noted that the Sheriff's assistants were careful in keeping a respectful distance from the woman who kicked out at the officers of the law.

"Aye, and I did nothing, Your Majesty. It was all the fault of that poor miserable worm of a husband of mine."

"Step forth, Master Lockwood," the Sheriff ordered.

A sheepish Master Lockwood, holding a piece of raw meat to his right eye, joined his wife. Like the royal officers, he stayed well away from Mistress Lockwood. Apparently, Master Lockwood had felt his beloved's wrath once that day already. At least, the discussion had been diverted from the royal melons.

"A shrew, Your Majesty, a veritable shrew, look at what she did to me." He removed the slab of meat from his eye.

His eye was certainly black. Penelope hoped that it was all makeup.

"Tell Her Majesty why I blackened your eye," Mistress Lockwood jeered. "You worm."

"Tell her!" the crowd shouted. "Tell her!"

Master Lockwood hung his head and mumbled something.

"Speak up, man," the Sheriff ordered.

"I wasn't able to perform my husbandly duties."

The crowd hooted.

"Dunk him." The women in the crowd cried. "Dunk him."

"Dunk *her*," the men in the crowd chanted. "Dunk her."

" 'Tis the custom for a shrew," the Lord High Mayor counseled. "The dunking tank is vacant at the moment."

"Dunk both of them," the Queen said, thinking it was quite a Solomonic decision.

Apparently the audience agreed for a cheer went up. "Huzzah!"

The Lockwoods were taken away to serve their hour in the dunking tank while rubes purchased leather balls to hurl at the target that would send one or the other of the Lockwoods plummeting from their perch into the cold water below. It was a harmless punishment. At one point or another, in one persona or another, most of the Faire participants served their time in the dunking tank, the pillory, or the scold's bridle.

"The final case is a dispute between playwrights, both seeking to honor Your Majesty."

A cry went up from the crowd. "The greatest writer in all England is coming."

The groundlings took up the chorus. "Ben Jonson is coming. Ben Jonson is coming."

"No, not Jonson."

"Christopher Marlowe?"

"Marlowe's dead, you silly piece of toad dung, knifed in a tavern brawl back in 1591."

"Marlowe's not dead. He came back."

"Well, by God's truth, he should be. Damnable atheist."

"If not Marlowe, who then?"

"It's Master William Shakespeare."

"Who?"

"That hack!"

"He'll never amount to anything."

Some of the loyal subjects continued to hoot as Master William Shakespeare bowed low before the Queen.

Apparently the atheist was not dead after all, for a young and smirking Christopher Marlowe, dressed all in black, bowed as well, managing somehow to make the gesture insolent. His hair was long and hung to his shoulders. He wore a thin mustache.

"State your cases."

"Majesty," Shakespeare said, "this upstart encroaches upon our performances, demanding time on our humble stage. Besides, he's supposed to be dead. After all, this is 1595."

"Upstart, indeed, Majesty. The name of Marlowe rivals that of Shakespeare, now and forever. We, my poor players and I, simply wish to use the stage on occasion so that the people may see a real drama, scenes from *The Tragical History of Doctor Faustus* and *Tamburlaine the Great.*"

"The stage is reserved for our use," Shakespeare cried. He was trembling. "Let him perform on the village green. He deserves no better."

Marlowe drew his foil and waved it menacingly. "Arm yourself," he shouted, confirming his reputation for brawling. "We'll decide this on the village green, indeed."

"Stop," the Queen cried, awakening Big Mike, who looked about for the danger. "Enough of this dispute." She pointed to Marlowe. "Never draw your weapon in our presence again." Penelope waited until the foil had been replaced. "And you," she said, turning her royal finger to Shakespeare, "there is room enough for both of you. Marlowe will not use your stage, but he may erect his own platform at the opposite side of the village. I don't care what year it is. We will have no more of this prattling. Are we understood?"

"Your Majesty is too kind," Marlowe said, bowing low once more.

"Jerk," Shakespeare muttered as he bowed.

"What was that all about?" Penelope asked as the players of their respective companies gathered about Shakespeare and Marlowe, and the crowd dispersed to their various amusements.

"They hate each other," the Lord High Mayor said. "The rivalry is intense."

"But . . . but," Penelope said, indicating the elements of a bygone England all about them, "this is just a game."

"Not for some, Your Majesty."

Penelope quickly discovered, as Carolyn before her, that a Queen's work was never done. After holding court, it was back to the Royal Pavilion for the afternoon combats. The stands were filled and the crowd cheered as the knights, on spirited steeds, approached the Queen.

Penelope gave her champion a scarf to wear upon his wrist during the joust. In return, the White Knight pledged both fealty and victory.

The Black Knight made the same pledges to the Queen and to his own lady fair, lowering his lance to receive a similar token from the dazzling beauty, Lady Allison.

Steel visors clanked shut in final salute, and the two knights cantered to their respective squires.

The knights thundered at each other, shields clanged, wooden lances splintered.

"A point to the Queen's champion," the Lord Mayor cried.

The White Knight had been awarded three points to the Black Knight's two points when the Queen's champion unseated his rival.

The combat continued on foot and was fought ferociously with shield, broadsword, and mace until the White Knight tripped the Black Knight—an act the Queen thought quite lacking in sportsmanship—and stood with his sword poised at the fallen enemy's throat.

Still, Her Royal Majesty cried on cue, "Well fought, brave knights!"

At this pronouncement a bevy of buxom young maidens rushed to offer refreshment and succor to victor and fallen alike.

"Methinks my champion loses only to gain the attention of those lusty wenches," Lady Allison said.

"Dost thou worry?"

"Nay, Your Majesty, 'tis harmless enough, this wenching," Lady Allison said. "Besides," she added, smiling, "he knows where to park his lance if he knows what's good for him."

With the jousting over for the day and her royal duties completed for the nonce, it was time to do some real work. "Where is Sir Robert?" Penelope asked.

"Gone a-drabbing, Majesty."

"Drabbing?"

"Whoring, Your Majesty. He's with the Queen of the Bawds."

CHAPTER
SEVEN

Divested of royal attire, the Queen returned to the Faire disguised as a lowly but comely wench. There was still an hour or two to track down Sir Robert Dudley and enjoy the various pastimes before the gates closed and the stouthearted Elizabethans began to party.

Penelope had left Sir Walter and his cloak parked on the bed in the RV and Big Mike in a deck chair, catching the waning rays of the late winter afternoon. Both pleaded the need for a brief nap before the evening's activities.

Her dress—borrowed from Kathy's wardrobe of years past, when she had been a serving wench—was certainly more comfortable than the ornate gown of the Queen, but still the royal melons were more exposed than Penelope would have liked. It was no wonder the Elizabethans had been such an earthy group and felt the need for the occasional chastity belt. Still, when in Rome or Olde England . . .

It was pleasant to stroll virtually unnoticed—Penelope did draw more than one admiring glance—through the mock village, stopping at one merchant stall or another to examine pewter mugs and goblets, fine hand-crafted jewelry, or maps of the shire and old London Towne.

A thunderstorm was building in the distance. Thick dark clouds roiled above the mountains. Jagged lightning bolts danced against the sky, but the peals of thunder were dull and muted when their rumblings reached the Faire. It might pass us by, Penelope thought, although she knew the unpredictability of desert storms.

In the growing shadows, strolling musicians entertained with lutes, lyres, recorders. Pretty young wenches with lilting soprano voices sang madrigals. Jugglers mesmerized little boys and girls. Other children laughed and played on the giant swing. Some still danced around the maypole under the tutelage of village maidens while their parents relaxed from the strain of keeping track of hyperactive youngsters.

A Puritan, Bible clutched passionately to his bosom, preached to a crowd of scoffing peasants, promising eternal damnation as he railed against strong drink, pleasures of the flesh, entertainment of all kinds, and licentious behavior—to no apparent avail, as the peasants were busily engaged in all of the various activities.

Penelope wandered on. She was passed by some of her rowdy subjects who were telling papist jokes. "Why did the papist cross the road?"

Penelope didn't hear the answer. Why *did* the papist cross the road?

A flower girl pinned a blossom to a woman's blouse and asked, "What are the cockles of the heart? Haven't you ever asked yourself what a cockle is?"

"Not really," the woman replied.

"And you, kind sir, do you know what a cockle is?"

He admitted ignorance.

What *is* a cockle? Penelope wondered. It was one of those words that you just knew. But what did it *really* mean?

Other questions fluttered through her mind. Why? What? Who? When? No. That couldn't be the journalistic order. I'll have to ask Andy, Penelope thought. Who killed the Queen and why? When was easy. Last Saturday night. How? With a dagger, of course. And where is Master Edwards with his record of sales? And my chastity belt? Answer the why and there's a better chance of finding who. The unanswerable questions sent Penelope reeling, giddy and light-headed, to a refreshment stand for a diet soft drink.

On the way to the Queen of the Bawds, Penelope found herself hopelessly lost. Once away from the spacious village green and the Royal Pavilion, it was easy to get turned around in the narrow and twisting byways of the Faire.

"Base metals to gold. The secrets of the universe. Base metals to gold." The chant came from a small boy who punctuated his cries by clanging a hand bell enthusiastically.

It was the second time Penelope had passed the alchemist's shop. Disgusted, she took the opposite path this time and found herself among the Soothsayers' Guild, where the astrologers and fortune-tellers held forth.

"Penelope," a familiar voice cried. "Over here." Empty Creek's Madame Astoria was lounging on cushions before the open tent, where she gave her astrological readings.

Had Alyce not been wearing a gown and bodice decorated with the signs of the zodiac, she might have been a harem favorite luxuriating on the cushions while awaiting a summons from her sultan. Young, pretty, and vivacious, Madame Astoria was Empty Creek's own resident astrologer and psychic, unlike all the others on Soothsayer's Row, who came expressly for the duration of the Faire.

"I'm lost."

"I know. I also know you're looking for Sir Robert, you bought a chastity belt, although it hasn't been delivered yet, and you suspect everyone." Alyce smiled and toyed with the single strand of her plaited blond hair.

"That's marvelous. What a good psychic you are."

"Not really. I saw you standing at the alchemist's looking perplexed. Quite a number of people are looking for Sir Robert. Master Edwards asked where you were staying. He wants to deliver your chastity belt. And you always suspect everyone."

"It's not for me," Penelope replied hastily.

"What's not for you?"

"The chastity belt. I ordered it for Laney. As a joke."

"I knew that. I'm psychic."

"You were with Kathy that night at the pillory. Did you . . . sense anything?" Although there were those who doubted and scoffed at astrology and psychic powers, Penelope was not among them. She had seen too many incidents of witchcraft and traditional medicine in Africa to discount any belief. And Alyce did have uncanny senses, rather like Mycroft, who, for example, always knew when Stormy was coming to visit.

Alyce hesitated. "Not really. We were kind of giggly. I gave her a back rub and then I had to go." She smiled shyly at Penelope. "I was meeting someone."

"Is he nice?"

"Very."

"Good," Penelope said, knowing that Alyce hadn't had much luck with men lately. The inability to look into her own future was a singular and curious lacking in Alyce's psychic and astrological prowess. "I'm happy for you."

"Thank you. I'd like you to meet him."

"I look forward to it, but for now, do your powers tell you where I might find Sir Robert?"

Alyce closed her eyes and furrowed her brow in concentration. "I'm afraid not," she said sheepishly, glancing up at Penelope, "although he's probably with the drabs, or that actress he's so fond of now that poor Carolyn's gone."

"Yes, that's what everyone says. I must be off and find them."

"Be careful, Penelope."

"Yes, everyone keeps saying that too."

"No, Penelope, I mean it. Beware the Ides of March."

"Now, where did that come from? Besides *Julius Caesar?*

"I don't know. It just flashed through my mind."

Following Alyce's directions—"Turn left at the banger shoppe, go over Kissing Bridge, and turn right at the juggling school"—Penelope easily found the drabs.

Belying their name, the drabs were anything but dull and cheerless as they picked on the hapless rubes who came within their purview. One pretty young drab offered a knotted rope to a blushing wife. "Give 'em a good beating. Show him how much you love him." The couple fled hastily.

"He'll love it," the drab called after them.

The Queen of the Bawds leaned from a second-floor window, bantering good-naturedly with any man who dared pause for a moment or two. "Come on up, but bring sixpence."

"Haven't got sixpence."

The drabs all laughed. "God's blood, Maud, he's a ha'penny man."

"No love for you tonight."

"No love for you tonight," the drabs joined in.

"Come to join the bawds, dearie?" Maud asked when Penelope waved to attract her attention.

Penelope shook her head. "I'm looking for Sir Robert Dudley."

The Queen of the Bawds frowned, hesitated a moment, and then ducked from sight. When the Queen of the Bawds emerged from the mock cottage, she beckoned to Penelope. "Let's take a walk."

They followed a twisting path through the narrow village streets to the Queen's Own Public House, an area reserved for Faire participants. When they had taken seats at a small wooden table away from the clamor, the Queen of the Bawds held out her hand and said, "I'm Allison McKenzie. That's my real name."

"I'm Penelope Warren. That's my real name too."

"How do you like being the Queen of the Faire?"

"I think I'd rather be Queen of the Bawds. Less responsibility."

Allison smiled. "We get to say anything we want to."

"What did you say to Sir Robert?"

"He was quite maudlin. We had a pint of ale together. I tried to cheer him up, but he's upset over Carolyn's death. Blames himself."

"Do you know where he is now?"

"I suppose he went to that actress who started it all."

"How?"

"Turned Sir Robert's eye. It's strange, the Queen and Dudley were quite happy until she came along."

Leaving Maud, Penelope went to the Shakespearean stage but the last performance of *As You Like It* had long since concluded and the players scattered to *their* amusements. Rosalind would have to wait until later. Penelope had no intention of breaking into a love tryst, maudlin or otherwise. Sir Robert and his Rosalind would turn up eventually.

As "last call" was being sounded at the various public houses, Penelope returned to the campsite and found Andy and Mycroft mulling over the elaborate straps and buckles of the chastity belt.

"What is this?" Andy asked.

"It's a chastity belt, of course."

"I know that, but what's it for?"

"Really, Andy . . ."

"I mean . . . I know what it's for . . . but . . . but . . . *who* is it for?"

"You're stammering, dearest."

"Penelope . . ."

"And you're blushing."

"You're impossible, sometimes."

"Yes, I am," Penelope said smiling wickedly. "Wouldn't you like to have the only key?"

"I should certainly hope so."

"Well, if it were for me, you would be sole custodian of the key, but it's not for me. I bought it for Laney as a joke, although I'm quite sure that inventive mind of hers will come up with a suitable game to play with it. Something along the order of the Dragon and the Lonely Maiden.''

"That's a relief."

"You sound disappointed."

"Well, I could be the knight who rescues the lonely maiden. Mycroft could play the dragon."

"Really, Andy, sometimes I think you're as crazed as Laney."

"It was just a thought," Andy said hopefully.

"Well, Mikey would be a pretty good dragon. . . ." She ruffled Andy's hair and then leaned over to kiss him. Just as she was warming to the moment, Penelope remembered one of Stormy's earliest and least memorable films, where she had played the princess in the sword-and-sorcery epic, spending much of her screen time chained to a rock at the edge of some cold and turbulent sea whose rushing tides threatened to strip her of the flimsy sacrificial garment she wore before the bumbling hero could effect a rescue. The memory of those cold waters lapping about her sister's legs chilled Penelope's enthusiasm for the moment at hand.

"Mmm," Andy said, reaching out to draw Penelope into his lap.

"Later, sweetie, I have work to do," Penelope said.

"But . . . but . . . it was just getting interesting."

"Blame Stormy."

"I never know what's going on," Andy complained.

"What are cockles?"

"Now, that I know."

"You do?"

"Of course."

Penelope thought he was being smug. "Well?"

"According to Webster's, one cockle can be a weed or a wrinkle or a bivalve mollusk, but the cockles of the heart. Now, that's quite a different thing entirely. They are the core of one's being. Like you, Penelope. You are the cockles of my heart."

Penelope decided to forgive his smugness.

The records of Master Edwards narrowed the list of possible suspects to no more than three or four hundred Faire participants over the years, to say nothing of the rubes who had purchased various implements of cutlery as souvenirs.

The members of the Military Guild were good customers of the ironmonger's, as were the Royal Knights, members of the royal court, those in the Merchants' Guild and the middle class, various pages, and court dandies. Shakespeare and Marlowe and most of the actors in their respective companies had purchased swords, foils, and an infinite number of stilettos, daggers, and bodkins over the years. Even Kathy appeared as the purchaser of what was described on the invoice as "one lady's dagger."

Penelope sighed and stacked Master Edwards's records neatly before pushing them aside.

"Find anything?"

"Only that the Elizabethans appear to be quite heavily armed. It's too bad the Cold War is over. We could easily repel a Russian invasion of Empty Creek."

"There's always Saddam Hussein."

"Mycroft could repel *that* invasion."

Some fin de siècle party this turned out to be.

It was customary, according to Kathy, for the Queen and

her Consort to make the rounds of the Saturday night parties, although it was a duty oft ignored by Carolyn.

But the pall of last weekend's tragedy lingered over the Faire. As Penelope, Andy, and Big Mike trekked from one gathering to another, they found each assemblage rather more subdued than they had been led to believe. It seemed the entire nation mourned the loss of their Queen, although few had truly liked Carolyn Lewis.

Even the famed wet T-shirt contest of the Peasant's Guild had been canceled out of respect for the former Queen, to Andy's rather evident disappointment. Penelope didn't mind a straying eye on occasion so long as it returned to her. After all, it wasn't Andy's fault that he was afflicted with careening hormones like most of the men and women who lived in Empty Creek. Penelope firmly believed it was something in the water. And the Peasants' Guild *was* comprised of the lustiest young men and women among the Faire participants, including the buxom serving wenches and the painted bawds—all among the prettiest women at the Faire.

Still, the peasants, grateful for her appearance, crowded around the new Queen to wish her well and Godspeed, thrusting flagons of ale at Penelope and Andy, and raising a cheer for Big Mike when it was discovered that he liked a wee dram or two himself.

A pretty young woman detached herself from the crowd and introduced herself to Penelope. "I'm Sally," she said, "but you can call me Butch. Everyone does. My husband started it when I cut my hair. I just like short hair right now, but he was disappointed when I cut it. I wear a wig for the Faire." She shook her head. "Men. Anyway, the nickname stuck."

"Men," Penelope agreed. Watching Andy's awe-struck eyes taking in the multitude of pulchritude, Penelope thought poor Andy would just have to make do with a rousing game of Pursue the Queen later, or perhaps that dragon business.

Watching Penelope watching Andy watching the women, Butch smiled and said, "The royal melons will suffice, Your Majesty."

Penelope blushed. "You heard about that?"

"He's my husband."

"He's a peasant rogue, doing that to me and on my first day too."

"Yes, he's all of that."

At the Merchants' Guild they were all talking about sales figures, Faire attendance, profits and losses. The Queen and her court didn't stay long. In real life Penelope had to worry too much about the vagaries of owning a small mystery bookstore as it was. She had no desire to spend a Saturday night concerned with profits and losses.

She did take a moment to thank Master Edwards for the prompt delivery of the records.

"Did you find anything?"

"Only that you appear to do a very thriving business."

Master Edwards beamed. "Indeed, I do. And the other?" he asked with a sly grin.

"I'm sure it'll be quite the conversation piece."

Kathy and Timmy were at the Performers' Guild, where the jugglers, strolling musicians, flower girls, and their companions were engaged in an enthusiastic game of Pass the

Wench, where two laughing, shrieking young women were hoisted up and passed over the shoulders of parallel lines of men as quickly as possible. The winner appeared to get a free pint of ale, but then, so did the loser. What's the point, then? the orderly portion of Penelope's mind asked. Who cares? the disorderly portion quickly responded. They're having fun.

Ah, the resilience of youth. Death chilled their lives briefly, passed on, and was forgotten until that dark hour before the dawn, when it was comforting to awaken from a nightmare and find the warm, reassuring presence of a loved one.

"Would you like to try it, Your Majesty?" Timmy asked.

"Perhaps another time."

"Where next, Your Majesty?" Kathy asked.

"To the military encampment, I believe."

"They're all anal retentive," Kathy said. "They really think they're in the army or the navy."

At the Military Guild, Her Majesty's troops sprang to attention. They raised a cheer for the Queen, pressed flagons of home-brewed ale upon her, and went back to debating the strategy for defeating the Spanish Armada the next time it showed up.

The Shakespearean Players were also subdued. You'd think they were performing *Hamlet* rather than *As You Like It*, Penelope thought, and just then Master Will introduced Richard Burbage, a stout-bearded man and the famed actor of the Elizabethan stage.

"I wrote *Hamlet* for him, you know."

"Yes," Penelope said, quoting Gertrude from the dueling scene. " 'Our son is fat and scant of breath.' "

Burbage laughed and patted his ample belly. "It must have been the ale. Nothing's changed in four hundred years. I still like my ale."

"Have either of you seen Rosalind?" Penelope asked.

"No one's seen her since the performance," Shakespeare said. "It's not like her. I'm getting a little worried."

"She's probably with Sir Robert," Penelope said.

"That cad."

Christopher Marlowe's Players were whooping it up in fine Faire tradition. If the Queen's assassination bothered them in the slightest, there was no evidence of it as they raised their tankards in a toast.

"To the royal melons," Marlowe shouted above the din.

Penelope blushed furiously, wishing now she had booted his atheistic butt from the Faire rather than offering a compromise.

"The royal melons," the rejoinder filled the room. A plaintive cry was added, "Show us the royal melons!"

"Certainly not," Penelope said. Her cheeks burned red with embarrassment and anger.

"Pay them no mind," Marlowe said with the smirk Penelope was quickly growing to dislike. "They're just having a good time."

"At my expense."

"No harm was meant. 'Tis the ale speaking."

"You can drop the Elizabethan prattle," Penelope said, her temper rising. "The next time, I'll take a two-by-four to his head." She stormed out.

"What was that all about?" Andy asked cautiously. Both he

and Mycroft had seen Penelope's temper on rare occasions and neither wished to be the target of her wrath.

"I don't like that odious man."

A streak of lightning slashed through the darkness. It was quickly followed by a loud clap of thunder. The storm gods had apparently made up their minds to torment the Faire.

The members of the royal court were waiting quietly when the Queen and her entourage arrived. They offered a polite toast to "Her Gracious Majesty," which Penelope accepted with a smile and royal nods to all in attendance.

Penelope tried one last time. "Has anyone seen Sir Robert?"

"He never came back, Your Majesty."

A cool wind rattled against the Royal Pavilion, announcing that the storm was upon them.

"We'd best retire, Your Majesty."

"I think that would be wise."

The court scattered to their shelters.

Penelope loved the fierce desert storms that suddenly descended with their violent winds, pelting rain, angry lightning, booming thunder. They were quite English in nature, the portents of great events as recorded in the *Anglo-Saxon Chronicle* and Elizabethan tragedy.

Mycroft did not share Penelope's enthusiasm for nature's tumultuous displays of energy. He didn't mind the lightning so long as an errant bolt didn't strike the cache of lima beans in the cupboard. He tolerated the loudest thunder although it was difficult to sleep with Mother Nature carrying on so. The wind was no big deal either, but . . .

Big Mike had an aversion to water applied externally in any form. Once, during a prolonged drought in Ethiopia, Penelope had kept the bathtub filled with water for emergency purposes. Since the bathtub was the fifth turn on the race-track laid out by the energetic young Mycroft, Penelope knew it was only a matter of time until the kitten baptized himself in the old-fashioned way by full immersion. And when Mycroft warmed up with a few laps around the living room, Penelope took up her station at the bathroom door, ready for immediate rescue. Penelope cringed as Big Mike hit the straightaway of the hall, building speed, leaping high above the water-filled tub. To this very night Penelope swore that Mycroft stopped in midair, defied gravity while he turned 180 degrees, hit the afterburners, landed at the door, and skidded into the sixth turn to tear through the bedroom, never dampening a dainty paw.

So, when Penelope and Andy paused for a moment on Kissing Bridge, Mycroft ran for home, deftly dodging the first fat drops of rain, arriving in time to see a shadowy black-clad figure disappear around the corner of the camper truck. As Mycroft waited on the steps, where he was sheltered from the storm, he pondered the piece of paper that was now taped to the door.

Penelope and Andy managed to make cover just before the cloudburst and stood laughing and panting while Big Mike meowed in an effort to tell them what he'd seen, but, alas alack, humans were quite dense on occasion—most occasions, in fact. Indeed, if not for their deftness in operating electric can openers, the majority of cats would probably have nothing to do with the human race whatsoever.

At any rate, there was another kiss, quite prolonged, before

Penelope and Andy finally turned and saw the missive on their door. Lightning lit the night long enough for Penelope to see the bloody dagger on the sheet of paper and the crudely drawn words *Beware the Ides of March*.

And then all was dark again.

CHAPTER
EIGHT

The new day was bright and clear, cleansed by the refreshing storm. As the sun climbed into the sky, spreading warmth and cheer over the tiny field that would be Olde England for another brief span of time, happy Fairegoers were greeted at the gate with welcoming speeches by the Lord High Mayor, the Lord High Sheriff, and Master Will Shakespeare.

The Queen's procession wound its way through the village crowded with revelers to the Royal Pavilion without incident. More speeches were delivered to the assembly. The troops paraded. Knights saluted. The Queen was presented to loud cheers. Her Royal Majesty, in turn, bestowed her blessing upon the gathering and the festivities, all the while wondering which of her less than loyal subjects had delivered the premonition of doom.

Penelope knew that one among the multitude of happy faces staring at her might be a murderer. Or, horrid thought, the killer might be even closer at hand—a member of the trusted royal court. And where was the elusive Sir Robert Dudley? Was he out there living in some grim fantasy sparked by history. After all, the real Sir Robert's wife, Amy Robsart, had died under most mysterious circumstances. At the time, centuries ago, many had believed poor Amy to be her husband's victim, killed so that he might marry Elizabeth Regina. But that had not come to pass. Still . . . the present Sir Robert might have killed the Queen in order to possess his latest love, sweet Rosalind of *As You Like It*.

Penelope shook her head. If she couldn't solve the present murder, how could she solve an enigmatic occurrence more than four centuries before? Besides, it was too difficult to concentrate with all the clamor about her.

"Where is the Royal Cat?" Her Majesty asked between the bellowing flourishes of her trumpeters.

"I saw him duck under the tent, Majesty," Lady Kathleen replied. "He appeared to be heading for the turkey leg stand."

"Again?"

"I'm afraid so, Your Majesty."

Mycroft was developing quite a passion for turkey legs. Penelope wasn't worried about Mycroft wandering about the Faire alone. He could take care of himself, as the unlucky canines had learned the previous day. Nor was she worried about him overeating. Although he enjoyed food as much as he did sleep, Big Mike was a gourmet rather than a glutton. Even when a feast of his beloved lima beans appeared before him, he ate only enough to stoke the fuel tank of his enormous body—no more—turning away from the delicacy, quite willing to save a few for the next meal. Penelope firmly believed he worried about a sudden and inexplicable blight striking down the lima-bean harvest and always wanted to keep a few in reserve.

Several courtiers, overhearing the Queen and Lady Kathleen's brief conversation, exchanged glances and raised eyebrows. Perhaps it was time to move the Queen from the warmth of the sun, cool her forehead with a damp cloth, and loosen her bodice. That was a consummation devoutly to be wished, Sir Francis Drake thought as he admired Her Majesty's shapely, if feverish, body. Briefly, he considered calling that gangling and awkward Sir Walter—and his stupid cloak—to the field of honor, dueling to the death for the hand of England's fair Majesty.

Similar thoughts skittered through the minds of the other courtiers and knights. The Queen's champion, the White Knight, thought the Queen would be quite stunning in her own suit of armor, rather like Ingrid Bergman in *Joan of Arc*. The Black Knight, on the other hand, thought Penelope would be magnificent in nothing at all. In contrast, Sir Francis Bacon, whose fetishes ran to cleanliness and an appreciation for fine wines, daydreamed of assisting the Queen in a bath of wine, just like Mary Queen of Scots had been reputed to enjoy. Perhaps a nice cabernet to start and then a crisp chardonnay for a rinse.

The Lord High Mayor and the Lord High Sheriff were each content with their own fantasies; the former would have preferred the Queen as an earthy peasant wench to pursue through green fields for a prolonged frolic in a bed of daisies. The Sheriff, probably because of the nature of his job, longed to clap the Queen in irons and lead her off to a lonely cell in the Tower of London, where he could woo her at his leisure.

In her first twenty-four hours of rule, it seemed the men at

court had taken Penelope to their hearts and vied for her attention to the great dismay of the ladies-in-waiting. Oh, they
had nothing against the Queen, knowing that Penelope and
Andy were an item not easily sundered. No, it was their own
men who were foolishly attracted to Penelope's grace, beauty,
and, yes, power.

Sir Walter Raleigh, who *did* enjoy the Queen's favors, was
for the moment quite taken with the lady-in-waiting on
horseback who was besting several knights in tests of skill and
dexterity with the lance. There *was* something about a power-
ful and athletic woman that excited the imagination, particularly when the lady-in-waiting smiled at Sir Walter even as
she dipped her lance in homage to the Queen.

Had the Queen but known she was the object of so many
interesting and varied fancies of the imagination, she would
have blushed right down to her toenails and probably sentenced the lot of them to icy cold showers. But the Queen was
preoccupied and performed her duties mechanically while attempting to impose some semblance of order on the chaos
that reigned in her mind.

Her first official act of the morning had been to drop a
dime—two dimes, in fact—into a pay telephone and dial the
number of Discreet Investigations, a service so circumspect
that the answering machine had no message, only a beep indicating that it was ready to receive whatever bulletin the cal-
ler might wish to leave. "This is Penelope," she said. "Call
me."

With that done, she was free to ponder the imponderable.

Who left the note? The Ides of March fell on the last Saturday of the Faire. But what did *that* mean?

Where was Sir Robert?

Who killed the Queen?

Who was Lothario?

Who, dammit, who?

Realizing she sounded like a crazed owl, Penelope smiled inwardly and turned her mind to more pleasant thoughts. Despite the chilling impact of the note and its bloody dagger, Penelope and Andy had managed to find solace in a simple and uncomplicated game of I Love You. Still, she felt better for having called Discreet Investigations.

Empire building came naturally to Big Mike.

As a young and fearless feline in Ethiopia, he had ruled the college campus as his own personal fiefdom, reigning over cats, wild dogs, jackals, hyenas, and other assorted critters with considerable aplomb. And then, plopped down in the desert of Empty-by-God Creek, Arizona, after a journey that took him from Dire Dawa to Addis Ababa, Cyprus, London, Washington, D.C., and Phoenix, Mycroft blinked once or twice, complained loudly about the indignities modern flight offered cats, and proceeded to establish another domain in and around the small ranch, where he lived quite happily with Penelope and Chardonnay, as well as Mycroft & Company, the Double B, and various other establishments in and around town.

Now Big Mike had staked out the green fields of England as his own personal territory, claiming this new world as his own, accepting the tribute of turkey legs and the adoration of fair young maids as no more than his due. But he was a polite cat too, and demonstrated his gratitude with soft mewing, purrs, and leg rubs.

Still, Big Mike could stand only so much attention and

there were those moments when solitude was required. Thus, Mycroft claimed several hidey-holes for his various retreats, each suited to the mood of the moment. His favorite, perhaps, was the shelf beneath the counter of the turkey leg stand, where he could drift off to slumber land amid the soothing aromas of roasting turkey. Another was a perch in a scrub oak near the village green, where he could quietly observe the variety of Faire activities without the fear of being disturbed by a parade of fools or the celebration of some obscure rite of springe.

But for serious sleeping Big Mike chose a backstage storage room for one of the lesser playhouses. Entrance was gained by leaping six feet to a windowsill, squeezing through a broken pane, traversing a number of stacked boxes, and springing to the top of a big wooden cabinet, where he could settle down in dark seclusion.

Now, *that* was a hidey-hole!

When Penelope, her royal duties at an intermission, arrived at the Shakespearean Playhouse, the actors were preparing for their performance of *As You Like It.*

Backstage, she found Rosalind easily. The actress had the aura of stardom about her, carrying herself with confidence just as Stormy did even though she still acted in those wretched adventure epics, knowing all the while that her break would come. "Hi," Penelope said, smiling at the young actress.

"I don't know," Rosalind said, attempting to brush past.

Penelope blocked her path. "I haven't asked the question yet."

"I still don't know."

"Perhaps we should start over," Penelope said. "Hi."

Rosalind destroyed her aura by bursting into tears. "I don't know," she wailed.

Penelope didn't know what to do.

Master Will Shakespeare rushed over. "What did you say to her?" he cried.

"Hi."

"Hi," Master Will said, remembering his manners. "What did you say to her?" he repeated.

"Hi," Penelope said, letting her exasperation show. "That's what I said. Hi."

"That's all?"

"And then she started crying."

"She's very high strung."

"I can see that."

"I don't know where he is," Rosalind sobbed. "He left me. Said I was in danger."

"Who left you?"

"What danger?"

"Bobbyyyyy! I don't know what danger."

"By Bobby, do you mean Sir Robert?" Penelope asked, patting the young woman on the shoulder.

"Yesss."

"The performance begins in ten minutes. We've got to calm her down."

"Let me," Penelope said, putting her arm around the actress's shoulder and leading her away through the throng of players startled by their heroine's sudden collapse.

Shakespeare, shaking his head and wringing his hands, looked after them dubiously.

Behind the wall of the outdoor playhouse, Penelope led the

distraught actress to a secluded bench. Rosalind sobbed quietly against Penelope's shoulder. Penelope herself had not cried so wretchedly since her eighth-grade homeroom teacher had married her seventh-grade homeroom teacher, thereby breaking her heart for an entire weekend.

"There, there," Penelope said in her most soothing voice, patting Rosalind's shoulder gently. "It's not so bad as it seems. Everything will be just fine."

"I don't know. . . ."

Penelope prepared herself for a new outburst of tears, but Rosalind surprised her by raising her head, sniffing, and wiping her eyes.

"Oh, God, I've got to go on in a minute. You don't happen to have a tissue, do you? Bobby said I could trust you."

Not knowing what the one had to do with the other, Penelope replied, "Yes, as a matter of fact, I do." There were hidden and voluminous pockets in the dress borrowed from Kathy that enabled Penelope to transfer everything from her purse that she might need. Along with a package of tissues, this included wallet, cosmetics and lipstick, a Swiss Army knife, several paper clips (useful for picking locks, if necessary), a map of the Faire (she was tired of getting lost), a Baggie of cat treats, a notepad and ball-point pen, sewing kit, a watch with a broken band, and two sticks of gum.

"Thank you," Rosalind said. After repairing the ravages of tears, sighing several times, and a final sniffle, she asked, "How do I look?"

"Beautiful."

"Really?"

Penelope nodded. "Ready for the performance of your life."

There was applause as the play began. "Oh, God, it's time," Rosalind said. "I have to see you afterward. Will you come back?"

"I'll meet you backstage," Penelope said.

Penelope watched as Rosalind joined Celia to await their cue. Rosalind closed her eyes, breathed deeply, whispered to herself, and then turned to smile at Penelope. "Thank you," she said.

"Break a leg," Penelope said.

Then Rosalind was onstage, quiet and composed as she replied to Celia's entreaty to be merry.

" 'Dear Celia, I show more mirth than I am mistress of, and would you yet I were merrier? Unless you could teach me to forget a banished father, you must not learn me how to remember any extraordinary pleasure.' "

Or a banished lover, Penelope thought as she turned away to resume the duties of the Queen. I wonder whatever happened to those homeroom teachers?

The Queen just had time to join Andy at the turkey leg stand for a quick bit of nosh before returning to her royal duties and the afternoon combats. Andy had been out in search of the Royal Cat.

"Did you find him?"

Andy shook his head. "I thought he'd be here, but he left some time ago. No one's seen him since. I'm worried."

"Don't be, sweetie, you know what Mycroft is like. He's just out doing some cat thing."

"I hope so."

Penelope took a bite of Andy's turkey leg. "That's good," she said. "No wonder Mikey likes it here."

The afternoon's royal procession included the Picts, who were scheduled to pledge their undying fealty to Elizabeth Regina. As the Queen and her consort passed their savage ranks, they were suddenly confronted by a statuesque, cat-wielding woman wearing a crown, furry boots that rose to her knees, and a beautiful if skimpy dress.

"What *are* you doing, sis?"

"I'm the honorary Queen of the Picts. Isn't that nice? They've seen all my films and they're going to hold a Storm Williams Film Festival after the Faire is over. And Mikey's been looking for you. He seemed quite put out that you weren't here."

"Has Dutch seen this getup?" Penelope asked, giving Mikey a chin-scratch by way of greeting.

"He thinks it's peachy."

"So do I," Andy offered.

Peachy? Lord, give me strength to get through this day.

Penelope did survive the parade of the Picts and their honorary queen, who received thunderous applause at her grand entrance, something Cassie aka Stormy had always been good at doing. Grand entrances were a specialty of hers.

Penelope also survived trumpet flourishes, the clang of armored combat, several royal proclamations, and Mikey coughing up a hairball on the royal lap.

When the jousts finally, mercifully, drew to a close, the Queen offered a last, even gracious, blessing upon the assembled company, left Andy in charge of Mycroft, and hurried off to meet Rosalind.

"We'll be fine," Andy said. "We'll meet you back at the campgrounds."

As Penelope returned to the Shakespearean stage, she passed Marlowe's company declaiming their lines loudly to a sparse audience. Hurrying on, she found the rival theater filled with a rapt and attentive crowd. The play was at its dénouement with the actors leaving the stage empty for Rosalind to deliver her epilogue.

Penelope listened, pleased to see that the epilogue had been adopted to accommodate the fact that Rosalind was played by a woman, not a boy, as had been the custom in Shakespeare's own England. That was progress.

" '. . . I charge you, O women! for the love you bear to men, to like as much of this play as please you; and I charge you, O men! for the love you bear to women, as I perceive by your simpering none of you hates them, that between you and the women the play may please. . . . I would kiss as many of you as had beards that pleased me, complexions that liked me, and breaths that I defied not; and I am sure, as many as have good beards, or good faces, or sweet breaths, will, for my kind offer, when I make curtsy, bid me farewell.' "

At Rosalind's curtsy, the audience followed her instructions, erupting into applause. During the ovation Penelope hurried backstage to be waiting when Rosalind came off after the last enthusiastic curtain call.

"From what little I saw," Penelope said, "you were magnificent."

Rosalind smiled shyly. "Thank you."

"Are you feeling better?"

"A little."

"Come on," Penelope said, "I'll buy you a drink. You are old enough to drink?"

"I'm twenty-two," Rosalind said, "a senior at ASU."

"I went to graduate school at Arizona State. It seems like a long time ago."

"Did you major in drama?"

"Lord, no. English lit. What made you think drama?"

"It just seems that most of the Faire participants are actors or frustrated actors."

"Yes, it does seem that way. I take it you are majoring in drama."

Rosalind nodded. "Bobby's my teacher and mentor. That's his real name."

"What is your name?"

"Sharon O'Bannon."

"Then I shall call you Sharon. I think it's a much prettier name than Rosalind."

As they strolled toward the public house, the crowd was thinning out although the Faire would not officially close for the weekend until six o'clock. There was still a clamor at the pillory, however, where some peasants were happily pelting a Puritan.

"The Queen issued a warrant for my arrest last weekend. She was going to put me in there on Sunday, but then . . . they must have forgotten, but I suppose the warrant's still good. I keep expecting the Sheriff's men to come for me."

"I shall issue a royal pardon."

"Thank you, but I don't mind. It's all a part of the Faire. Last year . . ." Her voice trailed off.

"Last year?" Penelope prompted.

"Oh," Sharon said, blushing, "Bobby and I were kind of fooling around one night and . . . well, I kind of wound up in the pillory. There was a full moon and it seemed to shine on just us. It was the first time he kissed me."

Penelope had never thought about a pillory as aphrodisiacal. Her own brief experience with it—and Lothario—had done nothing to dissuade her, but Kathy was rapturous and moon-eyed when she recalled Timmy's caresses during her imprisonment. "Perhaps I should try it with someone I care about," Penelope said.

"But you're the Queen. Surely *you* haven't been locked up in it?"

Penelope explained her brief encounter with the pillory and described Lothario. "Do you know him? He said he was an actor."

"Not with us. Perhaps with one of the other companies."

They strolled on, entered the public house, and found a semiprivate table near the back, away from the staring rubes.

"Do you love him?"

"Oh, yes, but . . . it's difficult. He didn't want to hurt Carolyn . . . so . . . he was going to tell her, but then she was killed."

Surely, Penelope thought, it would be much easier to tell Carolyn that their relationship was over. It would hurt far less than murder. It didn't make any sense, but then, the human mind seldom did. Perhaps they argued and Carolyn attacked Sir Robert.

"I hope this doesn't upset you, but your Bobby seems to be rather enamored of the ladies. Carolyn, the bawds. He was even making eyes at me yesterday."

"I know, but it's just temporary. He's having a midlife crisis. Besides, all of his best friends are women. He doesn't mean anything by it." Sharon looked about the public house. The other patrons paid no attention to them. She dipped into her bosom and withdrew a folded piece of paper and handed it across the table. "Bobby received this. He wanted me to give it to you."

Penelope took it but did not open it. "Beware the Ides of March."

"How did you know?"

"I got one too."

As she returned to the campgrounds, Penelope summed up the first weekend of her reign as something less than productive regarding the solving of the murder of Carolyn Lewis. Indeed, she characterized the entire two days as worthless in the search for truth. If anything, the situation was more confused than ever. Sir Robert was still missing. His new lady friend was reduced to helpless tears. Alyce had an ominous premonition that was well on its way to coming true. Someone had taped hate mail to the Queen's RV. Mycroft had a hairball.

What else could go wrong? Penelope asked herself as she approached the RV. It was locked and forlorn. Hmm. They should be here by now, Penelope thought. Surely Andy and Mycroft weren't out drinking somewhere. She had just inserted the key in the lock, when a hand clasped itself firmly around her ankle.

"Just act naturally," a hoarse voice ordered from beneath the truck.

Penelope did. She used her free foot to stomp on the arm that belonged to the hand.

"Ow! Goddamn, that hurt!" Sir Robert Dudley cried.

CHAPTER
NINE

"What are you doing under my RV?" Penelope asked as Bobby slowly and painfully crawled out, clutching a bottle of chardonnay with his good hand. At least, he was a polite visitor.

"It's my romantic nature," he said. "I've always admired Burt Lancaster in *The Crimson Pirate*."

Penelope hardly thought a streak of romanticism would be expressed by scuttling around beneath a vehicle like a mechanic in search of an oil change and a lube. "Burt Lancaster would be swinging from a mast, not skulking under a converted pickup truck."

"I didn't want anyone to see me."

"I gathered that."

Bobby was in the midst of a convoluted explanation of how he came to be under the RV, when Andy and Mycroft arrived, followed shortly by Sharon, who took a firm grip on Bobby and refused to let him go. Penelope gave up and simply invited everyone to dinner.

The last red streaks of the desert sunset had faded when Penelope led the little caravan into her driveway. Andy, who had been dispatched ahead to order Chinese takeout for four, had joined them in town and now brought up the rear. Bobby and Sharon were in the middle.

As Penelope unlocked the door and turned the lights on, Mycroft went into his established routine for returning home, beginning a meticulous inspection to ensure that nothing had been disturbed in his absence.

"Why do you have pennies glued to your door?" Sharon asked. "For luck?"

"It's a long story," Penelope said, depositing a now-wrapped chastity belt on the couch.

"Death follows Penelope Warren," Andy said helpfully. "A killer put them there."

"Don't start that again," Penelope said. "You'll frighten our guests."

"They're already frightened," Andy pointed out.

"That's true, but there's no need to make it worse."

"The wine is getting warm," Bobby said.

"I'll stick it in the freezer, but don't let me forget about it. I have to feed Chardonnay," Penelope said quickly adding, "my horse, not the wine."

"Can I help?" Sharon asked.

Although Penelope was beginning to feel like Miss Lonelyhearts in Nathanael West's novel, with everyone pouring their emotions out to her, she acquiesced, telling Andy and Bobby, "You're in charge of the wine and the food. We'll be back shortly."

Chardonnay, who had been fed by Laney and Wally over the weekend, whinnied happily at Penelope's arrival. She fussed over the horse, feeding her peppermint candies, stroking her neck, and brushing a bit of mane away from her eyes.

"She's pretty," Sharon said wistfully. "Someday I'd like a horse when Bobby . . . well, when Bobby and I get things sorted out."

"What happened after I left you? I thought you didn't know where Bobby was."

"I didn't, and I was getting really worried again until that little boy, the one who sells tomatoes at the pillory, brought me a note from Bobby telling me to meet him at your spot in the campgrounds. I felt better then."

"I wish I did."

Andy and Bobby had set the table and were busily engaged in killing the first bottle of wine, when Penelope and Sharon returned.

"We've just been having the most interesting discussion about the Queen," Andy said. "Did you know she had a succession of lovers?"

"Yes," Penelope replied, "it had to do with the politics of the period. Elizabeth found it simpler to have lovers than husbands."

"No, I mean Carolyn Lewis. *She* had a series of affairs. She had the final say in auditions for the various roles played at court. It was her very own version of the casting couch. She picked Dudley and he was expected to . . . well . . . you know."

"Why didn't anyone tell me?" Penelope asked. "Why didn't anyone tell the police?"

"The court is always very secretive and protective of the

Queen," Bobby said. "Whatever one might think of Carolyn, she *was* the Queen."

"Let's eat," Penelope said.

Big Mike had enjoyed Chinese food immensely until an unfortunate encounter with a red pepper that neither he nor Penelope had noticed until he had gulped it down, paused for a moment's reflection at the sudden burning sensation, and then gone into a series of most undignified grimaces and contortions before dislodging the offending morsel. Since then, Mycroft had been content with his bowl of liver crunchies which he now crunched with gusto.

There were moments when Penelope wished her own life revolved around a full bowl of liver crunchies and a warm bed. This was one of those occasions. After a bizarre week of being accosted at the pillory, make-believe, assorted encounters with strange creatures—one of whom was now seated at her kitchen table—and a singular lack of progress in her investigation, Penelope longed for the simple life. She was also dying to ask about Carolyn's former lovers, but sexual liaisons were not suitable topics for gracious dining. Muffy and Biff, her parents who were now long accustomed to rolling their eyes at each new adventure of their daughters', would not approve, and rightly so.

Penelope surveyed the little group sitting around her kitchen table. Out of costume and character now, it might be a quiet suburban gathering, two couples getting together for a quiet evening. Sharon sat close to Bobby, her eyes shining as she glanced at him, quickly returning his sad smiles. With his graying beard and longish hair, and dressed casually in jeans and pullover, Bobby looked exactly like what he was in real life—a professor of theater. Andy, as always, was a dear, even though he complained of a chill and refused to shed his cloak.

As Andy refilled their wineglasses after dinner, Penelope finally said, "All right, what's this about Carolyn's casting couch?"

"It's true. I was the latest in a series of Sir Robert Dudleys."

"Who were your predecessors?"

"The Lord High Mayor and the Lord High Sheriff, to name two."

"And there were others?"

"Practically everyone at court. When she tired of one, Carolyn demoted him and went on to the next. I thought that would happen to me this year, but Carolyn would have none of it. All I wanted was to be a poor player strutting and fretting my hour upon the stage with Sharon—"

"Yes, yes," Penelope interrupted, "tell me more about you and Carolyn."

"I didn't kill her."

Penelope nodded. "I didn't think you did, although you have been acting rather suspiciously."

"I was going to tell Carolyn that it was over between us, but then she was murdered and everyone looked at me as if I had done it."

"But he was with me," Sharon quickly interjected.

"Still, there was talk, rumor, innuendo."

"From whom?" Penelope asked.

"The Spanish ambassador. That's why I popped him. Drake, Bacon, Marlowe, Shakespeare. I overheard them."

"The Spanish ambassador said something about heavy metal."

"The music?"

Penelope nodded.

"I don't know what he's talking about," Bobby said, shaking his head. "And then I received the Ides of March missive and I was afraid Sharon might be in danger by association. So I kept away from her and just wandered around the Faire, visiting friends. I was careful not to be alone with anyone though."

"But surely you must have known you wouldn't be attacked in broad daylight."

"I wasn't thinking straight. What did you think when you found your note?"

"I took steps. Discreet Investigations will be the Royal Bodyguard. My very own Elizabethan secret service. I shall include you and Sharon, of course."

"Perhaps," Andy drawled, "perhaps, you should leave things to the police this time, Penelope."

"And what have they accomplished? Did you see one detective at the Faire this weekend?"

"Well, Dutch was there, of course."

"Only because of Stormy. He's acting very strangely for a police chief. It's not like him at all. I wonder what's going on."

"Penelope, what *is* going on?" Sharon asked. "The Faire was always so much fun, but now . . . what are we going to do?"

"We're going to find the killer," Penelope replied with a confidence that she didn't truly feel. As in Denmark, there was something rotten in the state of the Faire.

Alone, Penelope, Andy, and Big Mike cuddled on a rug in front of the fireplace.

Mesmerized by the fire, Penelope thought about love and relationships, her own because of the nice thing Andy was doing to make her feel warm and tingly, but others intruded too. Although she hadn't known Carolyn Lewis in real life, she remembered the photograph of the much-loved history teacher in the high school yearbook, a plain but not unattractive woman smiling for the camera and her students. But beneath the veneer there had been a tortured woman who believed herself to be the Queen of England, the Mrs. Hyde who interviewed her prospective lovers for the course of the Faire before going back to her staid existence, imparting her love of history to those lucky enough to be in her classes.

And there was Sharon who, although she didn't seem to realize it, was hopelessly in love with the man she described as teacher and mentor, a man in midlife crisis, a man entangled in love, deception, and murder. Yet Bobby seemed enamored of Sharon, looking upon her with great fondness even as he traveled among the bawds and made abortive attempts upon the person of the new Queen. But his best friends are women, according to Sharon. He could make worse choices. His best friends might be the obnoxious stage manager or that creep Marlowe.

Penelope sighed and snuggled closer to Andy, thinking, It began with a search for lyrical love poems, and now extended into a morass of sexual intrigue.

"Perhaps you should think about a Miss Lonelyhearts column in the newspaper," Penelope said. "I could give advice to the lovelorn. Forget about him—or her. Straighten up. Find someone new. Abstinence. Get thee to a nunnery. Take a cold shower. Solid advice like that."

"I'm sure your readers would find you a great comfort. What if I were to write in. What would you tell me?"

"To get a hormone shot, of course, and take your vitamins."

"Very sound." He kissed the tip of her nose.

Driving into Empty Creek the next morning, the weekend of Elizabethan fantasy seemed long ago and far away. It was another cloudless and beautiful winter's day in the desert. The air was still crisp in the late morning sun.

At Mycroft & Company, Kathy was in the back room unpacking the day's delivery, checking each title off on the packing slip. She poked her head through the curtained doorway and said, "Oh, good morrow, Your Majesty. You're here early."

"I couldn't sleep."

"*You* couldn't sleep?"

The truth was that Andy had not only loved her to sleep but had awakened her in much the same fashion. But Penelope had no intention of telling Kathy *that*. Instead, she said, "Oh, it happens sometimes."

"Does that mean you're going to be grumpy all day?"

"Of course not. I'm in fine spirits." To prove it, Penelope smiled and turned at the bell announcing the arrival of a customer. To prove it even further, she managed to retain the smile even when she saw the prospective book-buyer to be Mrs. Eleanor Burnham. "Good morning," Penelope said brightly.

"It's almost afternoon, and you know it, Penelope Warren. I've been waiting hours for you to get here. Have you heard?"

"Heard what?"

Mrs. Burnham looked about, put a finger to her lips, and motioned Penelope closer. "Carolyn Lewis," she whispered.

"Yes?"

"Carolyn Lewis was preaching revolution, sedition, and treason at the high school. That's why she was murdered. I've already told that nice Detective Burke. He had jelly stains on his shirt."

"I can believe that, but sedition and treason . . ."

"It's true. She told her students that it was the right of the people to abolish the government. I don't think she liked President Clinton very much. And that nice Mrs. Clinton."

"Does it go something like this?" Penelope asked, closing her eyes to summon up long-ago classes. " 'When in the course of human events, it becomes necessary for one people to dissolve the political bands which have connected them with another,' et cetera. 'We hold these truths to be self-evident, that all men are created equal . . .' "

"That's it, exactly!" Mrs. Burnham cried. "Communism!"

Penelope sighed, not knowing where to begin. "Communism is dead, Mrs. Burnham. Don't you read the papers?"

"Only the society pages of the *Empty Creek News Journal.*"

"Or watch television?"

"I like *The Golden Girls.*"

"Naturally."

"But communism isn't dead," Mrs. Burnham persisted, "not in Empty Creek, not with teaching like that in our high school."

"Carolyn Lewis taught history. She was simply quoting the Declaration of Independence."

"Whose declaration?"

"Ours. The United States'. Thomas Jefferson wrote it."

"Well, he must have been a Communist too. What are you going to do about it?"

After Mrs. Burnham left, Penelope shook her head helplessly. Treason, indeed. She was still shaking her head when Kathy announced she was going to the post office. It's the water. It *has* to be the water. I must get Andy to test it, do an investigative series. We'll probably find we're all being poisoned by some obscure chemical that causes an incurable eccentricity.

Penelope had just vowed never to drink the water again, when the stirring sounds of the University of Southern California fight song heralded the rather indiscreet arrival of Discreet Investigations. A beaming Justin Beamish, behind the wheel of his red Cadillac convertible with enormous longhorns for a hood ornament, waved happily at Penelope and pressed the horn for another chorus of "Fight On." Behind the diminutive Beamish, twin behemoths named Ralph and Russell towered, grinning self-consciously.

"Don't you ever call?" Penelope asked when Just Beamish—all five foot two of him—clumped into Mycroft & Company. He wore his customary cowboy hat, plaid western shirt, jeans, and snakeskin cowboy boots. He barely had time to remove a long black unlit cigar from his mouth before disappearing into Penelope's arms for a quick hug and a kiss on the cheek.

Released, Beamish beamed and said, "Not when we can enjoy the presence of your company, dear lady."

And then it was Penelope's turn to disappear into the massive bear hugs proffered by first Ralph and then Russell, or vice versa—it was difficult to tell them apart. "Hi, Penelope," each said shyly. "Where's Laney?"

Since Penelope knew that both Ralph and Russell were enamored with unrequited love for the Ravishing Redhead, she did not take this inquiry as an affront. "Why don't you call her?" Penelope suggested as she checked herself gingerly for broken ribs. "Ask her to come in for lunch."

One of the twins lumbered to the telephone behind the counter while the other sat cross-legged on the floor and beckoned to Mycroft. "Hey, Big Mike," he said, "how's it hanging?"

Big Mike, who if suddenly transmogrified into human shape would no doubt match Ralph's—or Russell's—six foot eight and nearly three hundred pounds, ambled over for a surprisingly gentle chin-scratch.

"She'll meet us at the Double B," the telephoning twin announced.

"Cool," his brother responded.

"Kathy's at the post office," Penelope said. "We can go as soon as she returns. Who's minding the stores?" she added. The question was directed to the twins. Ralph operated the mail drop that was Discreet Investigations. Russell, on the other hand, was in charge of the adult bookstore next door, where there was a plentiful supply of reading material, magazines, videos, adult toys, and marital aids.

"Mother," the twins chorused. Both twins had the word *Mother* tattooed within a red heart emblazoned on their massive biceps.

"I really must meet your mother one day," Penelope said.

In due course, Mycroft & Company was closed for an hour— Kathy didn't want to miss any of the fun—and the entourage trooped across the street to the Double B. If any of the tourists or snowbirds thought the little company of two giants, a dwarflike man, two pretty young women, and a twenty-five-pound cat more than passing strange, they had the good manners not to mention it.

Two tables were pushed together, places claimed, a chair between Ralph and Russell saved for Laney, and drink orders placed with Debbie—iced tea for Penelope and Kathy, beer for the twins, diet cola for Beamish. Big Mike had already claimed his stool at the bar and was lapping up his favorite nonalcoholic beer, courtesy of Pete the bartender.

"And now, dear lady," Beamish said, "how can Discreet Investigations be of service?"

"Well, it's probably silly, but . . ." Penelope quickly explained the situation. She had just finished her summary of the sketchy facts, when Laney arrived.

"Ralphie," she squealed, "Russie."

When Laney emerged from the hugs-and-kisses portion of the program, Russell said gruffly, "Got something for you."

"How sweet. A present? A billet-doux? What? Don't keep me in suspense."

"Catalogue."

Laney had long urged Russell to compile such a catalogue of the various wares available from his little shop. She was far too shy to shop in person, even for such items as the flimsy undergarments she favored. Laney personally kept the Empty Creek post office hopping with deliveries from one catalogue or another.

"One for Penelope and Kathy too," Ralph added.

"At last," Laney cried, taking a magazine-sized package wrapped in brown paper. "How discreet," she said, ripping the plain covering off. And then Laney quickly thrust the catalogue beneath the table. "Oh, my God," she said, her voice filled with awe. Her blush deepened until her cheeks matched the deep red of her flowing mane. Still, it did not keep her from peeping beneath the table. "Oh, my God," she repeated.

"I think we'd better open ours later," Penelope said to Kathy.

"I think Your Majesty is right."

Over lunch, Just Beamish determined that Penelope had done the right thing in contacting Discreet Investigations. "Until this awful business is cleared up, dear lady . . ."

"Your Majesty," Kathy prompted.

"Yes, of course, Your Majesty. Until the crime is solved, we shall be at your side during the course of the Faire," Beamish declared. "Inconspicuously, of course."

"Of course," Penelope said, wondering how they would manage such a feat.

Penelope was quite capable of taking care of herself, as everyone present knew, but it didn't hurt to be just a little cautious. After all, she didn't want to leave Mycroft an orphan. Still, wearing the regal gowns of Elizabeth Regina didn't leave much room for concealing her AR-15 semiautomatic rifle, the civilian version of the M-16 rifle she had learned to fire quite well in the Marine Corps. She smiled at the thought of having a gown made in the camouflage pattern of the Marine Corps utility uniform and slinging the rifle over her shoulder for the royal procession.

"Better not hurt my queen," Ralph said.

"Tear his little head off," Russell said.

"Oh, my God," Laney said from beneath the table.

———

It was not until much later that Penelope remembered her mail order catalogue. When she removed it from the plain brown wrapper, she said, "Oh, my God," and instantly decided to confiscate Kathy's copy. It wouldn't do to give the child ideas.

Although . . .

What an interesting device that appeared to be.

CHAPTER
TEN

As the clock ticked inexorably backward toward the year of our Lord 1595 and another two-day reign on the throne of England, Penelope took action. It wasn't much of an action in the greater scheme of the universe or the *Farmer's Almanac*, but the slight gesture changed the course of civilization in Empty Creek and had profound influence on the lives of Penelope's many friends and one enemy. There was a whole bunch of other stuff as well, but it didn't really matter.

Eyes squinched against the light that penetrated the curtains, Penelope rolled over in bed.

That was it.

An infinitesimal blip on the cosmos.

But it disturbed Big Mike and the very pleasant dream he was having about Murphy Brown. Bounced somewhat unceremoniously from his reverie, Big Mike registered a complaint, not loud by his standards, but just enough to penetrate Penelope's consciousness, causing her to slowly awaken and, ultimately, arise ten minutes earlier than she might otherwise have done.

Ten minutes that changed the world. Sort of.

Penelope and Big Mike went through their morning routine together, avoiding pleasantries until the aroma of strong coffee filled the kitchen. Big Mike, settled on the windowsill, sleeping in the warm sunlight, fell out of his lofty perch twice, disguising each indignity by nonchalantly washing his face as if to tell Penelope, I planned my descent that way.

Penelope knew better and could not restrain a discreet giggle or two. Big Mike was always falling out of windowsill beds like that.

Although she dawdled over coffee and took a long time in showering and dressing (she could not decide between the charcoal-gray sweater and the red, finally choosing the latter because it was the Queen's prerogative to wear red), Penelope and Big Mike still managed to be at the door of the Jeep when the morning breeze blew a piece of paper into the yard.

Ten minutes earlier the piece of paper was nestled against a saguaro cactus down the road apiece. Ten minutes later the breeze would have picked up again and sent the paper flying away again toward Laney's home.

As it was, the offending paper was not allowed to spend its allotted ten minutes in Penelope's front yard before continuing its journey and its destined demise as lining in a bird nest.

Oh, well.

But, as Penelope would point out much later, it would have happened eventually anyway, even all that other stuff.

At the moment, however, since Penelope was a firm believer in free will and not predestination (or littering her beloved desert), she plucked the paper from the ground and was instantly horrified to find the royal melons displayed prominently on a flyer advertising the Empty Creek Elizabethan Springe Faire.

"Have you seen this?" Penelope demanded, still ten minutes ahead of schedule, waving the flyer in Kathy's face.

"Yes, of course, we have a stack of them here. All of the stores do."

"We do? They do?"

"There on the counter, Your Majesty."

"Not anymore we don't, not by a long shot," Penelope cried, uncaring of the triple negative she had just uttered. She gathered the stack of flyers and stuffed them into the San Diego State University bookbag that served as her briefcase when necessary, hoping that the alumni association of her beloved undergraduate days didn't hear of this. It would be just like them to publish the flyer in all its glorious detail in the "Class Notes" column.

"What's wrong, Your Majesty?"

"Wrong! Look at that picture of me."

"I think it's a very good picture," Kathy said.

"I'm practically naked."

The photographer had captured the Queen at the Royal Pavilion as she leaned over slightly to offer a token to her champion knight. The double dose of sun screen did nothing to protect her from the camera's lens.

"Well, it *is* a little revealing."

"Revealing? Revealing! Oh, my God, I hope Muffy and Biff never see it. They nearly died when they saw Stormy's first film." In her younger, more free-spirited days, Stormy had been so eager to sign her first film contract that she had failed to notice the nudity clause and, as a result, her statuesque body had been revealed to film aficionados around the world, particularly in Germany, where a number of Storm Williams fan clubs flourished. Now, of course, that clause had been eliminated from her contracts, although the skimpy costumes in her usual roles were even more suggestive.

"I think Timmy may be writing an ode to the royal breasts, Your Majesty."

"Tell him to cease and desist. I will not have my breasts, royal or otherwise, immortalized in verse."

"Well, who got *your* chastity belt in a bunch?" Laney asked as she entered the bookstore in the company of Alexander, who quickly yipped greetings to all present, bestowing dog kisses as he scampered from Penelope to Kathy to Big Mike.

"Don't say another word, unless you want to be referred to in the next edition of the *Empty Creek News Journal* as the *late* Elaine Henders." Penelope knelt to greet Alex.

"She's upset about the new publicity flyer for the Faire," Kathy said, kneeling in her turn to give Alex a good tummy-scratch.

"Whatever for? It's quite a good picture."

"That's what I said."

"You've seen it too?"

"Penelope dearest, *everyone's* seen it."

Penelope dearest groaned loudly.

Having saved a dog kiss or two for his best friend, Alex hunkered down on the hearth next to Big Mike and together they surveyed the room to see what would happen next. Something usually did.

Whenever it came time to beard culprits in their respective

dens, Penelope invariably called Laney, who was always ready for a good adventure. Together they had survived numerous exploits. And here providence—it was the ten-minute rule bubbling right along, although Penelope didn't know it yet—had courteously provided Laney's presence, saving the time and effort of a telephone call and an impatient wait.

"We're going to Scottsdale for lunch," Penelope announced.

"We are?" Laney said. "Why?"

"To see the people who put this . . . this . . . thing out," Penelope said, brandishing a flyer. "It's right here in the fine print. 'Wonder Ideas, an Advertising Agency for the Twenty-first Century, Scottsdale.' I'll give them an idea or two that will carry them well into the twenty-second century."

Big Mike, who could take Scottsdale or leave it, stretched languorously. After all, he was a well-traveled cat who had peed on three continents (if England was to be counted as a part of Europe proper), several states, and the District of Columbia.

Alexander, who had left *his* mark only in states where romance writers met for one convention or another, had never been to Scottsdale and thought he wanted to visit that trendy little city very much. Thus, he went ballistic barking-wise, reminding all concerned that he was being left behind. Once the door was shut firmly in his furry face, he ran back and forth from the door to Kathy, yipping plaintively. Kathy translated his remarks as They left me. Did you see that? They left me!

After the noisy departure, and after consoling Alexander with a dog treat from the stash Penelope kept for his frequent visits, Kathy went beneath the counter and replaced the flyers Penelope had confiscated. It *was* a good picture of the Queen, and besides the Faire needed all the publicity it could get, a sentiment that would be repeated later in Scottsdale.

On the way to Scottsdale, Penelope and Laney sang along with Garth Brooks and his "Friends in Low Places," belting the chorus out with considerable zeal. At the conclusion, Penelope hit replay on the CD and they sang it again. This occupied the duo all the way from Empty Creek through Cave Creek and Carefree until they turned on Scottsdale Road. From there it was a straight shot through the desert down to Scottsdale.

"By the way," Laney said, "thank you so much for the chastity belt. That's why I stopped by this morning. We've been having ever so much fun."

"You didn't actually try it out?"

"Well, of course. Why not? The first thing I did—"

"I don't want to hear it," Penelope cried, putting her hands over her ears but not very tightly. Who could tell what delicious game Laney might have come up with this time?

"But I love it," Laney exclaimed. "There I am, the poor love-starved princess, languishing in my tower prison, guarded incidentally by a fierce dragon, when the gallant Sir Knight comes to my rescue."

"I knew it," Penelope said, "or, rather, Andy knew it. He suggested Mikey as the dragon."

"The man shows definite promise. Under my tutelage—"

"I don't think I could stand it," Penelope interrupted.

"Where is your sense of adventure?"

"It's sadly lacking of late."

———

Scottsdale was one of those places that competed with Empty Creek for the tourist dollar, usually winning the battle because it had more hotels, golf courses, art galleries, restaurants, boutiques, and bookstores. Its souvenir shops were filled with Indian jewelry, stuffed rattlesnakes, and T-shirts emblazoned with skeletons crawling through the desert and a slogan that read BUT IT'S A DRY HEAT. Scottsdale's various festivals were always bigger and gaudier than those in Cave Creek. Its Arabian National Horse Show was much larger and more prestigious than Empty Creek's own version. Still, Scottsdale was only Scottsdale while Empty Creek was Empty-by-God Creek Arizona and Don't You Damn Well Forget It, as Red the Rat frequently proclaimed while in his cups.

Empty-by-God Creek, Arizona, also had better hamburgers as served at the Double B Western Saloon and Steakhouse, a fact Penelope was quick to point out to Laney while picking a tangled snarl of healthy bean sprouts from where there should have been a big thick slice of red onion. Once the ingredients had been rearranged to their liking, however, both women scarfed down the burgers and steak fries with considerable zeal. They paid homage to their little hometown by drinking Empty Creek's own home-brewed beer, a mysterious concoction in which jalapeño peppers were an integral part of the recipe. As a result, sweat was pouring from their faces by the time they had finished their repast.

"The beer, at least, was good," Laney said, mopping delicately at her brow with a napkin.

"Excellent," Penelope agreed.

———

Wonder Ideas, an Advertising Agency for the 21st Century, was located on Main Street in the Old Town section of Scottsdale. A diagonal arrow pointed to the second floor above an art gallery. Penelope and Laney climbed the steps, found a door with a sign that said enter, and followed its instructions to find themselves in a light and airy suite that seemed empty of human habitation.

"Hello, Wonder Ideas," Penelope called.

"I'm in the bathroom," a disembodied male voice hollered back. "I'll be right out."

"Don't forget to wash your hands."

"Penelope!"

"I won't."

"Well, that's what Muffy always used to say."

"Still . . . oh, look, there's Carolyn as the Queen."

There was indeed a full-color photograph of Carolyn and Sir Robert Dudley. In fact, one wall of the office was lined with similar photographs from the Faire, all featuring Carolyn Lewis with a succession of Sir Robert Dudleys, the most recent with Sharon's Bobby. On the other walls, a variety of photographs depicted the various activities of the Faire.

"I washed my hands. See."

Penelope and Laney turned to find a lanky young man towering over them. He displayed a crumpled paper towel which he immediately tossed through a miniature basketball hoop with a very credible hook shot. It swished into the wastebasket below.

"Two points," he cried. "Quentin Parnelle, Wonder Ideas. You just caught me. Another ten minutes and I would have been gone. How may I help you?"

"You are Wonder Ideas?"

"Late of the University of New Mexico, once a lobo always a lobo, and now sole proprietor of ideas for the twenty-first century. Do you wish a ditty? I compose excellent ditties."

"Well," Penelope said, drawing herself to her full height. Although she was no shrimp, Quentin Parnelle was at least a foot taller. Penelope wished she had worn heels. "I am Penelope Warren, currently doubling as Elizabeth Regina."

Parnelle snapped his fingers. "Of course, the new Queen. I didn't recognize you in civilian clothes. You should have come tomorrow." He pointed to the wall. "You would be hanging there. You're being framed at the moment."

"I certainly am, but I don't want to hang on your wall, framed or otherwise, nor do I wish to adorn these flyers," Penelope said, pulling Exhibit A from her purse.

"What's wrong with it?" Quentin Parnelle took the flyer and examined it.

"Wrong? Just look at my picture."

"But it's a very good picture. I took it myself. You're very photogenic. Much better than Carolyn. I had to take hundreds of shots to get something usable, and because she kept changing Dudleys, I had to keep shooting. God, I dreaded those endless auditions. Every shot I took of you turned out very well."

"Well, I don't like it. You should have asked."

"But it's the rule. You're the Queen."

"Whose rule?"

"Someone's. I don't know. It's always been like that. The Queen is the focus of the Faire's advertising. Besides, we need some good publicity for a change."

"The question is, what are you going to do about . . . about . . . *it?*"

"Well, the insertion orders for the newspaper ads just went out and—"

"Newspaper ads," Penelope cried.

"And there's television of course—"

"Television!"

"Only cable. It's less expensive, but still reaches a very wide audience."

Penelope groaned.

"And radio."

That was some small consolation. At least radio wouldn't be showing the royal bosom to the entire Valley of the Sun.

"I wish there was something I could do. . . ."

"How about billboards?" Laney suggested.

"Argh!" Penelope wanted to scream. "And from my best friend too."

"I'm only trying to help. I think it would be good for business at Mycroft & Company."

"Why don't Kathy and I just go topless?"

"That would certainly bring in the business," Parnelle said. "I'd become a patron. Whatever Mycroft & Company happens to sell."

"Books."

"That's good. I like to read. Shall we get your advertising campaign under way immediately?"

"We shall not."

Fortunately, the telephone rang before Parnelle could present a marketing and advertising plan for the first topless mystery bookstore in Empty Creek.

"It's for you," Parnelle said, holding out the telephone.

Penelope raised her eyebrows quizzically.

Laney shrugged and listened to Penelope's half of the conversation.

"Hello . . . oh, hi . . . no, we're about to leave. Another ten minutes and you would have missed us . . . you what . . . oh, all right, I give up . . . yes . . . no, we'll be back soon . . . me too."

Penelope hung up, and sighing heavily turned to face her expectant audience. "That was Andy, my boyfriend," she explained for Parnelle's benefit. "He loves the flyer and wants to get an original print."

"See," Laney said, "I told you it was a good picture."

"The Sir Walter Raleigh who looks like Ichabod Crane?"

"The very same. Will you make a print for him? He'll pay, of course."

"My treat. A present for the Queen."

"Thank you, I think," Penelope said. "Now, you said something about auditions. Do you remember them all?"

"Not really," Parnell said. "There were so many over the years."

"Too bad. It might have been helpful in finding Carolyn's murderer."

"But Amanda does."

"Amanda? Who is Amanda?"

"My computer. I named her for an old girlfriend."

"What happened to her?"

"She married her basketball coach."

"How rotten of her."

"Not really," Parnelle said, "she was taller than me. A real beanpole. Our children might have been ten feet tall."

"Will you make copies of your records for me?"

"Sure," Parnell said cheerfully. "Let's get Amanda warmed up."

Penelope tucked the floppy disks safely into her purse, thanked Parnelle once again, and followed Laney down the stairs.

What with one thing and another—the return drive, attending to business matters at Mycroft & Company and to Mycroft himself, a shopping excursion for office supplies, drinks at the Double B, and an impromptu feast at the Duck Pond, the best Mexican restaurant west of the Mississippi River—it was rather late before Penelope, Andy, and Big Mike got home.

After feeding Chardonnay—and promising her a good romp soon—Penelope left Andy in the living room, watching the snippets of *Citizen Kane* occasionally interspersed throughout prolonged commercial breaks on the telly and went into her little home office.

She popped a floppy disk into drive A, summoned the files to her screen, and scrolled through the various and sundry records of the Empty Creek Elizabethan Springe Faire.

First Penelope charted the lineage of the prior Queen's succession of lovers. Armed with poster board, Magic Markers in various colors, and the assistance of Big Mike, Penelope traced the tangled meanderings of Carolyn Lewis's love life as the Queen.

Carolyn had assumed the throne in 1586 with the first Sir Robert Dudley as her constant companion, both at court and in the confines of the royal tent. The first years of her reign had been relatively normal, but in the fourth, the year after the defeat of the Spanish Armada, she had been unceremoniously dumped by her longtime friend for a serving wench.

That was the beginning of the troubles. Carolyn took her

loss hard and, in 1590, began taking one lover after another, exacting a measure of revenge at the conclusion of each Faire by becoming the dumper rather than the dumpee. Talk about the royal imbroglios of today. Charles and Diana were distant finishers in the peccadillo department.

Penelope paused. It was somewhere during this time frame that Carolyn had convinced herself she really was Elizabeth Regina, ruling her subjects with a high hand, demanding and receiving total fealty. Astounding, Penelope thought. Someone should have told Her Royal Majesty to buzz off. But, as Penelope had begun to learn, those who participated in the Faire had a rather tenuous grasp on reality at best. They really did think they were subjects of the English crown.

The next Sir Robert had then been demoted to Lord High Mayor, a post of considerable respect, responsibility, and honor, but not at the exalted level of the Queen's lover. He was followed in 1592 by the man who now played the Lord High Sheriff, and in 1593 by none other than Sir Francis Bacon, a fact that Sir Francis had curiously omitted in any discussions with Penelope. The break in routine had come when Sharon's teacher and mentor had assumed the post in 1594 and was commanded to reprise his role in 1595.

Penelope had just asked Big Mike what he thought of all this, when the telephone rang, interrupting what might have been a most interesting reply.

"Hello."

"Thank God, you're there. I've been calling for hours. Did you forget to turn your answering machine on?"

"I don't have an answering machine," Penelope replied. "I don't believe in them. Who is this anyway?"

"Quentin Parnelle. You've got all the files."

"Yes. You said that this afternoon."

"No, I mean, really, you have the only files now. My computer crashed ten minutes after you left."

"Well, don't you back up your files?"

"Yes, of course, but someone erased all of them. My computer man says it was done deliberately. Poor Amanda. She was poisoned by a virus. Who would do such a thing to her?"

Who, indeed?

CHAPTER
ELEVEN

Even the Empty Creek National Bank, that most conservative of local business establishments, displayed the notorious flyer prominently amid other, more decorous advertising for financial deals of one sort or another—interest rates, home and automobile loans, certificates of deposit. Fortunately, from Penelope's point of view, it was a small bank with only four teller cages and two counters where the flyer could be conveniently displayed. Unfortunately, from the same POV, nearly everyone in town patronized the bank, just as they did every other establishment. There was no escape from the advertising campaign of Wonder Ideas.

There were only two customers and the staff present when Penelope walked down from Mycroft & Company, entered the bank, and saw the flyers, but she felt every eye was focused disapprovingly upon her.

The president of the Empty Creek National Bank, Samantha Dale—"Sam" to her friends and customers—waved and beckoned to Penelope from the confines of her tiny office, rising to greet Penelope formally, offering her hand. "Hello, Penelope, we were just talking about you this morning at the chamber breakfast."

"Oh, Lord, I suppose I'm going to be drummed out in disgrace." Penelope was a member of the chamber of commerce, of course, but rarely joined in their activities because of the early hour at which they insisted on meeting.

"Not at all," Sam replied, "we're all quite proud of you and behind you all the way." She smiled. "After all, what's good for the Faire is good for Empty Creek and business."

That had not been the opinion when Sam became president of the bank some five years earlier. There had been fierce resistance to her appointment from the macho element in town, overcome only when the chairman of the bank's board of directors declared rather vehemently, and managing to achieve political correctness at the same time, "She's the smartest person we interviewed and we're going to damn well hire her."

Since then Samantha Dale had dazzled one and all with her knowledge, financial wizardry, and the steadily rising dividends paid to the bank's shareholders. Her detractors had long since stopped pointing to Sam's tall and slender figure and beautiful face framed by soft blond hair as the primary reasons she had been able to bewitch the board into hiring her.

But Penelope's endearing memory of Samantha, who was always cool, sophisticated, and elegantly dressed, came from a time two years earlier, when a sudden thunderstorm had doused the Empty Creek Arabian Horse Show. Trapped beneath a leaky awning, Penelope and Sam decided to take advantage of a brief lull to dash for the car—Penelope's Jeep was closest—and when they had reached shelter, Penelope glanced over at a soaked but laughing Samantha, wet hair plastered to her head, looking for all the world like a cheerfully drenched kitten. After drying out, they had driven to the Double B for a late lunch. Since then they had been close friends.

"How can we help you today?" Sam asked.

"There's no need for you to bother. I just have a couple of things to put in my safety deposit box."

"It's no trouble at all. I'll do it."

Penelope followed Sam to the safety deposit boxes, waited while she unlocked the gleaming bars that blocked entry to the room, and together they unlocked Penelope's box. Sam stood discreetly aside as Penelope dropped the floppy disks containing all the records of the Faire on top of her own collection of important belongings—honorable discharge from the United States Marine Corps, certificate of service in the Peace Corps, her degrees from San Diego State and Arizona State, the diamond earrings Andy had given her for Christmas last year—and which she refused to wear except for very special occasions—a calendar from an African witch doctor advertising the various spells and potions available with his services, and a thick assortment of photographs chronicling Big Mike's life from kittenhood on.

When the box had been returned to its cubicle, Sam asked, "Do you have time for coffee? It's been so long since we've had a chance to talk."

"I'd like that," Penelope said.

They crossed the street to Mom's Do-Nuts. Mom was actually a burly dad named Paul Bowers who always explained, "Who wants to eat Dad's jelly doughnuts?" Mom or Dad, the jelly doughnuts were a perennial favorite of the Empty Creek Police Department, so neither Penelope nor Sam was surprised to find Sam Connors and Peggy Norton inside, taking their break. Their black-and-white would be discreetly parked behind Mom's. Samantha always quipped that Mom's was the safest place in town and that all banks should be located near a doughnut shop as a deterrent to bank robberies. Her premise appeared to be true, because the Empty Creek National Bank had not been robbed even once since Mom's took up its watchful post across the street.

Greetings were exchanged with the usual confusion of having two Sams present, and then Sam the cop asked, "Any progress, Penny?" He used the diminutive fondly. Penelope and Sam had once dated briefly before Big Mike had chosen an unfortunate portion of Sam's anatomy to use as a scratching post during some amorous activities. The ensuing screech dampened all ardor and was the reason Big Mike was now banished from the bedroom whenever Cupid hovered in the shadows. It also explained why Debbie D did not have a cat.

Penelope told them of the mysterious computer crash.

"Tweedledee and Tweedledum should know," Peggy said.

"They're my next stop," Penelope said. "I want to see Dutch too." Since Penelope was still running ten minutes ahead of schedule, she didn't know that they were about to join her, along with most of Empty Creek's finest.

"We had a good time at the Faire," Sam said. "You make a great Queen."

As a thank-you, Penelope curtsied and then went to get coffee.

"I know you can't tell me if there were any financial irregularities in Carolyn Lewis's accounts," Penelope said when they were settled in at their own table.

Sam shook her head. "No, I can't tell you anything."

"I suppose she had just the usual," Penelope offered, "a checking account, a small savings account, perhaps a small investment or two, something safe."

"I suppose if I could tell you anything," Sam said with a smile, "that might sum it up very nicely."

Penelope shook her head. "Well, I'm stumped."

"Why don't you tell me about it? Perhaps I can help." Like a great many of Empty Creek's citizens, Sam was equally horrified and fascinated by murder, avidly following each rare instance of violent death.

Penelope summarized the case for Samantha, telling her of Carolyn's record at school and apparently dull personal life away from her duties as Queen; Lothario, Dudley's disappearance, the ominous notes; Carolyn's penchant for taking new lovers at each Faire; even the chastity belt.

Sam laughed. "That sounds just like Laney. I can hardly wait for her next novel. Her heroines always get into the most impossible situations. Rather like you. Do you like being the Queen?"

"On the record," Penelope said, "no." She stared wistfully into her coffee cup for a moment and then looked up and smiled. "But off the record, yes. It *is* rather fun playing make-believe. But don't tell anyone I said that. I firmly believe in term limits for the monarchy. I shall retire after the Ides of March."

"Yes . . . the Ides of March . . . what if . . . no, that's silly."

"What were you going to say?"

"What if Carolyn was killed because she *was* the Queen and not because of anything in her personal life?"

"A political assassination?"

"Exactly!"

"In that case, whoever did it would have to be totally bonkers. It doesn't make any sense. Who would be crazy enough to try and change the course of Elizabethan England four centuries later?"

"I don't know, but my favorite Shakespearean plays were always the tragedies. *Hamlet, Macbeth, Lear, Julius Caesar.* They were all about murder and the usurpation of power in one way or another."

"Someone in the royal court?"

"Dudley."

"But he has an alibi."

"What of the other Dudleys? It's midnight. Do you know where they are?"

Sam and Peggy waved good-bye as they went out the back door to resume their patrol of the quiet streets of Empty Creek.

"But why did Bobby get the Ides of March warning too?"

"I don't know. *That* doesn't make much sense."

"None of it makes any sense."

"Well, I'd better get back to work," Samantha said, looking at her watch.

"This has been nice," Penelope said. "I'll go back with you. I might as well get some cash for the weekend as long as I'm here. See you later, Paul."

They crossed the street and entered the bank, running right smack into Mrs. Eleanor Burnham fluttering about in her birdlike manner. "Ah, there you are, Samantha Dale, I've been waiting for you and Penelope Warren too."

Samantha smiled brightly. "Mrs. Burnham, how good to see you."

Penelope admired Sam's ability to quickly and cheerfully adapt, when the sight of Empty Creek's town crier made her want to do nothing more than run as fast as possible. I can always get money some other time, she thought. "I have to get back to the store. I'll see you all later."

Penelope turned, took one step, and stopped abruptly as the doors flew open and two men wearing red bandannas over the faces and brandishing a variety of firearms burst into the bank.

"This is a stickup. Nobody move!"

"Get up against the wall!"

"Everyone cooperate," Samantha ordered, following the standard operating procedure for this situation. A few thousand dollars was not worth anyone's life. "Do exactly as they want." But so much for the doughnut-shop theory, she thought glumly.

"We're all going to be killed," Mrs. Burnham cried.

"You just told us not to move," Penelope pointed out.

"Move!"

"Don't move!"

"Please, make up your mind."

The two men conferred briefly. "All right, you can move, but just to line up against the wall. No funny business, or else." He waved his revolver menacingly and dropped a ring of keys on the floor.

"Get 'em against the wall, Carl."

"Which one, Marty?"

"That one, for Christ's sake, away from the window."

"We're all going to be killed," Mrs. Burnham cried once more as she scurried to the wall.

"Hands up and keep 'em there."

Mrs. Burnham reached for the sky.

Samantha tripped a silent alarm.

Penelope scuffled the keys along the floor as she went to take her place against the wall.

The small radios attached to police uniform shirts all over town crackled suddenly as Sheila Tyler's calm voice transmitted, "Possible two-eleven in progress. Silent alarm at Empty Creek National Bank. Units respond code two."

Sam Connors and Peggy Norton were the first police officers on the scene since they had been standing in Mom's parking lot having a spirited and prolonged argument over whose turn it was to drive. When the call came in, Sam and Peggy looked at each other for an instant.

Hot damn!

Then they took off running, splitting up, each circling around to take up positions at opposite corners of the building, where they were hidden from the view of anyone inside the bank.

Everything at the bank appeared to be normal. The alarm could have malfunctioned or been accidentally tripped. There was a dirty black Camaro with California plates parked at the curb, but the engine was not running and there was no nervous getaway driver at the wheel.

Peggy and Sam exchanged a thumbs-up. They were ready. Peggy rehearsed her lines but she was undecided about the order. Police officers! Freeze! Or, as an alternative, Freeze!

Police officers! She had just chosen the former, when the cavalry arrived. Damn, every cop in town was going to be in on this bust if, indeed, it was not a false alarm.

Black-and-whites and unmarked cars were arriving from all directions. Penelope would have been impressed with the efficiency of the operation had she not been standing against the wall of the bank with her arms raised. Each car took up a different position until the bank was surrounded by police officers and detectives. A dozen shotguns had rounds jacked into their chambers. Tweedledee and Tweedledum were hopping about with excitement. Tweedledee had a bullhorn in one hand and his gun in the other. Dutch was there, speaking quietly into the radio, directing operations. Andy, who had seen police cars speeding past the *Empty Creek News Journal*, trotted up, followed by the staff photographer who had shot a roll of film before Andy had the chance to ask of Dutch, "What's up?" Any erstwhile bank robber inside, however, might look out and see nothing amiss.

Fat chance of Marty and Carl noticing anything. They were too busy arguing over which cash drawer to empty first.

"We're all going to be killed," Mrs. Burnham whimpered.

"Pretend nothing's happening," Penelope said calmly, wishing, however, that Mrs. Burnham did her banking with another financial institution.

"I never realized how tiring it was to stand with your arms up," Samantha said. "It doesn't seem like that in the movies."

"You guys shut up," Marty shouted.

"We're just passing the time," Penelope said.

"Well, don't."

As bank robberies go, Penelope thought this one resembled something that Donald Westlake's bumbling criminals might have planned. Penelope could just imagine the dialogue leading up to this moment.

Whatcha wanna do today, Carl?

I don't know, Marty, whatchu wanna do?

Let's go to Arizona and rob a bank.

Bonnie and Clyde they weren't. Penelope wanted to pat the little dears on the head and tell them how to go about robbing a bank properly. At the very least they should have invested in some decent ski masks if they were going to look directly into each of the bank's hidden cameras with their bandannas slipping every which way.

"Just take the green stuff."

"The quarters are good for the Laundromat. We never have enough quarters."

"We'll buy new clothes, for Christ's sake. Just take the bills."

"And video games."

"Take the quarters, then, but hurry up, will ya?"

"I'm hurrying."

"Ya wanta count it? See if we got enough."

"No, I don't wanna count it. I wanna get outa here now."

"Let's go, then."

"Nobody move for ten minutes. Anybody sticks a nose out the door gonna get hurt."

Good God, Penelope thought, who is writing their dialogue?

"Remember, ten minutes."

Marty and Carl backed through the doors.

"Oh, my, I thought for sure we were going to be killed."

A sigh of relief went up among the assembled customers and bank staff.

Penelope retrieved the car keys from the floor and held them up for Samantha to see.

"Theirs?" Sam asked.

"Yup," Penelope drawled.

Sam burst into laughter. "Oh, my God, what a pair."

A collective shout penetrated the bank. In fact, the policemen's delight could be heard nearly all the way to the next county.

"Freeze!"

"I believe help is at hand," Penelope said.

"I believe it is," Sam replied.

The next several hours put a serious crimp in Penelope's plans for the day. First everyone had to tell their version of the abortive robbery to a series of police officers and detectives.

Just my luck to get Tweedledee and Tweedledum, Penelope thought, instead of Dutch.

Then, like a game of musical chairs, everyone switched partners and repeated their tale of what was already known as the Great Empty Creek Bank Robbery.

When special agents from the Federal Bureau of Investigation arrived from the Phoenix office, the process was repeated once again. Penelope's luck held and she had to relate the day's events to the FBI's version of the Mad Hatter.

All the while, the curious among Empty Creek's citizenry—which was most of them—peered through the bank's windows at the law enforcement tableau. Between interviews Penelope waved and smiled at Andy, who stood forlornly on the outside, excluded from the proceedings because he was a newspaperman, along with a couple of TV crews from Phoenix. Apparently, it was a slow news day with little more than the usual world strife going on. First Dutch and then Samantha issued brief prepared statements, and that was it for the media.

The Phoenix TV crews were more than a little dismayed when Kathy arrived with Big Mike in her arms and the cat was immediately granted entrance to the crime scene.

Lola LaPola, one of the TV reporters—Penelope couldn't stand her eternally breathless reports and always switched to another channel when she came on—threw a hissy fit at that. "It's a goddam cat," she wailed, attempting to thrust her mike through the door. "I'm from the fourth estate."

"Big Mike's an honorary cop," she was told as the door slammed rudely in her face.

Big Mike immediately leapt to the teller's counter to survey the activity.

Marty and Carl turned out to be drifters from Fresno, California, on their way to some undetermined location in search of "kicks," financing their trip with ill-gotten gains. That information was relayed to Penelope by Peggy Norton, who was still excited from covering Marty and Carl with her 9mm Beretta while Sam put the handcuffs on them. "You should have seen their faces," Peggy whispered.

When Penelope and the others were finally released, Andy gave her a big hug. "Are you all right?" he asked anxiously.

"I'm fine, sweetie," Penelope whispered. "Do your job and then I'll give you an exclusive."

"We were at death's door," Mrs. Burnham told Lola LaPola, who was pushing through the crowd to Penelope.

"No comment," Penelope said, winking at Andy.

It was only much later, after Penelope had told all to Andy, he had gone off to write his story, the store had been closed, and she had finally gotten home that she realized with all of the excitement she had never gotten around to telling Dutch or Tweedledee and Tweedledum about the computer crash that might be of great significance. That pesky ten minutes was still bubbling along, maliciously disrupting everything in its path.

Penelope called Stormy and got a busy signal. She called Laney and got a busy signal. The Empty Creek grapevine was obviously buzzing. Gathering peppermint candies and scraps of lettuce, Penelope went off down the path with Big Mike to feed Chardonnay and the bunny rabbits.

When they returned to the house, leaving contented wildlife in their wake, Penelope tried phoning again. This time she reached Stormy, only to find that Dutch was still working, but told her tale of the bank robbery for the umpteenth time to Laney.

"Thank God, you're here," she cried when Andy drove up and entered the house, "but not another word about today. Promise."

"I promise," Andy said, going directly to the television set and turning it on. "I just want to see what Lola has to say about the robbery."

"Lola?"

"We had quite a nice chat after she did her remote. I thought we might have her to dinner sometime."

"Not on your life, sweetie. Not Lola-from-the-fourth-estate LaPola."

The sound came up on the television just in time for Penelope to hear Mrs. Burnham for the last time that day. "We were all going to be killed."

Penelope fled to the kitchen.

After dinner Andy did the dishes while Penelope lingered over her glass of wine in the living room. She had just about decided to give Dutch another call, even going so far as to cross the room to the telephone, but then Andy came up behind her and embraced her, kissing the nape of her neck and causing little blond hairs to stand on end. And when he began doing that other thing that always set her inner fires to raging, Penelope forgot all about police business.

It was too bad, because a life might have been saved.

CHAPTER
TWELVE

E ach weekend of the Faire featured a variety of different spectacles. Opening weekend had focused on the Queen and her royal court until the unfortunate demise of Elizabeth Regina. Penelope's own opening weekend was given over to royal jousts and combats. In looking over the Faire program—the misspelling of Ralegh's name still irritated her—Penelope found that Saturday and Sunday would star the Picts and the Celts. The following weekend—the Ides of March and the swan song of her reign—was devoted to the Peasants' Rebellion, the military, and the great playwrights, all of which seemed very tiring to Penelope as she urged Chardonnay into the scrub-covered hills above Empty Creek.

Chardonnay had not been ridden since Penelope assumed the throne and she obliged happily, snorting and tossing her mane, ready to flatten her ears and run.

"Hang on, Mikey," Penelope hollered.

Big Mike, who enjoyed riding as much as the next cat, was

perched in a saddlebag behind Penelope. He dug his claws into the leather and meowed loudly. Normally, Alexander would have been in the opposite saddlebag, yipping away, the fur on his tiny face blowing in the breeze, but Penelope hadn't been up to facing Laney's questions that morning and opted, instead, for some quiet time.

Higher and higher they rode until they reached Penelope's favorite clearing, where they could look down at the endless desert, pristine in the late morning. The little community of Empty Creek snuggled close to the base of Crying Woman Mountain. Even in the distance Penelope could pick out the house Stormy and Dutch now shared halfway up the slope of the dark and brooding mountain where the spirit of an Indian maiden lived and could be heard weeping by a chosen few. Penelope had heard the tortured sobs a number of times.

"Why is Dutch acting so funny?" Penelope asked of Mikey, Chardonnay, and the soft winter breeze. Mikey batted at a fly that buzzed past his nose, Chardonnay snorted and pawed the ground, the breeze held its tongue. When Dutch had finally returned her telephone call that morning, he had been abrupt, saying only that he was too busy to see her. When Penelope insisted, he had reluctantly agreed to give her a few minutes.

"It's not like him at all, guys," Penelope said to her friends, leaning forward to stroke Chardonnay's neck. Then again, murder and bank robbery, however inept the perpetrators, were highly unusual events for Empty Creek. Were they prelude to the Ides of March weekend, Penelope wondered as she leaned back to scratch Mikey's chin—there was no need to provoke jealously among her feline and equine friends. She needn't have worried. Big Mike was quite content to stare out at the horizon, pondering his own thoughts.

High above, a hawk circled, gliding through the sky, riding the wind currents gracefully with outstretched wings. Penelope shielded her eyes as she looked up at the predator, knowing its sharp talons and beak could instantly kill an unsuspecting mouse or small rabbit. And yet it was so beautiful. And ominous?

Grim portents were not limited to Shakespearean tragedy. *The Anglo-Saxon Chronicle* also pointed to famines, eclipses of the moon and sun, strange celestial lights, comets such as never seen before, and pestilence as harbingers of momentous events—the deaths of kings and bishops, fierce battles, the invasions of the Danes and Normans.

"All very well for literature," Penelope told the wind, since it seemed to be the only one listening. Chardonnay was munching a leaf and Mycroft was now teetering precariously on his hind legs as he went after the fly again. "But not for real life and certainly not for this Queen, however modest my reign."

Still, a visit to the Royal Astrologer might be in order. Just as a precaution, of course.

"Let's get to work, guys."

Another ten minutes passed as Chardonnay balked, at first reluctant to leave the juicy leaves and then, when given her head, she took the wrong path. The brief interruption should have put the universe back on schedule, but, perversity being what it is, it didn't.

"Dutch is expecting me."

"He's on the warpath," Sheila Tyler warned. "Oops, that

may be politically incorrect." She stroked Big Mike's head fondly after he leapt to the counter.

"I won't tell anyone."

"Let's just say he's in an extremely bad mood."

"Well, I'll just have to cheer him up. Right?"

Wrong.

Sheila buzzed the counter door open and Penelope entered the inner sanctum of the Empty Creek P.D. to follow a meandering path through the warren of hallways, office cubicles, and the bullpen, where desks were separated by room dividers, to Dutch's office, losing Big Mike along the way because he had stopped off to investigate some clues in the little office shared by Tweedledee and Tweedledum. Since they were out, Penelope saw no harm in letting him rummage through an old jelly doughnut wrapper or two.

"What?" Dutch shouted in reply to Penelope's light tap on his closed door.

Penelope took a deep breath, put on her game face, and opened the door.

"My, aren't we grumpy today," she said, claiming the privilege of beloved sister-in-law-to-be and the chair in front of his desk.

"I could have stayed in L.A. if I wanted to fight crime waves."

"But, then, you would have never met the beautiful and charming Warren sisters. Especially me."

"Most especially not you!"

"Why, Dutch, whatever could I have done?"

"You're pigheaded, obstinate, meddlesome, and won't listen to reason," Dutch exclaimed.

"Is *that* all? I'm practically a candidate for sainthood in my own lifetime."

"And as for your sister—"

"What has the inestimable Stormy done to incur your wrath?"

"She agrees with you, goddammit!"

"Of course she does. I'm right."

"Right about what?"

"Everything."

Dutch groaned. "I give up."

"Please, don't," Penelope said with a grin. "I love it when you're so macho, and here you are wearing my favorite shoulder holster too. I'm getting all excited."

Dutch truly surrendered and offered a shy, conciliatory grin in return. "Does Andy know you lust for my body?"

"Not your body, silly, your shoulder holster. I just love the way your gun hangs upside down like that."

"All right, all right, what do you want?"

"Nothing."

"Then why are you wasting my time?"

"I have something to give you. I was going to tell you yesterday, but then Marty and Carl happened by—how are they doing, by the way?"

"Complaining about the food. Get on with it."

"Well, anyway . . ." Penelope presented the facts of the computer crash and the mysterious erasure of all of Quentin Parnelle's backup disks briefly and succinctly, thinking when she had finished, I would make a very good lawyer. Certainly better than Robert Shapiro and Marcia Clark, who, to her mind, both tended to ramble.

"That's it?" Dutch asked rather skeptically. "A computer

crashes and you think it's linked to the Lewis murder? It seems a little coincidental. Computers crash around here all the time."

"Around here," Penelope observed dryly, "it's probably operator error. Anyway, that's what I was doing at the bank yesterday. I have backups in my safe deposit box and I have a set for you . . . *if* you want them."

Dutch sighed and held his hand out.

Penelope passed the floppies across the desk.

"Won't you give it up, Penelope? And convince Stormy too. I really think you're in danger out there. Stormy, too, now that she's running around as queen of the pickles."

"Picts."

"Whatever."

"I thought you said she looked peachy, or words to that effect."

"I did, but she could do that at home, not out there with some crazy running around killing women who pretend to be queens."

"What's your favorite Stormy movie?" Penelope asked.

"All of them."

Dutch had a complete set of Stormy's cinematic career on video, all neatly aligned between bookends on his desk. Penelope suspected that during less trying times in the fight against crime he spent his afternoons watching them.

"I like them all too, of course, but I think if I had to pick a favorite, it would be her first." *Biker Chick* was a blatant ripoff of *The Magnificent Seven* in which Stormy had played a tough, Harley-riding moll, leading her intrepid band of women warriors on a crusade to clean up a corrupt California beach town.

"And you're going to clean up the mess at the Faire?"

Penelope nodded. "With your help, of course."

"Somebody get this cat out of my wastebasket!"

Penelope recognized the thundering voice, of course.

A loud clatter echoed through the Empty Creek police station, followed by another . . . and another.

Oh-oh.

"I thought things were a little too quiet around here today," Dutch said as he followed Penelope to the disaster scene.

Penelope quickly put the chain of events straight. Mycroft had been dozing peacefully in the wastebasket, minding his own business, when Burke and Stoner returned. Tweedledee's loud shout had startled Mycroft, who then leapt straight up, overturning the wastebasket in the process. Still half asleep and startled again by that crash, Mycroft had landed in the in basket and knocked that to the floor as well. Now Big Mike was on the desk, hair standing on end, hissing fiercely, daring Burke and Stoner to duke it out.

"You shouldn't frighten Mikey like that," Penelope told Tweedledee. "How would you like it if someone started shouting at you when you were asleep?"

"My wife does it all the time."

"I can just imagine."

"Aw, boss, I didn't do anything. He attacked me, and look at the mess. I just got all those papers sorted out too."

"Well, sort 'em again, and when you're through, I got some computer disks for you to work on."

All right, Dutch!

Penelope and Big Mike—quite recovered from his abrupt awakening—found Alyce Smith in her guise as Madame Astoria, basking in the glow of new love and the aftermath of any number of passionate kisses so recently exchanged with a young man Penelope would have recognized as a rather fickle Lothario had she but arrived a few minutes earlier, ten minutes earlier to be precise.

Still warm and flushed from her encounter with love's softer side and looking forward to the evening when she planned to allow herself to be seduced—after a suitable passage of time and playful resistance, of course—Alyce greeted Penelope and Mycroft rather breathlessly.

Despite being allergic to cats, Alyce nuzzled Mycroft for several moments, a respite designed to allow a little more time for the unnatural rosiness to leave her face. "Mikey, my favorite cat," Alyce crooned.

Mikey, knowing he was everyone's favorite cat, purred.

Rising to face Penelope, Alyce said, "Ah-choo!"

"Bless you."

"Thank you. Ah-choo!" Alyce rubbed her tearing eyes and said, "I hate being allergic to cats."

"Better cats than men."

Oh, how true, Alyce thought, how very true.

Penelope was always amazed at the state of modern astrology and psychic counseling. Except for a large framed poster depicting the signs of the zodiac and an astrological calendar, the nicely furnished little office might have been that of an accountant. Everything was computerized.

Oh, Alyce did interpretations by dealing the cards of the tarot and often utilized her psychic abilities by holding some object provided by her client, but when it came to astrology she turned to the computer, punching in the exact date, time, and place of birth, and faster than you could say "Double,

double, toil and trouble; Fire burn and cauldron bubble," the printer began unraveling the mysteries of the universe. If witch hunts were ever renewed, floppy disks would be used for kindling at the stake.

"Would you like some coffee?" Alyce asked. "Or tea?"

"Thanks, no," Penelope replied, "just a question answered."

"If I can."

They sat on the couch where Alyce did her tarot readings. Penelope took the Ides of March warning from her purse and handed it over to Alyce. "I received this shortly after you told me to beware the Ides of March."

Alyce glanced at the bloody dagger and said, "You don't think I did it. . . ."

"No, no, of course not, but I wondered what made you say that."

"I don't know. It just popped into my mind. That happens sometimes."

"Not a chance remark you might have overheard somewhere, one of the playhouses, something like that?"

"Nothing happens by chance," Alyce said. "When we were visiting at the Faire, I felt a sudden chill come between us and then it was gone and the words just came." Alyce closed her eyes and held the piece of paper tightly between her hands.

Penelope waited, feeling like someone had stepped on her grave.

"It's here," Alyce whispered.

Chills ran up and down Penelope's back and her flesh crawled. She reached out and touched Mikey's soft fur. He gazed up at her with quiet, understanding eyes as if to say, Don't worry, I'll take care of you.

Alyce shuddered and opened her eyes. "Something . . . someone . . . I don't know . . . I'm sorry."

"Don't be." Mycroft's body was warm and reassuring beneath her hand.

"May I keep this?" Alyce asked. "Perhaps . . ."

Penelope nodded. "Don't lose it. It may be evidence in Carolyn Lewis's murder."

"It is," Alyce said. "I'm sure of *that.*"

Well, that sure put a damper on the day, Penelope thought as she strolled back to Mycroft & Company, feeling a killer's eyes looking at her from some hidden vantage point. Penelope looked back several times, gave alley entrances a wide berth, and looked both ways—twice—before carrying Big Mike across the street.

"What's wrong, Your Majesty? You're so pale."

"Am I?" Penelope pinched her cheeks.

"I hope you're not coming down with something."

"I'll be fine," Penelope said. "Why don't you take the rest of the afternoon off? You've been working too much lately. Go walk barefoot through the park with Timmy. Or something."

"I don't mind staying."

"There's nothing wrong with me. Go. Have fun."

"If you're sure . . ."

Penelope smiled. "I'm sure."

Penelope spent the afternoon in front of the hearth, sitting in the big and soft Victorian chair, going through the backlog of publisher's catalogues that had been building since she became Queen, ticking off the novels of new authors that sounded interesting, the latest offerings from old favorites, or new editions of the classics, getting up to serve customers, make recommendations, and ring up sales.

Big Mike stretched out on the rug at her feet and slept most of the afternoon away, getting up only to help serve customers, make recommendations, and ring up sales.

It should have been a very pleasant—and productive—afternoon.

But . . .

Several times Penelope glanced up from her work expecting to see someone staring at her through the window. Once she hurried to the door and looked down the sidewalk in both directions, but all was normal with not a potential killer to be seen anywhere.

"This is maddening," Penelope said. "And silly."

Mycroft agreed. It certainly disturbed a hardworking cat's need for rest. And besides, anyone with half a nose could tell there was nothing out there.

Yet.

The western sky was the color of blood when Penelope locked Mycroft & Company for the night and headed for home with Big Mike.

Driving up to the dark house and parking, Penelope found herself reluctant to get out and face a quiet evening in solitude, although with Big Mike she was never truly alone except when he reverted to his wilder instincts and insisted upon a nocturnal excursion, spending the night prowling through his domain. Occasionally, he was gone for two nights and the intervening day, but he always came back, tired and happy, plodding up to the door, meowing loudly all the way to announce his return. *Just wait till you hear what I did.*

Sitting in the darkness, Penelope told herself it was silly, but the uneasiness remained. Something . . . someone . . . She wondered what Alyce was doing tonight. Did she have the warning note close at hand? Was it sending her grim vibrations?

It was a deadline day for Andy and the *Empty Creek News Journal,* and he would not be dropping by tonight. It was usually late by the time the paper was put to bed and so they spent those nights apart.

Dammit, why tonight?

She got out of the Jeep and went to the door, feeling somewhat like she was checking into the Bates Motel. She looked around nervously, still feeling as though someone was watching her, half expecting a crazed, dagger-wielding Anthony Perkins to leap from behind the stately saguaro cactus in the yard. The pennies glued to the door were a stark reminder that a killer *had* once visited her home on several occasions.

Inside, she filled the house with light.

It didn't help.

She started a fire, then went to the kitchen and poured a glass of wine. Returning to the living room, she leaned back against the couch, kicked off her shoes, put her feet up, and sipped the wine.

It didn't help.

Finally, she gave up and went to the telephone, wondering whether to be coy, flirtatious, seductive. She decided on honesty as she dialed the number.

"Newsroom, Anderson."

"I don't want to be alone tonight."

When Andy arrived he was more than a little worried. Penelope Warren was a very calm, determined, independent, and self-sufficient woman as he knew only too well from long experience. It wasn't at all like her to issue a call for even the slightest help.

Penelope reassured him that she was fine, that nothing was wrong, and that she wanted only his company. It was just a little lie, she told herself, and he was much better than a night-light in the bedroom.

They shared a dinner of leftover spaghetti and salad and afterward cuddled in front of the fire and, well, one thing led to another and . . .

Then, sometime during the night, Penelope boarded a dusty African bus driven by Anthony Perkins, who leered as she paid her fare. When she turned, Penelope found every seat on the bus, except one, was taken by Anthony Perkins. She took her seat and placed the box with the two squawking chickens inside on her lap. I must be going to market, Penelope dreamed as the bus started down the bumpy dirt road.

The bus followed the narrow road along precipitous heights in the stark Ethiopian highlands, twisting and careening perilously close to the crumbling edge.

Suddenly Penelope's wedding ring slipped from her finger and bounced out the window and over the escarpment. Stop the bus, Penelope pleaded, I have to get my wedding ring. But it took a long time before Anthony Perkins would pull to a stop, and when he finally did, Penelope clambered off, only to be left standing on the edge of a great and lonely wasteland with no idea of where to begin looking for her wedding ring.

When Penelope awakened with a start, she realized she had forgotten her chickens.

Now, what in the hell does all that mean?

CHAPTER
THIRTEEN

The sun seemed to match Penelope's and Big Mike's storied sluggishness for once, taking what appeared to be an inordinate amount of time to rise above the dark mountain hulks of the eastern horizon. But if the sun was reluctant to appear—perhaps it had more urgent business over Kansas or Nebraska—it pacified aficionados of the dawn by sending coming attractions. A soft rosy glow edged the jagged line of the distant mountains, casting pink streaks higher and higher, turning orange and then red, slowly dispelling darkness and fears. It was going to be a glorious weekend for all things Elizabethan.

The Queen and the Royal Cat missed it, of course, lying abed, a delicate pale arm snaking from beneath the blankets at regular intervals to hit the snooze alarm, although the tantalizing aroma of coffee—brewed by automatic timer—filled the RV.

By the time they finally made it to the starting point of the first royal procession of the weekend, the sun had concluded its affairs in the Midwest and was hard at work dismissing the last vestiges of the desert night's chill.

The Queen was greeted with a chorus of enthusiastic "Good morrows" which she returned as best she could between sips of the dark, life-giving liquid in a not-so-royal coffee mug.

Sir Robert Dudley joined the Queen. "Break a leg," he said.

"And the same to you," Penelope replied sleepily. "I'm glad to see you. I was afraid you might not come."

"I'm not going to let some nut scare me away. Besides, you and Sharon might need my help."

The hullabaloo of the staging area fell unnaturally silent as the Elizabethans turned to stare at an advancing apparition.

Oh, my God, Her Royal Majesty thought.

It was a sentiment expressed throughout the milling crowd that would eventually form the royal procession as one after another noticed what seemed to be a goodly portion of Birnam Wood advancing upon their number.

"It's the Royal Bodyguard, Your Majesty," Lady Kathleen said helpfully.

"Yes, I can see that."

So could everyone else within a mile or two, although it might be a little difficult to pick out the Royal Bodyguard's tiny commander from any great distance.

Justin Beamish wore green tights, brown leather boots, a green jerkin, and a feathered green cap cocked at a rakish angle. Buckled about his waist was a broadsword. The scabbard trailed in the dust. He was flanked by the massive twins, similarly attired all in green, and armed with long, heavy staffs.

They approached the Queen and bowed in a carefully choreographed and oft-rehearsed movement, gracefully doffing their caps in unison.

"What is all this?" Penelope asked.

"Why, I'm Robin Hood, of course, and these are my merry men of Sherwood Forest, Little Ralph and Little Russell."

They *are* the forest, Penelope thought, not unkindly, for she was grateful for their presence and their willing devotion to the cause of keeping the royal bod from harm. But they looked like massive green oak trees wearing little green caps. "Indeed," Her Majesty said, including all of the trio in her radiant and regal smile. "You look very, very nice." She had decided not to tell them that they were some four centuries off the mark.

Beamish beamed. "We wanted to be inconspicuous, of course," he said, "blend in with the crowd, so to speak."

Her Robin Hood wore an elegant pencil-thin mustache beneath his feathered green cap that might have sent Jimmy Buffett to rewriting his song if only he happened to chance by the Empty Creek Elizabethan Springe Faire or buzzed the green fields of Merrye Olde in a seaplane. But of course he wouldn't do that. The nearest seaplane landing was . . . well, Penelope didn't know *where* the nearest seaplane landing might be.

"But . . . but . . . it's not period," the stage manager stammered.

"It *is* English," Beamish pointed out rather sternly and with more than a trace of disdain in his voice, "is it not, dear boy?"

Penelope thought he sounded rather like Noel Coward.

"English, right!" Ralph or Russell growled sounding exactly like Ralph or Russell. He waved his massive staff like a toothpick.

"Ah, yes, right," the stage manager agreed hastily. He had no desire to anger the Queen again, and God knows what these two would do to him. "English, very English, indeed. Shall we begin?"

A cannon boomed, sending a big puff of white smoke roiling across the lake where sea monsters and various other demons were said to dwell.

A distant voice cried, "Let the pageantry begin!"

The trumpets blasted flourishes.

The drummer boys of Captain Sneddon's Companie of Foote beat a tattoo.

Ralph and Russell smiled shyly at a pair of pretty young serving wenches who seemed to welcome their attention if the radiant smiles issued in return were any criteria.

Big Mike dug furiously at an itch that required his immediate attention.

All seemed well as Penelope took her first royal step—she had dismissed the sedan chair—back into the sixteenth century once more.

"Penelope, wait for me!" Laney cried.

The royal procession came to an abrupt halt, which was actually a good thing because Big Mike, preoccupied with alleviating his itch, wasn't about to give ground to Captain Sneddon's proud companie, or anyone else for that matter, and a little feline mayhem might have been committed on a passing leg or two were it not for the fortuitous interruption.

The Ravishing Redhead, clad in an ornate blue gown of the period, rushed up breathlessly, freckled bosom heaving. "Look," she panted, "isn't Alexander adorable?"

"I'm not sure adorable is the correct word," Penelope said as she knelt to pat Alexander's head. A head, lapping tongue, and fiercely wagging tale was all that was visible of the little terrier. His body was covered by a suit of chain-mail armor.

"He's just the cutest little knight I know," Laney said.

"He's going to rust if he keeps up this slobbering," Penelope said.

"He's just happy to see you and Mikey. He really wants to be a knight. He told me."

"Well, then, he shall be Sir Dog." Penelope rose. "Now, can we get this show on the road?"

Sir Cat and Sir Dog followed the Queen's banner, proudly leading all the rest of the royal procession.

Wending its way through the quaint little Elizabethan village, the royal procession made it to the Royal Pavilion without mishap. The Queen waved and smiled at her many cheering subjects. She was followed at a respectful distance by her two loyal courtiers, Sir Walter and Sir Robert. Robin Hood and his merry little band hovered close behind, although merry was probably not the correct word to describe Little Russell and Little Ralph, who glared and scowled at the crowd, daring anyone to attack *their* Queen.

Relieved that the procession was uneventful, Penelope was in quite a good humor until she entered the Royal Pavilion to be greeted by the glare of television lights, the ever-breathless Lola LaPola in her version of Elizabethan costume, and the catcher for the Empty Creek High Gila Monsters. At least, she was glad to see *him*—until she noticed he was clutching a stack of the dreaded flyers.

"Here she is," Lola said, sounding like Bob Barker announcing Miss America, "Elizabeth the First, Queen of England." She rudely muscled the young baseball player aside, no little feat considering his bulk.

That's Queen of *All* England, you silly twit, Penelope thought rather ungraciously as she smiled grimly for the camera, noting that Lola LaPola had committed a faux pas, a big-time boo-boo, a major league social blunder: her dress was red.

Only the Queen was allowed to wear red. Everyone knew *that*.

Still, the hapless television newswoman might have gotten away with it had she not planted a fat, juicy kiss right on the lips of Sir Walter who—much too late—hastily backed away, knowing he was now in B-I-G trouble.

"Thank you so much for inviting me, Andy," Lola gushed in her usual breathless manner. "This is going to be ever so much fun. And such a great story too. Television is my life."

Penelope agreed, glaring at the bright red splash of lipstick on Sir Walter's lips. It *was* going to be oodles and oodles of fun.

"Excuse me," Sir Walter said, suddenly discovering there were pressing matters of court to attend to. He quickly joined the members of the Royal Bodyguard at the hors d'oeuvres and popped a grape into his dry mouth.

Now, green and red are most complementary colors normally, but not when the green is born of jealousy. And much to her surprise, Penelope found that she seethed most uncommonly with jealousy. With any other woman in the entire world (Daryl Hannah was, of course, a notable exception) Penelope would not have felt the slightest twinge of jealousy's ugly bite, but with Lola Television-is-my-life LaPola, the green monster caused her to see red.

She turned back to Lola and smiled sweetly. "How can I help you, Lola dear?" she asked.

"Well, first, just a little background information and then I'll spend the rest of the day with you. I want to see and do and experience the full flavor of the Faire."

And so you shall, dearie, Penelope thought, so you shall. "Anything I can do to help," she said.

"Well, how are all these people chosen? Are there applications and auditions, that sort of thing?"

Auditions. *And* applications! I should have thought of that before. Thank you very much, indeed, Lola. The hint provided by the television reporter was almost enough to make Penelope consider a reprieve. Almost.

Penelope answered Lola's many questions about the Faire and her role as Queen. Then she waited patiently as the reporter did four different standups, bullying her camera crew on each one.

"Well," Lola finally asked brightly. "What's next?"

"You're under arrest," the Queen said. "Take her into custody," she ordered.

Yes! A long-suffering camera crew gave the Queen a hearty thumbs-up.

"What for?"

The Lord High Sheriff explained, "Only the Queen is allowed to wear red at court. This is a most grave offense."

And only the Queen is allowed to kiss Sir Walter, Penelope thought.

"You can't be serious."

"Most serious, indeed, madam." He waved his assistants forward. "What is your pleasure, Majesty?"

"The pillory, I believe."

"The ducking stool," the cameraman offered.

"Burn her at the stake," the woman in charge of lighting said.

"How about the rack?" the cameraman said, getting into the spirit of things.

"Or the iron maiden," the lighting woman suggested in her turn.

It seemed that Lola LaPola was not popular among those with whom she worked.

Poor Lola. Deserted by her colleagues, she looked to find a friendly face at court to plead her case. "Andyyyyyy . . ."

Andy, no fool he, ducked behind the massive frame of Little Ralph or Little Russell.

"You can't do this to me," Lola said backing away.

Oh, no?

Seized by the Lord High Sheriff and his assistants, Lola LaPola was ceremoniously restrained in the irons so thoughtfully provided by Master Blaine Edwards and dragged off to await her fate, her camera crew gleefully recording every delicious moment for the evening news.

Penelope turned to the baseball player. "Now, what is all this?"

"I'm the delegate assigned to get your autograph on these for the team and coaches. We voted you our honorary captain." He pointed to the stands across the field of combat. The Gila Monsters rose in unison and cheered.

Penelope blushed and sighed, wondering if her portrait would eventually grace the bedroom wall of every male adolescent in town. "Oh, very well," Penelope said, going to the royal writing table.

"This is for me, Henry Danning, but you can call me Hank."

Penelope patiently signed flyers for the starting lineup, the subs, the coaches, who should have known better, and finally for the principal, Van Costen, who *really* should have known better.

"How good is your arm?" she asked after the last autograph.

"The best."

"Accurate?"

"Yep."

Penelope whispered brief instructions in his ear and then slipped him a couple of dollars.

He grinned and said, "Then, will you marry me?"

Penelope turned to scowl at Sir Walter once more. He was still hiding behind one of the twins. "Probably not," she said, thinking it would serve Sir Walter right if the Queen took up with a younger man, "but I'll think about it."

Since the Queen's magistrates had spent a very busy morning sentencing one malefactor after another for a series of high crimes and misdemeanors, Lola had to wait quite a long time before her turn in the pillory arrived. She was thrust into a fenced enclosure—the Elizabethan version of a holding tank—where she lifted manacled hands to wipe away the twin tears that streaked her pretty cheeks. As a local celebrity, her famous face was easily recognized by most of the passing crowd, who then lingered to watch.

"What did she do?"

"Wore the Queen's colors."

"Why, the brazen hussy."

"But I'm innocent," Lola wailed, "I didn't know."

Her crew waved to her as the camera rolled.

"I'll get you for this," Lola shouted.

"How much are those tomatoes anyway?"

"Nooooo!"

Quentin Parnelle delivered a handsomely framed photograph of the Queen. Penelope accepted it, although with the memory of *that* kiss still rankling, she wasn't at all sure that Andy was going to receive it anytime soon. Lola LaPola, indeed.

"What is the procedure for auditions?" she asked after thanking him for the photo. After all, it wasn't his fault.

"Everyone fills out an application, listing the kind of roles they might like to play, the guild they might like to be in, stuff like that. Then the guilds conduct the auditions and make recommendations to the Queen. Carolyn was always the final arbiter, as you will be next year."

"Not very likely," Penelope said. "Do you have the applications?"

"Yes. They're in storage."

"Are you sure?"

"After what happened with the computer, I checked. They were still there, but I moved them to another storage locker, just in case."

"A good idea. I'd like to see them Monday. I'd have you bring them out here, but I'm not sure that's wise."

"You're not really going to put me in that horrid thing, are you? This is just a joke, right?"

"Nay, madam, 'tis no joke."

The charges were read by the Lord High Sheriff himself. "Guilty of wearing the Queen's colors. Guilty of kissing Sir Walter Raleigh without permission. Guilty of breathless and vapid reporting . . ."

"Breathless," Lola shrieked. "Vapid?"

"A shrew and a scold too," the Sheriff continued. "Guilty of rudeness to sundry gentle folk," he concluded. "Bailiff, do your duty."

The bailiff, who didn't think Lola was at all vapid, was gentle as he placed her wrists and slender pale neck in the waiting enclosures and lowered the crossbar, brushing her shoulder with his lips.

"Stop that," Lola cried, stamping her foot angrily.

On the pretext of arranging her hair, the bailiff shielded her from the rabble eager to see her pelted with rotting tomatoes, and stole another kiss from her full lips.

"This isn't fair," Lola protested, wiggling her hands helplessly.

"I'm a great admirer of yours," the bailiff said.

"You are?"

"I think you're beautiful and not at all vapid."

"You do?"

"If you'll have a drink with me, I'll intercede with the Queen on your behalf."

"You will?"

The young man nodded solemnly.

Lola, preoccupied with her travails, had failed until this moment to take any real notice of her surroundings or the people therein. Now she looked into the deepest, brownest, most gorgeous eyes she had ever seen. The rest of him was pretty damned good too. "Oh, yes," she said breathlessly.

The bailiff turned and shouted, "A boon, Majesty, I prithee." He rushed to the Queen and flung himself to his knees.

A startled Queen motioned him to rise.

"Nay, Your Majesty, I shall remain at your feet and beg mercy for yon gracious lady, the loveliest vision I have ever seen."

Penelope, always a sucker for matchmaking, immediately softened, and looked to the loveliest vision who waited with quivering lips for the outcome of her champion's intercession.

"Her transgressions were serious."

"Most serious, Majesty, but unintentional."

"One tomato."

"I shall throw it myself."

"No missing."

"My aim will be unerring. I thank Your Most Gracious Majesty."

"And see that she gets out of that red dress."

The bailiff grinned. "As quickly as humanly possible, Your Majesty, I can guarantee it."

"I'll just bet you can," Penelope said, breaking character and laughing.

The bailiff rose and went to the little urchin's basket and rummaged around for the softest, ripest tomato he could find.

Lola waited with faint knees, willing it to be over so that she could look into her hero's eyes again at an extremely close range. She watched as he wound up, unwilling to lose sight of him even as he threw, closing her eyes only as the tomato hurtled toward her.

"Huzzah!"

Pirated, unedited videotapes of Lola LaPola's ordeal would be circulating among all the major—and minor—media outlets throughout the Valley of the Sun in time to make the late news.

Ah, the sweetness of a tormented camera crew's revenge.

By that time, however, Lola would not care. She would be happily dancing the night away in the arms of a certain young bailiff.

Penelope slipped away after the parade of the Picts and Celts, if it was possible to slip away while the inconspicuous Robin Hood and his merry men were shadowing her every move from a discreet distance, and went to the RV to change. But, as she was passing Soothsayer Row, she glanced over to give a wave to the Royal Astrologer, who happened to be kissing Lothario at that moment.

Stunned, Penelope jumped behind the alchemist's shop and peered around the corner. Lothario released Alyce, gave a fond pat to her bottom, and slipped between the curtains of the tent where she did her readings.

Looking back to ensure that the Royal Bodyguard was still with her, she took a circuitous route that brought her up behind Alyce. Putting her finger to her lips, motioning Alyce to silence, Penelope tiptoed to the curtains and thrust them aside.

Startled, the Empty Creek chief of police looked up. "What are you doing here, Penelope?"

"That's my line, Dutch," Penelope said. "And with *him* too!"

CHAPTER
FOURTEEN

B efuddled by an amused Venus working her magic from afar, the ever-so-close presence of Harvey Curtis, and not having had time to consult the stars, deal the tarot cards, or otherwise seek enlightenment on the current situation, the Royal Astrologer simply entered the tented enclosure and asked, "What's going on?"

"That's what I want to know."

Ralph and Russell burst into the tent with Justin Beamish right behind.

"Are you all right, Penelope?"

Sir Dog scooted between Penelope's legs and barked excitedly, setting his armor to clinking. He was followed by a somewhat more dignified Sir Cat, sans armor, but with his normal terminal case of curiosity.

"Is there anyone else you'd like to invite, Penelope?" Dutch asked, throwing his hands up in disgust.

"As a matter of fact," Stormy cried, ducking through the curtains. "Why weren't you at my parade?"

"There's my little knight," Laney said, entering the fray. "Isn't he cute?"

"Penelope," Sir Walter said, "I can explain everything."

With everyone crowded into such a tiny space and all talking at once, Alyce's little consultation chamber was beginning to resemble the Tower of Babel. Penelope decided it was time for a little of Elizabeth Regina's storied wisdom in dealing with her subjects.

"Quiet!" she roared in her best parade-ground voice. "Everyone out, now," she commanded when all attention was focused on her. She pointed to Dutch and Lothario. "Except for you and you!"

The tent slowly emptied.

"Well," Penelope said, hands on royal hips.

Dutch groaned.

"I can explain," Lothario said.

"Somebody better."

"He's a cop," Dutch said. "Harvey Curtis."

"A cop!"

Lothario nodded sheepishly. "How do you do?"

"Undercover," Dutch said. "I sent him undercover to keep an eye on you and see what he could discover about the murder."

"An undercover cop," Penelope laughed, "and the first thing he does is try to get my phone number."

"I chewed his butt good for that," Dutch said.

"Did you chew his butt for fickleness too? Asking for a date and the next thing I know, he's out cavorting with the Royal Astrologer."

"Well—"

"No, no," Penelope interrupted, "don't tell me. You're having a midlife crisis. There's a lot of that going around."

"How can I have a midlife crisis?" Harvey asked. "I'm not even forty yet."

"Never mind," Penelope said. "Since you've been snooping around undercover, at least tell me you've learned something useful."

Harvey looked to his boss for instructions.

Dutch nodded. "You can tell her anything. She's practically one of us."

"Well, thank you very much, Dutch. That's the nicest thing you've ever said to me."

"Don't let it go to your head."

"Well?"

"Nothing," Harvey said.

"Nothing?"

"That's it. No one wants to talk to me. Except Alyce, of course. She tells me everything."

"Some undercover cop you are."

"I'm still trying."

"There's always Rainey and Stoner. I've got them working overtime on the computer."

"Somehow, I don't find that a comfort. Have they found anything."

"Not yet. They've done all the obvious things. Run the names for wants and warrants. That kinda stuff, but nothing yet."

William Shakespeare and Richard Burbage were having some minor creative differences over the interpretation of the selected scenes from *Hamlet* being offered as a change of pace for those in the audience who desired tragedy rather than comedy. They should have stuck with the comedy, since their creative differences erupted during an intermission with an overflow audience eagerly awaiting the famous duel scene.

As the playwright, Master Will thought his interpretation of certain soliloquies in his greatest creation were correct and proper. As the star player, Master Richard believed *his* was the proper interpretation.

"You sounded like Clint Eastwood. Is that what you're going to do now? Go ahead, Laertes, make my day. Or how about Kevin Costner for a change? You haven't imitated him yet."

The burly Burbage was beside himself. "I'm not imitating anyone, you . . . you . . . toad's behind."

"Hmm, now, let's see. That wasn't Costner. No, let me guess. I have it! Sylvester Stallone!"

"You *are* a hack," Burbage cried. "Sometimes I think Marlowe did write your plays!"

"Marlowe!" Master Will shrieked. "Marlowe couldn't carry my quill pen to market! I'll show you how it should be done!"

"All right, then, you do it!" Master Richard shouted.

"All right," England's greatest playwright shouted back, "I will!"

Thus it was that England's greatest playwright stormed on-stage—to the astonishment of the assembled court of Denmark—grabbed a foil, struck what he believed to be the most melancholy of poses, and only belatedly realized he didn't know his lines, or anyone else's for that matter.

"Revenge!" Master Richard shouted from beneath the stage, having decided at the last moment to play the ghost of

Hamlet's father, although the murdered king's last appearance had been a number of scenes earlier. "Go ahead," Burbage thundered, "make my day!"

Master Will made everyone's day. By the time he had stumbled and stammered his way to his final death throes and Fortinbras, King of Norway, entered to haul off the bodies, the players and the audience were in gleeful hysterics.

At the back of the outdoor auditorium Penelope held her sides and wiped tears from her eyes, but even as she laughed a serious thought ran through her mind. Someone better get those two to make up before the next performance.

"They're dolts."

Penelope turned to find a blurry Christopher Marlowe standing beside her. "Funny dolts," she said, still wiping the tears away.

"You should stop by our little company. See what real drama is like."

"Perhaps I will," Penelope said. "I've always been fond of Faustus."

"We'll be expecting you, then," Marlowe said, moving off, throwing one last disgusted, even malevolent, look toward the Shakespearean stage.

Penelope fully expected to make an appearance at Marlowe's presentation, but with one royal duty or another to attend to, time slipped away somehow, and when a respite arrived, all the theatrical performances had ended for the afternoon.

And that really pissed Marlowe off.

A bright-eyed but subdued Lola LaPola returned to the Royal Pavilion hand in hand with her bailiff. She was now clad, quite becomingly, in a gray off-the-rack dress from the purveyor of fine Elizabethan fashions just down the street from the ironmonger's, whose own fashions had so recently adorned her wrists.

"Good morrow, Your Majesty," Lola said. Her bailiff had provided some brief instruction in Elizabethan language as it related to court and other sundry matters, primarily having to do with getting his newly found love out of the gray dress too, a procedure he had been led to believe might be welcomed—in time.

Lola dipped into a graceful curtsy. The bailiff bowed.

"Rise, loyal subjects," the Queen said. "May I offer you some refreshment?"

"Alas, Majesty," the bailiff said, "there are pressing judicial matters to attend."

"I suppose you're going off to throw tomatoes at some other poor young woman now," Lola said.

"I shall think only of your tomatoes, dearest blithe spirit. Until I return, only the thought of you will sustain me throughout hard toil."

For a bailiff, Penelope decided, he had a definite poetic flair. "Will you join me, Lady Lola?"

"Thank you," she said, staring wistfully at her departing young man.

Members of the court and the Royal Bodyguard politely provided a space for the Queen and Lady Lola at the bar.

"Your pleasure, Majesty?"

"A glass of white wine, I believe."

"And the gracious lady?"

"I'll have the same, please." She turned to the Queen. "I must apologize. I'm not always so rude and pushy. It's just that television news is a very competitive business. We're always fighting for airtime and I want to be a good reporter, not just another pretty face on the screen." She shrugged her shoulders and smiled ruefully. "Sometimes I can be a real bitch, I guess. I'm sorry."

"I apologize too," Penelope said. "I was pretty bitchy too. There was no reason to send you to the pillory like that."

"Oh, I'm glad you did. I wouldn't have met Lynn otherwise. Isn't he terrific?"

Penelope smiled and raised her glass. "To new friends," she said.

"New friends."

"It's strange, isn't it?" Lola said after their toast. "If it hadn't been for the bank robbery, I wouldn't have met Andy. He wouldn't have invited me to the Faire. I wouldn't have bought a red dress. You wouldn't have sent me to the pillory. What a strange series of events. And just think, someday friends will ask how we met and I'll reply, 'Well, I was in a pillory and Lynn was heaving a rotten tomato at me.' That's the kind of story that could get us on *The Newlywed Game*."

"And if I wasn't at the bank robbery . . ." Penelope suddenly felt a strange and ominous premonition. "I would have . . ."

"What is it?"

"I don't know." Penelope shrugged her shoulders helplessly. "Something."

Sir Walter slowly emerged from the royal doghouse, but only after a prolonged period of suitable groveling and pleas for forgiveness. "All I did was invite her to the Faire. How was I to know she was going to kiss me and send you into a jealous rage?"

"I was not in a rage."

"Yes, you were."

"No, I wasn't."

This continued throughout the evening as they went from one Faire party to another, "Keeping up appearances," as the Queen said, "for my loyal subjects."

The Queen and her entourage had diminished by two since Alexander had been allowed a sleepover. The Royal Cat and Sir Dog were back at the RV, having a slumber party. Still, Robin Hood, Little Ralph, Little Russell, in company with their serving wenches, made for quite a formidable entrance at each stop on the royal tour.

By the time they reached the Peasants' Guild, poor Andy was more than a little exasperated. "Sometimes, I'd like to take you over my knee and give you a good spanking, just like Kate in *The Taming of the Shrew.*"

"Brute," Penelope said, although the suggestion certainly had interesting possibilities. "You wouldn't dare."

"Would too."

"Would not."

The Queen's entourage was further diminished by the loss of Robin Hood, who remained with the peasants, happily ensconced in the lap of a buxom young bawd.

At the Merchants' Guild, Andy took to sulking, keeping the corner of his eye on Penelope to see if it was having any impact.

Penelope ignored him, laughing gaily with a variety of merchants and their ladies.

At the Military Guild, Andy decided to see if jealousy

might work, although that emotion had sent him scampering to the royal doghouse to begin with. Unfortunately, the pretty little camp follower he picked was betrothed to a rather large knight who was having nothing to do with Sir Walter's plan for reconciliation with the Queen. Poor Sir Walter retreated in disgrace, hoping that his brief and unsuccessful encounter had gone unnoticed.

But his amused Queen bestowed the Order of the Royal Smirk upon him.

The remaining members of the Royal Bodyguard tried to keep watchful eyes on the Queen as the round of the village continued, but there were bouts of giggling, punctuated by increasingly longer silences as the twins received favors from their young maidens.

But then, just as they approached the Shakespearean Players party, Penelope overheard a whispered plan.

"You guys watch," Little Ralph or Little Russell said, "and we'll . . . then, we'll watch and you guys can . . ."

Master Will Shakespeare and Master Dick Burbage were still feuding when the Queen and the now-disconsolate Sir Walter entered. They stood at opposite ends of the party, each surrounded by a coterie of sympathetic followers, and glowered at each other over tankards of ale.

The royal decree to shake hands was summarily ignored. It was a grievous breach of conduct, but Penelope decided to ignore it until the morrow. But then, by God . . .

Sir Walter looked from one group to the other, but he was at a loss for a plan in this divided house and decided to stay with Penelope as she approached the neutral party, which seemed to consist primarily of Bobby and Sharon.

"What news, Your Majesty?" Sir Robert Dudley asked.

Penelope shook her head. "I was hoping you could tell me. Any sign of the Ides of March?"

"Nothing. I'm beginning to think it's just a prank."

"Let's hope so."

"Did you see the performance today?" Sharon asked.

"Oh, yes," Penelope replied with a laugh which earned her a few scowls from the opposing camps. "It was hilarious."

"Thank God, Ophelia was dead."

"I assume you played Ophelia."

"She was magnificent," Bobby said, "just the right blend of insanity born of lost love."

Andy could sympathize. He was beginning to think that he would have to rend his garments, wander friendless through the encampment, crying his woes to the heavens, to regain his former lofty position in Penelope's heart.

"Marlowe was delighted," Sharon said.

"Oh, God, I promised to attend *Faustus* today, but I forgot."

"He won't forgive you for that. He's entirely too intense. I think he's nutso city."

"His ink pot isn't quite filled."

"Well, it must be difficult to play a lesser role. You know what writers are like," Penelope said, looking over at Shakespeare.

Arriving at Marlowe's company, Penelope regretted defending Marlowe. He was a jerk and Sharon was correct. Marlowe greeted the Queen with a cold and haughty intensity unmatched anywhere in her small kingdom.

"Apparently, there is not enough buffoonery with the Hack to amuse Her Majesty tonight," Marlowe said.

"I apologize," Penelope said, "I meant to come, but there simply wasn't time. I'll be there tomorrow though."

"It doesn't matter. If Your Majesty is content with second-rate performances by a third-rate playwright . . ."

"There's no need to be rude."

Marlowe airily waved her off. "My time will come. The world will finally recognize that Hack for what he is and applaud Christopher Marlowe as he so richly deserves."

Feeling distinctly unwelcome—and rightly so—Penelope said, "Until the morrow, then."

Marlowe turned away. "More ale," he shouted, "we'll toast the world's greatest playwright."

Outside, the first chink in the royal armor appeared when Penelope said, "You know, I believe that man really thinks he's Kit Marlowe."

Sir Walter, frantic to leap on any scrap tossed in his direction, replied, "I agree completely. There's a tenuous hold on reality out here as it is, but he's too . . . too . . ."

"Intense?"

"Exactly."

Penelope turned away to hide a smile.

Behind them, Marlowe's company of players roared their toast to the heavens. "Christopher Marlowe. The greatest playwright in all Christendom."

Having decided that Andy had suffered enough penance, Penelope skillfully led the royal party in the direction of Kissing Bridge. She slowed her pace slightly as they approached the bridge, waiting for Andy to seize the moment. The pace slowed to a crawl at the summit of the bridge.

What a dunce. I have to do everything.

Penelope turned abruptly and said, "Well?"

"Well what?"

"Aren't you going to kiss me? This is Kissing Bridge. No one is allowed to cross without a kiss."

"Even if you're mad at me?"

"Especially if I'm mad at you."

The stream that flowed under the bridge bubbled and gurgled softly as Andy took Penelope in his arms for the first time that day. As kisses went, this one was tentative at first, but as time went on, it climbed steadily on Penelope's smooching scale of one to ten, surpassing one famous kiss after another in her memory, sending temperatures rising until she was quite ready to send it to the Empty Creek Kissing Hall of Fame for permanent enshrinement.

Indeed, there was quite a lot of memorable kissing going on at that precise moment. The Royal Bodyguard, having lost track of whose turn it was to do what, were spooning enthusiastically at a discreet distance from the Queen and her consort. Lola sighed in the arms of the bailiff as he softly brushed her eyelids with his lips. Bobby held Sharon in a mentorlike embrace until she tweaked his ears and planted a great big smack on his lips. Robin Hood was quite lost in the tender if somewhat smothering embrace of the young bawd. Even Dutch had been forgiven for missing Stormy's triumphant parade as Queen of the Picts and he was the grateful recipient of some rather savage and unqueenly endearments. After all, the Picts weren't exactly civilized. As for Laney and Wally . . . well, they were embroiled in some Laney-like activities having to do with tattoos devised in the name of research.

All was well with the world if Venus and Cupid were going to have anything to do with it.

"Wow," Penelope whispered with awe when Andy finally released her.

"Am I forgiven now?"

"Oh, yes," Penelope said rather breathlessly, sounding just like Lola LaPola, who had uttered the same words only a few moments earlier. "Take me home. Work your dastardly will with me."

They rushed from Kissing Bridge with unseemly haste.

Doing his German shepherd imitation, Alexander barked furiously as Penelope and Andy waved good-bye to the Royal Bodyguard, who seemed in dire need of some guards of their own. Well, perhaps not.

After a few perfunctory pats on Alexander's head, he was ordered back to his own slumber party in no uncertain terms as Penelope quickly shucked royal raiments and clambered into bed to await Andy's dastardly will.

She didn't have to wait very long.

And what a will it was.

Penelope struggled to emerge from a deep and blissful sleep as distant cries penetrated the love bower.

"To arms! To arms!"

"Yes, dearest," Penelope said clearly, "I have two arms, thank you."

"Humph," Andy replied.

Penelope rolled over, vaguely aware of a barking dog.

"To arms."

The cry came from the military encampment.

The distant wail of a siren intruded on sleep. It was joined by a second and then a third.

The closing sirens set Alexander to howling. That wild,

mournful yowl was a great help in assisting Penelope back to consciousness, since the terrier had taken up a station next to her ear when he let fly. She bolted upright and bumped her head on the low ceiling.

"Ow!"

Big Mike bounded to the door, ready for action.

"Whazzat?" Andy asked, fumbling for his glasses before realizing he must have been dreaming, since he didn't wear glasses.

"Something's happened," Penelope said, struggling to pull her jeans on, slip into her loafers, find her sweater, and open her eyes simultaneously.

"What? What's happened?"

A shout from the village answered Andy's question.

"Murder."

CHAPTER FIFTEEN

In the greatest of all theatrical traditions, the Faire opened its gates on Sunday morning, but no one's heart was truly in it. The cannons boomed out their announcement of another day of festivities, but the booms were leaden and muted. The trumpeters blared flourishes—quite stridently some thought, others believed rather urgently. Lacking their usual lilt, the flourishes seemed a desperate call to fun.

Early Fairegoers were greeted by Elizabethans of all ranks who distributed tiny flowers for the women and challenged their men to be merrye on this day of all days. The jugglers and magicians performed, delighting young children. Despite the apparent jollity, however, the gaiety was that of well-rehearsed lines and oft-proven routines.

Even Big Mike and Alexander were listless after the long night, and moped around, waiting impatiently for the Queen to take her throne so they would have a friendly lap where they could catch up on their sleep.

The Royal Pavilion buzzed with rumors and gossip.

Penelope, going on adrenaline and caffeine, tried to keep things on schedule, encouraging her subjects not to dwell on the tragedy of the night before, but to perform to their utmost for the rubes.

It was good, sound advice, and Penelope wished she could follow it herself, but dwell she did.

From a distance, Penelope irrationally thought, the scene in the village had looked like a mob of Transylvanians milling about, waving torches, screwing up their courage to storm Dr. Frankenstein's castle (or was it Count Dracula's?). It was much too early—or late—to be playing movie twenty questions, particularly since some unseemly affair had evidently struck the Empty Creek Elizabethan Spring Faire once again.

Penelope and Andy raced across the bridge into the village and pandemonium.

"What happened?" Penelope cried as a sleepy and disheveled Royal Bodyguard circled the wagons around her.

"Don't look, dear lady," Just Beamish said.

"Dead."

"Who's dead?"

"Don't know. One of the actors."

Oh, God, not Sharon. Please, not Sharon.

"It's awful, Your Majesty." Kathy was shivering and huddled close to Timmy, who had his arm around her shoulders.

Sharon and Bobby rushed up, only to be blocked by Ralph and Russell.

"It's okay," Penelope said, granting entrance to the royal circle.

"What happened, Penelope?" Sharon had tossed a jacket

over a white nightgown. Bobby's hair was sticking out in all directions of the compass and then some.

"I don't know yet, but I intend to find out." She grabbed a torch from a passing pikeman and strode with determination to the back of the tavern, where uniformed policemen were holding back the curious Elizabethans, all of whom seemed to be waving one of the torches that had been stockpiled for the Peasants' Rebellion. Her protectors quickly followed.

The garish flickering lights revealed a dark, lifeless form on the ground.

My God! It's Richard Burbage.

Robin Hood fainted dead away. Fortunately, his pretty young companion was there to catch him.

Despite the gravity of the situation, Penelope had to smile at the memory of Justin Beamish coming to his senses, speaking the always popular line for fainting victims. "Where am I?"

"Jeez, Justin," one of the twins said, "wait'll Mom hears about this."

"Don't move, sweetie," Justin's companion said, cradling his head in her lap.

Beamish looked up ruefully at Penelope. "I've always been a little squeamish," he said. "In college I fainted during a health class. They were showing a movie on natural childbirth."

"At what point in the film?" Penelope asked as she knelt beside him.

"The title."

"Don't you worry, sweetie, when I have your love child, we'll just get an extra bed for you. You can faint all you want."

Penelope looked at the young woman in amazement. The Faire up to this point had obviously agreed with Beamish.

"I'm Sarah. I'm a bawd. At least, I used to be. Now I'm going to be Maid Marian. Isn't he darling?"

The clang of dueling broadswords brought Penelope back to the reality of knightly combat in the warmish Arizona sunlight. She sympathized with Beamish and understood why cops resorted to black gallows humor at a murder scene. It was a way to cope with the specter of death, and the reminder of one's own mortality. Although she wasn't given to fainting at the sight of blood, natural childbirth movies, or bodies, Penelope was always shaken when confronted with violent death, which was happening all too often of late. Somebody had better hire a fat lady to sing. And soon too.

During a break from mortal combat, royal proclamations, and other duties, Laney and Wally entered the Royal Pavilion. "God, you look exhausted," Laney said.

"I was up most of the night."

"It's terrible. I hurried right over after I heard. I know you're going to be busy and I thought I'd take Alex off your hands."

"He hasn't been any trouble," Penelope said. "He and Mikey slept the morning away in my lap. Kathy just took them over for a bit of turkey leg. They'll be back soon."

"What happened?"

"Much the same as before."

"Who do you think could have done it?"

"According to the authorities, William Shakespeare is a distinct possibility."

"My God!" Laney exclaimed. "Not Shakespeare!"

Penelope nodded, took a deep breath, and began the explanation Laney would require.

Poor Richard Burbage had apparently been killed by a bare bodkin he didn't see coming, although the medical examiner had refused to make any hasty assumption on the spot.

Will Shakespeare had discovered the body behind the tavern and raised the alarm.

The Bard of Avon was distraught over the loss of his friend and the greatest actor of his day. He was also more than a little drunk. He was *also* a prime suspect.

"My God," Shakespeare bleated like a stuck piglet, "I'll be next and I haven't written my greatest plays yet. Or my will. What will the British Museum do without my will?"

Dutch twisted the piglet's tail. "What were you doing out here so late?"

"I was thirsty and didn't have anything back at the RV except orange juice. I know a little board in the back wall that's loose. I figured I'd just grab a bottle or two and pay for them in the morning."

"Decent of you."

"Burbage and I discovered it. That's probably what he was doing when . . . when . . ."

"When you killed him," Larry Burke offered helpfully.

"I didn't kill him," Shakespeare wailed. "He was my friend."

"Isn't it true that you argued violently this afternoon at the theater?" Dutch broke in like Matlock circling his prey. He had been quickly briefed by Penelope.

"Yes, but—"

"Isn't it also true that the argument continued well into the evening?"

"Yes, but—"

"Isn't it true that he called you a horse's ass?"

"Yes, but—"

"That must have happened after we left," Penelope told Dutch. "They weren't speaking when Andy and I were there."

"Don't interrupt," Dutch said.

Burke leapt into the brief silence. "Isn't it true," Tweedledee said, "that you followed him and stabbed him in the back?"

"Yes, but . . . no, wait, you're confusing me. This is entrapment. I want my lawyer."

" 'The first thing we do,' Dutch said, 'let's kill all the lawyers.' "

Shakespeare groaned.

"Henry VI Part 2," Penelope said. "Act Four, Scene Two. I have a sweatshirt from the Folger Shakespeare Library with that quotation on it."

"Penelope, you're my friend, tell them I didn't do anything. You believe me, don't you?"

"I want to, but . . . motive, opportunity, drinking, well, it's the stuff murders are made of."

"That's it. I'm closing the Faire down," Dutch said after Shakespeare went mute and was hauled off by Tweedledee and Tweedledum to call his attorney.

"You can't do that."

"And why not, Miss Smarty Pants?"

Miss Smarty Pants? Was he regressing to childhood under

the stress? "Because . . . if you do, we'll never find the murderer. You don't really believe Shakespeare did it. The man would have to be stupid to argue publicly with Burbage, lie in wait to kill him, pretend to discover the body by accident, and sound the alarm to one and all within fifteen counties of his dirty deed. All he had to do was sneak quietly back off to bed and let someone else find the body, probably not until morning. By then he could have arranged a perfectly good alibi."

"If the Faire's closed, there'll be no more murders. At least, not out here."

"I have a plan," Penelope said.

"What is it?"

"I was afraid that would be your next question," Penelope, who had been thinking it might be a good idea to have the ironmonger make up a whole bunch of iron-plated, dagger-proof bodices and doublets for the Elizabethans, said.

Undaunted, Penelope said, "Well, we should have a plan."

"I'm listening."

Penelope decided upon another tack. "What about all the lost revenues? A lot of those people depend on the concessions for their livings."

The economic argument prevailed. After all, Dutch had to answer to the city fathers and mothers on the council. They would look upon the city's copious loss of revenue with dismay if the Faire were shut down for something so trivial as murder.

"All right," Dutch said finally. "But you watch your six. Hear?"

"I hear."

"Good," Dutch said, "now I'm going to bed."

That seemed as good a plan as any.

It still did as Penelope finished relating the details of the second murder to Laney and Wally.

"What an awful thing to happen during your reign," Laney said. "Or anyone else's, for that matter."

Big Mike and Alexander returned in the company of Lady Kathleen. Refreshed by their long naps in the Queen's lap and sustained now by good, hearty English fare, they were ready for a snooze.

As the Queen resumed her place on the throne, Alexander was carried off clutched to the bosom of the Ravishing Redhead while Mycroft took a good five minutes kneading and arranging the folds of the Queen's gown to his satisfaction before he nodded off again, purring his contentment with the world, sounding just like a small motorboat. Penelope stroked his fur gently, thinking—perhaps it was a wish—I'd make a great cat.

The Elizabethan stage was dark, both in memory of Richard Burbage and because his understudy was the victim of food poisoning (some tainted parmesan cheese he had sprinkled all too liberally over his pizza of the night before, he believed).

Marlowe, graciously for once, offered to fill the void, and the Queen quickly accepted the offer, promising once more to attend the performance, fully intending to keep her word this time.

"Thank you," Marlowe said simply. "My poor players would appreciate a visit from their Queen."

When it came time to dispense justice on the village green, Her Most Gracious Majesty granted clemency to three shrews, a pickpocket, and a blasphemer, much to the disappointment of the long-suffering victims of shrewishness, the assembled Elizabethans, the rubes, and the little urchin who sold the tomatoes who had all gathered for some good old-fashioned wench pelting.

After ordering the shrews to kiss and make up with their husbands in front of God, Her Majesty, and the assemblage—three deeds entered upon reluctantly, but finally accomplished with great enthusiasm by the blushing shrews and helpful commentary and much appreciation by the kissing connoisseurs in the audience—they were admonished to "go and shrew no more."

For the pickpocket, the Queen found inspiration in the epitaph of H. L. Mencken—Andy's hero—and he was ordered to "forgive some sinner and wink your eye at some homely girl" for the duration of the Faire.

For the blasphemer, Penelope wanted to draw upon her Catholic school background and have him recite a few Hail Marys, but of course that wouldn't do in antipapist Elizabethan England, so she plucked a lovely blossom from the tray of a flower girl, gave it to him, and said, "Contemplate the wonders of God."

Feeling quite pleased with herself, the Queen, her faithful bodyguard, and their inseparable companions—the Royal Consort, and the Royal Cat—retired in search of refreshment to cheers led by the Lord High Mayor "for Her Majesty's mercy in granting pardon to all who are worthy of forgiveness."

After bangers and ale, the royal party returned to the pavilion to find Master William Shakespeare earnestly proclaiming his innocence to Sir Francis Bacon and anyone else who would listen.

A much-chastened playwright bowed as Penelope approached. "I didn't do it," he said upon rising.

"I don't think you did," Penelope said gently. "It looks bad, but . . . who is your lawyer?"

"George Eden."

Penelope nodded approvingly. George was the Gerry Spence of Empty Creek. An outlandish dresser, Policewoman Sheila Tyler, his significant other, had taken to numbering each of his garments so that shirts, ties, and jackets matched—when he bothered to glance at the numbers, which was seldom. He had once confided to Penelope that he dressed that way only to keep Sheila's mind off his real vices of scotch, cigars, and golf.

"He's good."

"Otherwise those idiot detectives would still be questioning me. Don't they eat anything but jelly doughnuts?"

"I don't think so." She turned to Sir Francis. "I've discovered that you once played Sir Robert to Carolyn's Elizabeth."

Sir Francis took a quick gulp of ale. "I wondered when you would find that out."

"Did you?"

"Of course not. I liked Carolyn."

"That's not what I've heard."

"It's a damnable lie. Who would tell you such a thing?"

"No one. I just made it up to see your reaction. It's not nice to keep things from the Queen."

"It was common knowledge. Everyone knew."

"Yes, but I've found this to be a most recalcitrant group

when it comes to a little honest disclosure. Are you now or have you ever been the Queen's lover?"

"Things get complicated sometimes," Bacon said.

"I'll bet that damned Marlowe is gloating."

Penelope made another mental note to attend the performance of Marlowe's players, but her brain was fuzzy with fatigue and as she tried to sort everything out, Marlowe got lost again. "Never mind," she said, "the Shakespearean stage will open again next week."

"At least," Shakespeare proclaimed, "he won't be able to usurp the Ides of March. They're mine, or will be when I get around to writing *Julius Caesar.*"

That remark momentarily restored clarity to Penelope's gray matter, but she decided not to say anything about the bloody-dagger note. We'll just keep that little secret from Shakespeare and the court for the moment and see what happens.

Penelope brightened at the sight of Ben Jonson in the company of his lovely Celia entering the Royal Pavilion. She had quite forgotten about Leigh and Burton. "Do you dislike Ben Jonson too?" she asked of Master Will.

"Of course not," Shakespeare replied. "He wrote the loveliest introduction for my first folio."

"Where have you been all weekend?" Penelope asked, impatiently waving for them to rise.

"Ben, here, has had the flu. I've been nursing him back to health," Leigh replied. "Poets are so frail sometimes. He shouldn't be out of bed, really, but after we heard what happened . . ."

"A terrible thing," Ben said, "just terrible. I don't know

what's happening anymore. The Faire was always such fun, but now . . ." He threw his hands up.

Penelope wanted to do the same, but there were royal duties to perform. Damn, these jousts go on forever. The thought of going to bed with a good book was ever so tempting. Not Shakespeare though. Or Marlowe or the gloomy Sir Walter, not even the nice love poems of Ben Jonson. As she took her place on the throne, Penelope banished all Elizabethans, vowing never to read anything earlier than the nineteenth century ever again. That'll show them, by God.

The Queen was joined by Sir Robert Dudley and the fair Rosalind, who had nothing to do for the nonce with her stage darkened by untimely events.

"Where have you been?" Penelope asked.

"We dropped by Marlowe's playhouse," Sir Robert answered.

"Was he gloating?"

"He was quite civil for a change," Sharon replied, "although he tried to recruit me again."

"Again?"

"Oh, yes, he's been after me the whole Faire to join his company, but he never wrote any good roles for women."

"No," Penelope agreed. "He didn't."

The afternoon dragged on interminably. Penelope put herself on autopilot, smiling and waving at all the proper moments with only a little prompting from Lady Kathleen as she tried to organize and make sense of the chaos swirling about the Faire, but to no avail.

With the last regal wave of the afternoon, Penelope determined that there was nothing to do except go back to the beginning.

But what was the beginning? Not Carolyn's death. That was too late. What happened prior to her death? That was the key. It had always been where the explanation would be found. Every plumber's apprentice knew that, as Miss Foley always used to say in freshman lit.

Tired, hungry, and thirsty after a night and a day that had dragged on far too long, Penelope, Andy, and Big Mike were escorted to the RV by the members of the Royal Bodyguard and their ladies. Trudging along determinedly, Penelope was the first to see the note taped to the door which was becoming a regular bulletin board.

Not more of that Ides of March stuff, she thought as she approached the door to read the latest missive. The message was painfully scrawled in large block letters by someone obviously printing with the wrong hand.

CATCH ME IF YOU CAN MISS QUEENY.

Oh, good God, Penelope thought, recognizing the parody immediately, the centuries are certainly getting confused. It was a paraphrase of one of the notes sent to the Metropolitan Police by Jack the Ripper. Every plumber's apprentice knew that too.

"I just hate cocky murderers," Penelope said.

Disrespectful too. Queeny, indeed.

CHAPTER
SIXTEEN

While waiting for Quentin Parnelle to deliver audition applications, Penelope went back to the beginning. When that proved futile, she skipped on over to the middle, but that was maddening too, with its damnable questions. Who killed Richard Burbage? Why was he killed? What was the connection between the actor and the Queen?

Penelope wrote the questions on a legal pad, optimistically leaving space to write the answers. As she waited for inspiration, she doodled. Since she couldn't draw anything beyond stick women and men with frizzy hair and block houses for them to live in, this consisted mainly of a bunch of circles and squares and elaborate question marks.

Frustrated, then, Penelope paced the house, taking one deep breath after another, willing herself to tranquility, trying to curb impatience, all to no avail. Tranquility thought it was pretty funny, hilarious in fact, while Impatience grabbed her in a headlock, threw her to the mat, and quickly pinned her for the count of three, or whatever it was they did on those bogus wrestling shows, as jumbled thoughts raced through her mind.

Big Mike watched from his perch on the kitchen counter, probably figuring there was no good reason for everyone to get worked up.

On her third circuit of the house, Penelope was so desperate, she even briefly considered exercise as a means of stimulation, but quickly gave that idea up. She didn't have time to start running at this late stage.

She called Dutch and was pleasantly surprised when she got through immediately. "Anything?" she asked hopefully.

"Nothing. Burke and Stoner are still on the computer, but if there's some great revelation there, they haven't found it."

"What about Burbage?"

"Lived quietly in Paradise Valley. A production manager for a printing company. Performed in little theater productions around town. Survived by parents, two sisters, and a brother. They know of no reason why anyone would want him dead."

"Not much to go on," Penelope said, "let's hope the applications give us something to go on."

"Hang on a second . . . yeah . . . okay . . . Penelope?"

"I'm here."

"So is Parnelle with the records. I'll send him out to your place with a set and get Burke and Stoner to looking through them, but you're our best bet. You've met most of the players."

"A lot of good that's done so far."

"Why don't you come over to the house later? I'm going to knock off early. We can compare notes."

"Let's hope we have something to compare."

Penelope and Mycroft went outside to wait for Parnelle. Although there were neighbors not too far away, the house might have been plopped down in the midst of a vast desert wasteland. That was the reason Penelope had bought it. There was a sense of splendid isolation. The desert scrub blocked sight of all human habitation and muted the sounds of their presence. The desert was like that, swallowing the frail accoutrements of mankind whole without so much as even a burp.

Penelope and Mycroft sat on the stoop, contemplating the solitude, each in their own way. For Penelope, it washed over her, cleansing her, offering serenity, a respite from the problems at hand. Big Mike, with his greater sensory powers, saw something vastly different, a natural environment teeming with life and a constantly changing tableau of mysterious dramas running their course on a sandy stage. He followed the progress of the universe with twitching nose, swiveling ears, and avid curiosity.

Their reveries were interrupted by the sound of Quentin Parnelle's car making the next-to-last turn leading to the little ranchette. He beeped the horn when he swung into the driveway.

"Back to work, Mikey."

Mycroft turned and looked up at her quizzically, as though to ask, What do you think we've been doing?

"My God, you live out in the wilderness," Parnelle said. "Aren't you afraid of snakes and stuff?"

"Not much."

"Snakes are definitely not my thing," he said, looking around cautiously.

"It's too early for rattlers."

"I know that, but do they?"

Penelope laughed. "Some lobo you are."

"I'm a city lobo," Parnelle replied as he opened the trunk to reveal two cardboard storage boxes. "Where do you want them?"

"The files are categorized by guild, by year. Military, musicians, actors, and so on. That should help. Good coffee."

"Thanks. By the way, I've been meaning to ask. Who would have had access to your offices? From the Faire, I mean?"

"Practically anyone. A lot of the people come and go, especially actors."

"Why actors?"

"Publicity stills. That sort of thing. Most of them are really actors, you know, waiting for their big break." Parnell grinned. "Unlike you, they want their photographs all over town. They're always after me to put them in the ads and flyers. Wonder Ideas is kind of their hangout away from the Faire."

Penelope and Mycroft spent several hours snooping through audition applications, looking for the right connection. Had the nature of their quest not been so serious, it would have been quite delightful prying about, discovering, for example, that Kathy had listed her occupation as actress/bookseller/student and that her goals included a desire "to be as well read as Penelope Warren" and to have a film career "like the great Storm Williams." I'd better warn her about the nudity clause.

Our Leigh of sexy-librarian fame listed among her hobbies "reading, movies, and belly dancing." In fact, she had helped finance her education by dancing professionally in a variety of Greek restaurants. "How about that, Mikey?" No wonder Burton Maxwell traipsed after her so helplessly in love. He was, no doubt, mesmerized by the swiveling jewel in her navel.

As for the quiet and unassuming companion to Leigh, Penelope discovered he had once jumped out of airplanes for no good reason while serving with the 82nd Airborne Division at Fort Bragg.

Richard Burbage had played Oscar in *The Odd Couple* in a number of revivals around town. That's certainly a leap to Hamlet, Penelope thought. But there was little else of interest in his résumé. He began as a spear carrier and worked his way up to the great Shakespearean roles over the years. He had never auditioned for the role of Sir Robert Dudley either.

Before taking up commerce in Empty Creek, William Shakespeare had been a licensed pharmacist.

The Spanish ambassador was a computer programmer. That sparked Penelope's attention momentarily, but working her way through the applications, she found that the computer field was quite a popular profession in one way or another among those who spent their weekends at the Faire, including a number of the actors. And why not? There were any number of good jobs in the field. And besides that, any ten-year-old nowadays was perfectly capable of hacking away destructively at Amanda.

Christopher Marlowe's application was sketchy and indicated a single-minded devotion to the theater and an ambition to write tragedies as great as his namesake's. Under publications he listed the titles of forty unpublished, unproduced plays, all under the pseudonym of—no kidding, Penelope thought—Christopher X. Marlowe. That was dedication, all right.

The most recent Sir Robert Dudley had been a Peace Corps volunteer in South America and still traveled widely in South and Central America every other summer. We'll have to get together and share stories, Penelope thought.

Bobby's travels also prompted a longing for Africa. Penelope wanted to go back to that wondrous continent, but often wondered if she would like to revisit Ethiopia. Drought, famine, war, revolution—all had devastated the mountainous nation. It would be too sad. But it would be equally sad not to go back. Penelope always bawled at the end of *Out of Africa*, when the graphic flashed on the screen saying that Karen Blixen had never returned to her beloved Africa.

"Oh, Mikey, we have to go back someday."

Penelope was still brushing tears from her eyes when she read—rather blurrily—that Sir Francis Drake was an avid balloonist.

Sir Francis Bacon had been a rock musician in high school and college and had begun life at the Faire in the Musicians' Guild before being promoted to Sir Robert Dudley and then demoted again to his present role at court.

Alyce Smith had majored in psychology for three years at NYU before dropping out to take up her profession as astrologer and psychic consultant to Empty Creek's elite.

All of this was certainly interesting, but useless in unmasking a killer.

"Newsroom, Anderson."

"I want to go back to Africa."

"Have you been watching *Out of Africa* again?"

"No," Penelope sniffed. "Just thinking about it."

Penelope took the latest missive to Madame Astoria, who sneezed right on cue as Big Mike clambered into her lap for a little seance, probably looking to commune with a few lima beans from the beyond.

"Another one?"

"Not a threat this time. He's feeling pretty damned sure of himself. Or she. I suppose it could be a woman."

"No, it's definitely a man," Alyce said. "A very troubled man. I'm positive."

"Anyone who goes around killing people is troubled," Penelope pointed out.

Alyce shook her head. "That's not what I mean. He's tormented, tortured, fighting some demons from within."

That narrows it down some, Penelope thought. All we have to do is find someone walking around, tilting at demons. "Anything else?" she asked.

Alyce shrugged. "I haven't been much help. Everything is dark and clouded. That happens sometimes. I can't force it."

"How is Harvey?" Penelope asked as a change of pace, knowing full well how the universe dug its heels in doggedly whenever someone tried to force it to do something. It was just like a cat in that way. When Mike was just a kitten, Penelope, having read somewhere that cats could be taught to do tricks, had tried to teach him to jump through a hoop and fetch. Mikey had just looked at her with an incredulous expression that told her all she needed to know about cats and the universe. You're kidding, right?

That erased Alyce's frown. "He's wonderful. I'm teaching him astrology."

"See if you can teach him to jump through a hoop," Penelope suggested. "Or fetch."

Alyce's smile grew. "I've already done that."

"Good girl."

Penelope and Big Mike returned to Mycroft & Company to find a disdainful Christopher Marlowe browsing among the Storm Williams memorabilia. Kathy looked relieved at Penelope's entrance.

"I've been waiting for you," Marlowe said.

"I didn't know. You should have called for an appointment."

"Why haven't you come to our performances?"

"Oh, Lord!" Penelope exclaimed. "I forgot again. I'm sorry, but there was just too much going on. I'll attend this weekend for sure. I promise."

"My players grow angry. They don't like being ignored by their Queen."

"I apologize, but they have to understand . . ."

"Now that we have been restored to our rightful place in England's theater, we must have a command performance. It's imperative. Else we are relegated to the royal dung heap. Is that what I must tell my company the Queen thinks of England's greatest playwright and those who perform his masterpieces? I have served the crown loyally in many ways. I deserve better treatment from your hands, Majesty."

Penelope thought a third apology to be more than a little redundant. Still, she *had* promised. Oh, what the hell? Actors had such fragile egos. "Please extend my deepest apologies to your troupe and tell them they shall have their command performance."

"On the main stage?"

"Yes," Penelope said with a sigh. "On the main stage."

"They will be pleased." Marlowe turned to the poster of Storm Williams starring as Princess Leogfrith in *Return of the Amazon Princess*. The poster showed the poor Amazon, bound and dangling above a pit of snarling tigers. "Your sister, I believe."

"Yes," Penelope said, thinking, Go ahead. One smart-ass remark and you're dead meat.

She was somewhat disappointed when Marlowe said, "She makes an excellent Queen for the Picts. They don't deserve her. I don't like Picts. They're savages."

"Oh, they're not so bad. You just have to understand them."

"Perhaps," Marlowe said, turning away from the poster. He took Penelope's hand and raised it to his lips before she could protest. "Until the weekend, then?"

"Yes," Penelope said, retrieving her hand. His lips were cold.

Marlowe smiled at Kathy. "Adieu, fair lady."

The Queen and her lady-in-waiting stood at the counter and watched as Marlowe crossed the street, passed in front of Madame Astoria's, and disappeared down the street.

"Well."

"I'm glad you came. He was coming on to me. He's creepy."

"I'd just as soon kiss a snake as Christopher Marlowe. Andy would be history if his lips were that cold."

———

When Samantha Dale popped into Mycroft & Company that afternoon, Penelope was not at all surprised. Sam was an avid reader and a very good customer, often buying ten or twelve books at a time, only to return a week or so later complaining that she had nothing to read.

"Your Majesty," Sam said with her usual radiant smile.

"Oh, stop it, I'm not feeling very majestic today. I wish this were all over. I'll be very glad when I can go back to being plain old Penelope Warren."

"I can just imagine. It's a shame about that poor actor. Do you have any leads?"

"No more than with Carolyn. I've been going through records like crazy. I feel like I know the life history of everyone ever connected with the Faire, but—"

"Nothing?"

"Less than nothing. The killer apparently succeeded in destroying whatever it was that needed to disappear and now he's, well . . . catch me if you can."

"I'm sorry, how did Jack the Ripper enter this discussion?"

Penelope told her of the latest note.

"He's clever and he's playing games with you. Which makes me wonder. What if there were nothing incriminating in the records? What if he erased them just to confuse everyone?"

"And here I am wasting my time looking for something that doesn't exist."

" 'Fair is foul . . .' "

" 'And foul is fair . . .' " Penelope smiled. "Nothing is as it seems. Thank you for reminding me of that."

"You're quite welcome," Sam said, looking over the bookcases. "Now, what's good? I have absolutely nothing to read."

After telling Kathy to close the shop early, Penelope and Big Mike drove past Dutch and Stormy's house to the very top of Crying Woman Mountain to the little park with the expansive vista of all Empty Creek and the desert to the north.

A cold breeze swirled around the mountaintop and Penelope zipped her Windbreaker as she went to the low stone fence that surrounded the park. Looking down from the heights, the mock Elizabethan village seemed tiny and remote, innocent in the rays of the sun sinking toward the horizon.

After Sam left carrying a shopping bag filled with books, the refrain she had started rang through Penelope's mind like one of those songs that, once hummed idly, persisted and wouldn't leave.

" 'Fair is foul, and foul is fair.' "

Even after trying to imagine everything backward, the puzzles of both murders seemed as incomprehensible as ever.

Mycroft sat quietly on the wall, moving slightly, approvingly, beneath Penelope's soft touch as she smoothed his windswept fur.

"We've been thinking about it too hard, Mikey. It's time to let it go and see what happens." Again, it was excellent advice, and Penelope wished she could follow it.

Stormy was reading scripts when Penelope and Mycroft arrived. Big Mike hopped right into his favorite aunt's lap.

"Mikey, give me a kiss. Hey, Penny."

"Hey, yourself, Cassie. Anything good in that pile?"

"There are a couple I like. Myron wants me to do this one." Myron Schwartzman was Cassandra's agent, the very same man who had created her stage name, Storm Williams (under the influence of strong drink), while reminiscing at the Polo Lounge about the great tassel-twirling burlesque queens he had seen in his youth.

"Myron is certainly a great judge of immortal film roles for women."

"Oh, Myron's not so bad. I'd still be doing swimsuit commercials without him. Take a look."

Penelope took the bound film script and read.

Legs

An Original Screenplay

by

Stanley White

FADE IN:

MAIN TITLES OVER a drawing board as an unseen comic book artist quickly sketches with bold, firm strokes, creating VANESSA DIAMOND, a heroine of the epic tradition. As the artist adds details, we see that Vanessa has long, blond hair, a beautiful face, a statuesque body, and long, slender legs that go to forever.

"What drek," Penelope said.

"It's me. I can wear a fedora. Keep reading."

MAIN TITLES CONTINUE as we see drawings of the tough and voluptuous private detective kick-boxing three villains into submission, slapping the cuffs on them, and turning them over to the police.

MAIN TITLES end as we DISSOLVE to color and our comic book heroine becomes real—Legs Diamond, Private Investigator.

VANESSA(sultry)

What's yours, baby?

"Humphrey Bogart in drag," Penelope said, tossing the script aside. "What's your other choice?"

"Dracula's kid sister."

"Do Humphrey," Penelope said, thus unwittingly launching Stormy's career in an unlikely sleeper as Vanessa "Legs" Diamond, a move that would eventually lead to two sequels and a prequel, a Vanessa Diamond fashion line, a Super Bra commercial, an appearance on Jay Leno, and full-page ads in *Variety* and *The Hollywood Reporter*.

"What do you think, Mikey?" Auntie Cassie asked.

Mikey apparently agreed with Penelope's choice of starring vehicle, although he always fell asleep during Stormy's movies—after the popcorn was served, of course. He didn't really care for popcorn much except as small missiles to be propelled about the room by a mighty whack or two, somewhat resembling a hockey player delivering a slap shot. Still, he liked to be consulted about these lofty matters and demonstrated his approval by knocking Dracula's kid sister to the floor—along with *Warrior Women on Mars*, *Slaves of the Exosphere*, and *Monster of Munich*—as he made room for himself in Stormy's lap.

"Well, that's settled then."

And all before dinner too.

Which was slightly delayed, as Penelope insisted Dutch repeat the statement he had made (after a kiss for Stormy and a sedate sisterly buss for herself) to get the conversation off to a lively start.

"Say what?"

Dutch looked more than a little pleased with himself, although he hadn't done the actual work.

"The cause of death was Chondodendron tomentosum," Dutch said. "Curare. The dagger was tipped with poison."

Just like the foil tipped with poison that killed Hamlet, Penelope thought. It seems the killer has a flair for the ironic. "Well," she said, "I have a news flash or two for you, then."

"Dudley has traveled widely in South and Central America," Dutch said, "where the plant that produces curare is indigenous."

Penelope nodded approvingly. Tweedledee and Tweedledum had noticed it too. "And Shakespeare was once a pharmacist," she said.

And everyone had forgotten the cat, a situation not to be tolerated, and one easily rectified by a rather loud complaint from Big Mike.

CHAPTER
SEVENTEEN

As the Ides of March approached, Penelope kept a sharp eye out for any signs of the sheeted dead running amok in the streets of Empty Creek, flaming meteors streaking through the sky, potential eclipses of the sun or moon, or dark clouds raining blood.

But nothing. Empty Creek and its environs were sorely lacking in heavenly signs of any kind other than the usual. The sun came up. The sun went down. The moon rose and fell. The sparkling night skies were clear and cold. The days were warm and pleasant. It was all too ho-hum for the Ides of March.

Penelope did see an airplane—several actually—skywriting an advertising message for some beer or another, but since they were somewhat to the south and she was late noticing their presence, the letters were already breaking up into little clouds of their own. The message was also upside down when viewed from Empty Creek. All of this meant that Penelope couldn't decipher whatever it was that was writ so large. She doubted it said Watch your six, Penelope, anyway, and so she was unable to count it as a portent. It did remind her that she was out of beer, which was something.

For his part, Mycroft didn't give a whit for the Ides of March (or any other old portents either) and quite wisely kept his eyes, ears, and nose focused on the ground, where he found all sorts of interesting things, including a mouse befitting of royalty which he promptly chased into the house and just as promptly forgot after it was settled in.

"Oh, dammit, Mycroft," Penelope complained, "why did you do that?"

"It's what a cat does, sweetie," Andy said.

"Then you catch it."

"Do you have any mousetraps?"

"Traps!" Penelope cried. "You're not going to trap it?"

"How else am I going to catch it?"

Penelope shrugged, conveniently relegating the problem to the Hunter of the Species. "With your hands, or something, but don't kill it," she warned.

"It might have the bubonic plague."

"Then sweep it out with a broom or something, but no traps," Penelope said firmly. "Mice have mothers too."

Thus it was that the Hunter of the Species, armed with a broom, crept through the house in search of the royal mouse, helped only by an occasional shriek from Penelope.

"There it goes," she would cry.

"Where?" Andy would cry in turn, broom poised at port arms.

"There!"

Big Mike, the only true hunter in the house, watched all this with a great deal of amusement. He could have pointed out the royal mouse's various hiding places, but no one bothered to ask him.

Now, Penelope wasn't afraid of mice—or much of anything else, usually, with a few possible exceptions like giant rutabagas falling from the sky. It was just that she didn't think mice should live in houses with real people and cats. What if it *did* have the bubonic plague, although it seemed unlikely that something so plump and cute could be afflicted with a deadly disease. Still, Penelope wondered if her plague inoculations—she *was* afraid of needles and people who drew blood too—might still be current. Probably not. The Marine Corps and the Peace Corps were long ago and far away.

"There!"

"Where?"

This continued throughout dinner, the cleaning-up, the relaxation on the couch, and the late news, where Lola LaPola—not quite so breathlessly anymore—presented part one of a promised three-part series on staying in shape. Part one focused on aerobics classes with Lola traveling from one health club to another to hippety-hop along with the fitness instructors. Since Lola seemed to be in quite good shape, as evidenced by the form-fitting pink shorts and matching bra top she wore, Andy was entranced and forgot all about the royal mouse for a moment. At least until Penelope, feeling that old green monster intruding once again, hollered, "There!"

"In a minute, dearest," Andy said mildly, his eyes riveted to the screen. "I want to see if anything falls out."

By the time Lola promised part two on pumping iron "and now back to you in the station," Penelope had caused a few things of her own to fall out, which diverted Andy's attention from the rest of the evening news quite nicely.

Much later Penelope murmured, "Exercise sure does make you sleepy."

"We'll have to do more of it," Andy whispered, throwing his arm around Penelope and drawing her even closer—if that was possible—before falling asleep.

Penelope was quite ready to nod off herself when she heard *it*, and continued to hear it, one of those irritating things that prevented sleep, like a persistent drip from a faucet or trying to remember, as James Thurber once did, the name of a New Jersey city with two words in it.

In succession, the royal mouse nibbled away on Mikey's liver crunchies, played in the bedroom curtains, and generally rustled about, having a fine old time.

What the hell *was* the name of that town, the one with two words in it?

Andy and Mikey blissfully slept through the nocturnal activities while Penelope listened to each annoying sound, all terribly magnified in the quiet night, growing more exasperated with each agonizing moment of sleep deprivation.

Finally, she threw a sharp elbow into Andy's ribs, feeling only a slight remorse that he wasn't the true culprit, but there was no use in trying to reason with Mycroft at this hour. The only other choice was to get up and read Thurber's *My Life and Hard Times*, and it was too cold to be wandering around the house.

"Oomph," Andy said.

"Name some towns in New Jersey."

"Passaic," Andy mumbled, "Hackensack."

"No, towns with two names."

"Perth Amboy."

"I hate it when you do that," Penelope said.

"Murmph," Andy replied.

Master William Shakespeare and Sir Robert Dudley were hauled in for questioning by the first team, the second team, and the third team. Dutch even had each of the not-so-prime suspects print *Catch me if you can* with their left hands. All that proved was that it was awkward printing with your left hand when you were right-handed.

"Of course I gave it up," Shakespeare shouted during his session. "Do you know how boring it is to count little pills all day long? Good God, no one in their right mind would want to be a pharmacist."

Right mind, indeed.

"This isn't probable cause," George Eden interjected. "My client hasn't practiced pharmacy for years. And besides, curare is used primarily by anesthesiologists in surgery."

"It used to be used in electroshock therapy too," Shakespeare said. "Maybe it still is. I don't know. It's out of my expertise now."

"It's all circumstantial anyway," George said. "You've narrowed your list of suspects to anyone who has ever been in South or Central America, and most of the medical population in Arizona. I'd say that was a quite sizable group to deal with." He paused dramatically. "I'm sure a jury would agree."

And the damnable part, of course, was that George Eden was right. Even Tweedledee and Tweedledum had to agree with him.

As for Bobby, forgoing his right to have an attorney present and his right to remain silent, he was adamant in his protestations of innocence. "I wouldn't know a curare plant if it walked through that door right now."

I wouldn't either, Penelope thought later while reading the transcripts of the interrogations, but I'd know how to find it if South America is anything like Ethiopia, where shopping for luxuries was done on the street or sitting on the veranda of a hotel, sipping gin and tonics while one street vendor after another offered cigarettes, whiskey, gold, silver, ivory, and, on one memorable occasion, a shotgun. Penelope had always supposed that special orders could be placed as well, although she was quite satisfied with her mail order account at an excellent bookstore in Edinburgh, the Christmas and birthday packages from Muffy and Biff, and generally living on the economy.

"Whiskey, madam?"

"No, thank you, but I would like a bottle of curare, please."

"Yes, madam, coming right up."

That's how I would do it if I happened to be in South America and happened to want some curare.

But, according to Bobby, no such thought occurred to him.

Penelope wanted to believe him for Sharon's sake, but . . .

Bobby and Sharon had argued and she went back to Tempe, spending the night there alone until Bobby came straggling in apologetically, well after Burbage's body had been discovered.

No wife, no horse, no mustache, and no alibi.

And not nearly enough probable cause for an arrest or to take to a preliminary hearing.

Always loyal to the citizens he served, Tweedledee opted for Bobby as the guilty party.

"Nah," Tweedledee disagreed. "I think it's the pill pusher."

"Former pill pusher," Penelope pointed out.

"Yeah, but he had the argument with the victim."

"So, you're so smart, who do you think it was?" Tweedledee asked.

"I have no idea," Penelope replied honestly. "Yet."

"So what do we do now, boss?" Tweedledee asked.

"Keep an eye on both of them," Dutch said, "and while you're at it, if you happen to see a headhunter with a bow and arrow, grab him."

"Huh?"

"Oh, never mind."

"I see it," Andy cried triumphantly, grabbing for the broom.

My hero.

"Oh, damn, it's gone again."

Some hero.

Penelope went through the transcripts again and again, looking for the slightest indication of guilt, but found nothing. After all, Shakespeare *was* a prominent member of the Empty Creek business community, belonging to the Chamber of Commerce and Rotary, participating in any number of social and charitable events during the year, and it wasn't his fault that he had made a mistake in his youthful choice of career. Penelope supposed it *was* boring to count little pills all day long.

Bobby was a little eccentric, but that was accounted for by his status as both a professor and a sometime actor, to say nothing of his continuing midlife crisis. At least he didn't have leather patches on the sleeves of his tweed jackets. Penelope had met any number of cheerfully eccentric teachers during her undergraduate and graduate school days. That wasn't a crime, nor was joining the Peace Corps or going to South America.

"I'm sorry, Mikey," Penelope said, tapping the pages of the transcripts neatly together, "they just don't fit."

Mycroft took the Fifth Amendment. He had lost all interest in the case when Penelope wouldn't let him play with the transcripts.

But if not Shakespeare and Dudley, who at least had plausible reasons for possessing a knowledge of curare, then . . . who could it be?

Oh, no, Penelope thought, I'm not going to start sounding like an owl again.

Ensuring that the mouse had adequate water and food to sustain him through the day, Penelope and Big Mike left for work. It was as good a place as any to wait for the Ides of March, but not distracting enough to keep her mind from murder, but that was natural enough since nearly every book in Mycroft & Company dealt with murder in one fashion or another, as well as much of the world's great literature. Samantha was right. Shakespeare's greatest plays revolved around murder. Kings and emperors were murdered so others could take their place. Did someone kill Carolyn to clear the throne for another?

"But that's absurd."

"What's absurd, Your Majesty?"

"Oh, I'm just talking to myself," Penelope said. "Ignore me."

Kathy nodded understandingly. Dealing with royalty could be trying on occasion.

"Why would anyone kill the Queen to take her place? Who would want it? And what did Burbage have to do with it?"

"Yes, Your Majesty." Kathy went right on ordering books from the publishers' spring lists.

Penelope caught Bobby in his office at ASU. "Tell me about Carolyn Lewis."

"Again?"

"I'm afraid so."

Penelope asked the same questions and received much the same answers, and when she replaced the telephone, came to similar conclusions. Carolyn Lewis was Dr. Jekyll and Mrs. Hyde, consumed with power and an apparent lust for men she didn't really like while serving as the Queen. At school she reverted to being a dedicated teacher.

And what does that tell me? Penelope asked herself.

Absolutely nothing, she answered.

"I'm going to visit Master Will Shakespeare," she told Kathy. "I'll be back shortly."

"Not you too, Penelope," Master Will groaned when she burst into his office. "I'm innocent. I didn't kill anyone."

Penelope held up her hands. "I just want some information."

"I should call George."

"I'm not the police."

"You might as well be."

"We both want to find the killer. Help me."

"Well . . ."

Reluctantly at first, and then more enthusiastically, Shakespeare cooperated, repeating everything Penelope had already heard and read.

Penelope closed her eyes and listened intently, hoping for one tiny little thread of something, anything, that might point her in a new and more profitable direction. Is that too much to ask? she wondered.

Apparently.

"Well, thanks anyway," Penelope said when Shakespeare had finally concluded.

"I'm sorry, you know, really sorry. The argument just escalated. I made a little suggestion and he went off into one of his fits of artistic temperament. Artists! They're all like that. Actors, painters, writers."

"Even playwrights?"

"Especially playwrights," Shakespeare admitted sheepishly, "but I didn't kill him."

And so the week slowly passed, punctuated by parts two and three of Lola's report on physical fitness, the continuing search for Harold—if he was going to hang around, the damned mouse might as well have a name—and Penelope's growing sense of frustration with her inability to clear the muddied waters swirling around the two murders. Penelope determined once again to stop thinking about it, hoping that the answers would come naturally, like Perth Amboy. And then she realized that she hadn't even come up with Perth Amboy. Andy had done that, and in his sleep too.

Penelope waited with poised elbow, struggling to keep her own eyes open, until Andy was sound asleep.

Whack.

"Oomph."

"Quick, who killed the Queen and Richard Burbage?"

"Daryl Hannah."

Oh, well, it was worth a try. Penelope settled in, pulled the cover up to her nose, and closed her eyes. She was almost asleep when she sat straight up and delivered another elbow to Andy's rib cage.

"Arrgle."

"That's for dreaming about Daryl Hannah."

After watering all the plants outside in preparation for the weekend, Penelope went through the house with her sprinkler can, providing the same service for the indoor plants.

And there he was.

You're busted, Harold! Up against the pot.

The royal mouse looked up at her with big brown eyes and twitched its whiskers nervously, no doubt fearing its meal ticket was over.

He was very cute.

"No, you can't stay, I'm sorry," Penelope said, hoisting the plant and humming "Born Free" while she carried it outside.

Harold wiggled his nose at Penelope.

"Oh, to hell with it."

Penelope went back into the kitchen, filled one small bowl with liver crunchies, another with water, and took them back to Harold.

"In the future, Harold," Penelope said, "dinner is at seven. Don't be late."

She decided that capturing and releasing the royal mouse with a hearty Godspeed and enough sustenance to host a party was the only real accomplishment of the week, unless you counted Lola LaPola dropping a barbell on her instructor's foot during part two as any sort of accomplishment, which Penelope did.

"And, as for you," Penelope said, "you're supposed to keep mice out of the house, not herd them in."

Mycroft just looked at her with that quizzical expression he liked so much, doubtless wondering who had hidden *her* catnip.

But, at least, the Ides of March had finally arrived, or would at midnight.

"Well, Mikey, this should be an interesting weekend."

CHAPTER
EIGHTEEN

The Peasants' Rebellion of 1595, as it would come to be known in the annals of the Empty Creek Elizabethan Spring Faire, rewrote history, taking liberties such as never taken before. It was traditional for the long-suffering peasants to rebel on the last weekend of the Faire. After all, they had been bowing and scraping to their betters for more than a month of weekends, providing amusement for all by their frequent trips to the dunking tank and the pillory, and generally suffering the lot of . . . well, peasants. At no time in prior years, however, did the peasants rise to the occasion so much as to have greatness bestowed upon their insurrection by a grateful Queen.

There were all of the usual activities associated with the Faire—the royal procession, proclamations of one sort or another, theater presentations on the various stages, jousting, and combats on the field of honor. After all, the rubes expected their amusements. But after the last joust, the peasants ran amok.

Until then, however, it was business as usual. Attendance at the Faire seemed higher than ever. The same morbidly curious people who slowed to rubberneck the wreckage of automobile collisions on freeways now swarmed to the Faire, only partly to see royalty, the upper classes, and the gentry get theirs.

All of the usual suspects gathered at the Royal Pavilion.

The two largest members of the Royal Bodyguard were in a corner, showing their wenches what looked suspiciously like a mail order catalogue from an adult bookstore. The wenches giggled and blushed, nodding with unseemly enthusiasm.

The smallest member of the trio was plucking discordantly at a lyre as he sang for *his* pretty young wench, and happily accepting the grapes she popped into his mouth—probably to shut him up, for his voice matched his playing ability.

The ever-loyal Sir Walter Raleigh kept his place at the Queen's side. The Royal Cat, however, had disappeared again, off to one of his favorite hidey-holes, no doubt.

At the bar in their accustomed place, the Lord High Mayor and the Lord High Sheriff called for another flagon.

Sir Francis Bacon was in earnest conversation with the Spanish ambassador, disputing some difficult philosophical point.

Sir Francis Drake swashbuckled about, posing grandly for the rubes.

Knights clanked in their armor, squires close at hand to help if the occasion should arise.

All was well in Elizabethan England, except Sir Robert Dudley and Master Will Shakespeare were missing.

Penelope closed her eyes and savored the sounds of the

royal court at work and play. I will miss this a little bit, she admitted to herself. If not for the circumstances, it would have been fun . . . no, it was fun, but . . .

Penelope opened her eyes with a start. It *was* the Ides of March, after all, and it wouldn't do to go about with her eyes closed.

Lola LaPola entered the pavilion hand in hand with her bailiff. Although she wasn't in costume, she curtsied as the bailiff bowed to the monarch. "Your Majesty," Lola intoned gravely and not at all breathlessly. That was certainly progress. Lola hadn't been breathless since part three of her story on physical fitness. Since it had covered the popularity of running, a little breathlessness there could be forgiven.

"Not another piece on the Faire?"

"Oh, no, this is just for fun. I'm told that the last weekend is always worth seeing." She smiled at her bailiff. "But I've got a camera crew on call. Just in case. Has there been any progress?"

"No, I'm sorry to say."

The Royal Bodyguard seemed relieved when the Queen said their services would not be needed for the moment. The three pretty maidens seemed even more pleased. "Thank you, Your Majesty," they chorused.

Now, as she strolled through the Faire with her very own companion, Penelope again realized that she would miss all the folderol of the royal procession, greeting her subjects, the booming cannons, the flourishes of trumpets, the brightly colored sights and delicious smells.

"It has been fun, hasn't it?"

"Yes," Sir Walter said wistfully, "although I never did get to lock you in the pillory. Look what it did for Lola."

"Andy, I swear, sometimes you act just like a man."

"But I am."

"Of course you are, sweetie."

They strolled on, Penelope cleverly picking the path that would take them across Kissing Bridge.

"In public?" Sir Walter asked, glancing around nervously at all the people watching their progress.

"I am the Queen," Her Most Gracious Majesty replied, "and the Queen wishes to be kissed."

A loud cheer went up as Sir Walter kissed her. It was only a nine (pretty damned good) on the kissing scale, but would have been a ten, or even an eleven, except for the onlookers, who embarrassed Sir Walter.

"I shall never forgive James the First for what he did to you," Penelope said, sounding just like Lola used to. "Perhaps we should stop by that old pillory tonight before it's too late."

"Marlowe, Marlowe, Marlowe."

The selected scenes from *The Tragical History of Doctor Faustus* had just concluded, with Marlowe playing the title role.

The scruffy band of actors chanted until the audience joined in. Their performance had been good, and Marlowe had been excellent as the tragic hero who sold his soul to the devil for knowledge, but overall, the performance had not been up to the standards of the Globe players. Still, what harm did it do to let Marlowe have his moment of glory?

Shakespeare had been in such a funk that he had showed

up in civilian clothes. At least, he had finally made an appearance backstage to wish his actors and actresses a good "break a leg." But Sir Robert Dudley was still a no-show.

Penelope went backstage to congratulate Marlowe, but he was not to be found. "Where is Marlowe?" Penelope asked Helen of Troy, although she doubted that hers was a face that would launch a thousand ships. Two or three modest rowboats perhaps, maybe even an old Mississippi River paddle steamer, but a thousand ships? That was stretching it. Still, Marlowe had been most earnest as he begged, " 'Sweet Helen, make me immortal with a kiss. / Her lips suck forth my soul; see where it flies! / Come, Helen, come, give me my soul again.' "

"Oh, Kit is always taking off unexpectedly. He does it all the time."

"Do you know where he goes?"

"Not really," Helen of Troy said. "You might try the campsite. He likes to hang out there when we're not onstage. He gets awfully depressed sometimes. I don't think his shrink is helping much."

Penelope felt the first chills run up and down her back. Depression was sometimes treated with electroshock therapy, and curare used to be injected to lessen the convulsive symptoms associated with that treatment.

Marlowe?

No, that was crazy.

Upon the return to the Royal Pavilion, the Queen noticed that the members of her court were rather more nervous than when she had left. The rabble were beginning to gather out-

side, awaiting the last clang of broadswords and the close of
games for the day.

"I beg pardon, Your Majesty," Lady Kathleen asked, looking about furtively, "may I be excused?"

"Of course, child, but why?"

"To don my disguise. I've seen these peasants' rebellions
before. They act just like . . . peasants."

"But you used to be a peasant."

Kathy smiled. "I know. I was terrible."

"Why don't you just go and hide in my RV?"

"Oh, but that wouldn't be playing fair."

After Elizabeth Regina bestowed the last royal benediction of
the day and praised her loyal knights for having fought well
and good, the cry went up.

"Rebellion!"

The Queen's person, of course, was sacrosanct, as was Sir
Walter's, by royal fiat. While the other members of her court
and the gentry were hotly pursued through the narrow streets
and over hill and dale by the rake- and pitchfork-wielding
rabble, the Queen had nothing to worry about, particularly
since the Royal Bodyguard had been made honorary peasants
at the urging of their new female friends.

But just where *was* the Royal Bodyguard? They were late
getting back, delayed no doubt by an all-too-enthusiastic par-
taking of lusty Elizabethan pastimes.

Thus, as the Lady Kathleen, now wearing peasant's garb,
tore past, skirts hoisted, pursued by a shouting band of rabble,
Penelope had only to stand back out of harm's way and wish
the speeding Lady Kathleen greater fleetness of foot.

Unfortunately, her good wishes went for naught, as Kathy was run down far short of the church door, where she could claim sanctuary. Swiftly manacled, she was brought back to await her turn in the dunking tank, the pillory, or perhaps both, unless she was willing to grant a favor or two to her captors. It was well known that a pretty young maiden could beseech her captors, and clemency might be granted in exchange for a kiss or two.

"My Lady might be granted reprieve if . . ."

Playing her role to its fullest, Lady Kathleen bravely flared her nostrils and declared with a heaving bosom worthy of any of the Ravishing Redhead's heroines, "Never! Do your worst."

"But one sweet kiss for a poor juggler . . ."

"Never, sirrah, not for a worm's belly like you."

"Take her away," Timmy said gleefully, for it was indeed Lady Kathleen's very own juggler who had denounced her disguise and now condemned her. "After an hour or two in the pillory, perhaps I'll visit My Lady again."

The Lady Kathleen was marched off in the firm grasp of two huge and grinning peasants.

It appeared that the Lady Kathleen was to end the Faire as she had begun it—doing penance—but Penelope had to smile, knowing that Kathy would make poor Timmy pay for his enthusiastic denunciation for the remainder of the year.

Unfortunately, the Queen of the Picts enjoyed no amnesty from the rebellion. She was paraded through the village wearing the bridle of a common scold, while a host of washerwomen, fishwives, and harlots taunted her. "To the ducking stool."

Going to meet her fate, Stormy looked at Penelope with

wide blue eyes, perhaps imploring her older sister to intercede on her behalf. She also tried to holler, but her speech
was stifled by the contraption about her head and mouth.

Penelope hadn't even known they had a ducking stool.
Perhaps the peasants had installed it especially for their rebellion. Besides, Stormy ought to be used to this sort of thing,
what with all the scrapes she was always in onscreen. She had
been in peril more than the legendary Pauline, although she
had never been tied to the railroad tracks. Probably that was
coming. And anyway, a good ducking might teach Stormy
some manners and make up for that time she had pushed Penelope out of the swing.

The most hated figures of all, the Lord High Sheriff and
Royal Tax Collector, along with his minions, were prized prisoners. They were all herded into the royal hoosegow to await
their turn in the pillory. No mercy for them.

Penelope noticed that Lola was already in line to purchase
a tomato or two to hurl at her bailiff in some small measure of
revenge. She would have waited to see how Lola's arm measured up, but it was growing late. Penelope glanced at the
sky. There was still time to visit Marlowe's encampment and
find Mycroft before darkness fell. And besides, there wasn't
one single portent to be seen anywhere.

The rabble was shouting for the Royal Tax Collector to be
brought forth when the Queen turned to Sir Walter Raleigh
and said, "I'm getting worried about Mikey. Why don't you
check and see if he's having a turkey leg and I'll check the
banger shoppe?"

"Is that wise? Perhaps we should go together."

"There's plenty of daylight left, and it'll be faster this way.

I'll meet you back here in an hour. By then Robin and his little band will be back."

"Well . . ."

"Everything will be fine, sweetie."

Penelope had just turned past Soothsayer's Row, noting that the Royal Astrologer's booth was closed, when she was greeted by an apparition in the guise of what appeared to be either a tree or a beekeeper plastered with leaves.

"It's me," the apparition hissed.

"Me who?"

"Dudley. I'm in disguise. I'm the spirit of the forest."

"I can see that."

"It throws the peasants off. They don't expect the upper classes to be running around looking like trees. They think I'm one of them."

"Do they often dress up as trees?"

"For the planting festival. That's tomorrow. Sharon is disguised as a milkmaid, but I can't find her. Have you seen her anywhere?"

"No, but if I do, I'll tell her a tree is looking for her."

"Thanks."

Penelope watched in amazement as Sir Robert Dudley tiptoed off. He'd better hope that Sir Dog doesn't see him, Penelope thought.

"No, we haven't seen him, Your Majesty," Penelope was told at the banger shoppe. She continued on her way, calling out every so often. "Mikey, Mikey."

Penelope tried the campsite. Big Mike wasn't at the RV waiting impatiently for an early infusion of lima beans. At least, there was no note on the door. Yet, Penelope thought grimly.

Marlowe's spot was easy to find. Some few of his band were there, drinking ale and toasting their triumph. They rose to greet the Queen. "May we offer Your Majesty some refreshment?"

"Thank you, no. I'm looking for Marlowe."

"Oh, he should return soon. He had some important matters needing his attention before the evening's festivities."

A boom box blared a screeching heavy metal song—if such cacophony could be termed song.

Idly, Penelope punched a button to change the station. And again, despite the protests from Marlowe's crowd. And again.

All the stations were set to heavy metal stations. Penelope returned the radio to its original station.

"I'm not much of a fan," Penelope said. "Do you like it?"

"It's all we listen to," a young actor replied. He had played the devil, Mephistopheles, in the play. "Marlowe says everything else is crap."

The chills were back, racing along her spine. "Thanks," Penelope said, hoping that he didn't hear the catch in her voice. It was time to find Mikey and get the hell out of Dodge. "Tell Marlowe I was looking for him."

"He might be off playing his flute," Helen of Troy said, "or perhaps practicing his calligraphy."

"Flute? Calligraphy?" Penelope thought the actress was much prettier without her stage makeup—fresh and sweet-faced. She could launch at least five hundred ships, and burn a few towers at the same time.

"Oh, yes," Helen of Troy gushed. "He's a true Renaissance man. Skilled in all the arts. You saw his performance today. And so handsome too."

"Yes, he was very good," Penelope said. Perhaps too good, she thought. Good enough to fool us all. "Well, I have to go now. I have to find my cat."

"We'll see you later tonight, then," Mephistopheles said, "at the Star Chamber?"

"Yes, sure," Penelope said, backing away cautiously. She turned and hurried off, looking back over her shoulder several times and wishing she hadn't been quite so cavalier in dismissing the Royal Bodyguard and sending Sir Walter off in the opposite direction. It was the same feeling she had experienced leaving Alyce's psychic parlor.

He was watching her.

And the Star Chamber. What was that all about? The Star Chamber was a medieval kangaroo court appointed by royal authority that met in secret without a jury. Confessions were coerced through torture and its judgments were severe and arbitrary. Did I appoint a Star Chamber, Penelope wondered, without knowing about it? One of those endless decrees they're always pushing at me to sign? Sometimes the politics of the Faire was too deep to fathom.

From the distance, a roar went up as another hapless gentleman or gentlewoman went to the pillory.

Penelope hurried on, her mind racing faster than her feet. "Mikey," she called, "Mikey."

If all music except for heavy metal was crap, why would Marlowe be off somewhere playing a flute? And why was Carolyn's radio set to a heavy metal station? What reason would Marlowe have to kill the Queen? He had never been a

Sir Robert Dudley. He might want Richard Burbage dead—he was a rival of Marlowe's own company. But the Queen?

There was an explanation, but it was just too crazy. Dutch would laugh her right out of town, but what if . . .

Whole bookcases were filled with weighty volumes proving that William Shakespeare did not write his plays. Among the several most likely candidates proposed as the true author of the Shakespearean canon was one Christopher Marlowe. There were those scholars and others who argued that Marlowe's death in the tavern brawl was faked in a kind of Elizabethan witness protection program as a reward for Marlowe's service as a spy in the service of Elizabeth Regina.

Crazy. Crazy. Crazy!

Those who advanced Marlowe's candidacy for the role of the Bard of Avon pointed out, usually quite vehemently, that Will Shakespeare's appearance on the London theater scene coincided quite nicely with Marlowe's demise and thus Marlowe was Shakespeare.

Penelope didn't really care who had written the plays. All that mattered were the plays themselves. But . . .

If Carolyn told Marlowe that he couldn't return from exile . . .

But that was no reason to kill someone.

Was it?

It was not until Penelope passed behind the lesser stage that she was rewarded with an answering meow. Actually, Big Mike said, "Meowurgle." That was what he always said when awakened from a deep sleep. "In here," he meant.

Penelope peered through the dusty window, but the inside of the room was dark. "Mikey?"

"Meowurgle."

Penelope found the door and the light switch of the storage room. A sleepy Mycroft peered down over the edge of his hidey-hole.

"What are you doing up there?" Penelope asked, knowing full well it was a dumb question.

Big Mike stood and stretched leisurely in one direction and then repeated it. There was a muffled clank and the rustle of paper from the top of the cabinet.

Penelope climbed up on a chair. The top of the cabinet was still too high for her to see over, so she felt about with her hand and found a cold glass vial. As soon as she saw the label, she dropped the vial as if it had suddenly transformed itself into a cobra. One glance was all she needed to know what it was. And there might be fingerprints.

She rummaged about the top of the cabinet and found the paper. It was crinkled and warm from Mikey's body, but the message could be clearly read.

Who will be next Miss Queeny?

It wasn't exactly the best calligraphy Penelope had ever seen, but the pen and ink set she found next was certainly capable of producing a Beware the Ides of March note.

"Mikey," Penelope exclaimed, "you've done it again."

Big Mike, still a little sleepy, wasn't quite sure what he had done but, recognizing the tone in her voice as the one that usually heralded an offering of lima beans, he was willing to accept any and all credit.

"Let's get out of here, Mikey, and find Dutch." Or Tweedledee and Tweedledum. Lothario. Anyone.

But just then, the room was plunged into darkness.

CHAPTER
NINETEEN

Unaware of what had befallen their Queen and the royal cat, the peasants' rebellion continued apace. Lola LaPola proved to have a very good arm indeed, and accurate too. Had she not been otherwise occupied, Penelope would have been quite proud of Lola's unerring toss and the collection of another anecdote for *The Newlywed Game*.

Penelope would also have taken a great deal of pride in the stoic and brave manner in which Lady Kathleen met her fate in the pillory.

And when the young juggler, unable to bear the sight of his beloved tormented, leapt in front of the tomato meant for said beloved's beautiful face, Penelope's breast would have fair burst with pride. She was, after all, a hopelessly incurable romantic.

Stormy, too, would have evoked similar emotions when she gave as good as she got during her rescue by the Picts.

But since the Queen was quite preoccupied with her own troubles, she learned nothing of all this until much later.

The fight was furious, if all too brief, and punctuated by murderous squalls when someone twisted Big Mike's tail by mistake. Penelope landed one good punch and two or three other glancing blows on her assailants before someone tripped her and she landed heavily, knocking the breath away momentarily.

It was enough, however, for the Queen to be rendered helpless. An elaborate scold's bridle worthy of the Queen was quickly fastened about her head, stifling speech, and cold irons locked about her wrists.

Rough hands hauled her to her feet.

"Murmph," the Queen said as the lights were turned on. What the hell is going on? she wondered as she confronted her captors.

Marlowe leered at her. Helen of Troy was there, attending to one of the minor devils from the play who had made the obvious mistake of tangling with Big Mike in the darkness. There were also two scholars and a friar—all from the production of *Faustus*—and Master Edwards, the ironmonger, who smiled at her. What was he doing here? Were they *all* killers?

"Murmph," the Queen repeated, shaking her chains, looking around for Mycroft. He seemed to have made his escape. He'd better not be hurt, Penelope thought.

Marlowe drew close and whispered, "Don't expect your friends from the constabulary to help. I've arranged a little diversion for them." He turned to the others. "Take her away."

The din and hullabaloo of the Peasants' Rebellion receded as Penelope was marched off through the eerily empty village streets.

Big Mike, hunkered in the shadows, ears flattened, tail twitching ominously, watched them go. Had anyone noticed him rise and slowly begin his stalk, they would have thought him a lion cub practicing his creeping through the grass of the African plains, but they would have been wrong. This was no cub and he didn't need any practice.

All of Marlowe's company was at the small village green at the opposite end of the village, well away from the tumult of the Peasants' Rebellion. The devils and scholars and priests were there. So were the Good Angel and the Evil Angel, along with the Seven Deadly Sins. There were a few others Penelope didn't recognize, hangers-on from one guild or another. All rebels now.

The crowd parted and the Queen was jolted to see Alyce and Sharon, similarly manacled and silenced. They looked helplessly at her as Penelope was pushed forward.

"The Star Chamber is now in session," Marlowe intoned solemnly.

He had donned a magician's robe, and Penelope thought he looked like the Wizard of Id. She waited for him to say something like "Frazzle the friggle pump," or whatever it was the Wizard of Id said during his conjuring.

"You are charged with high treason and crimes against the arts," Marlowe said, "and judged guilty. There is no appeal."

That's Newt Gingrich, you silly twit, Penelope wanted to say, but all that came out was "Nugabrich." Despite Marlowe's declaration, Penelope turned and looked appealingly at Helen of Troy.

"Isn't this fun?" Helen gushed. "You never know what's going to happen the last night of the Faire."

Penelope frowned. At least, she thought she frowned. It

was difficult to tell with the brank over her head and mouth. These fools don't even know what's going on, she decided.

The sequence of events was coming clear to Penelope, or she thought it was. Marlowe had waited for Carolyn in her tent, passing the time by listening to *his* music. Missing the Queen there, he had confronted her on the village green. When his petition was unsuccessful, he had killed her.

I probably saved *my* life, Penelope thought, by allowing Marlowe's plays to go on that first day. But that wasn't enough for Marlowe, and he had murdered Burbage to disrupt the Shakespearean players.

There were some other few details to be worked out, but along with the calligrapher's kit and the curare, Penelope had all the probable cause she needed to effect a citizen's arrest. Now there's a thorny little rub that needed some work, and damned quick too, if the crazed glint in Marlowe's eyes was any indication.

In quick succession Sharon was adjudged guilty of refusing to join Marlowe's actors, and Alyce equally guilty of witchcraft and alienation of affections. It got a little confused along about there, because Marlowe alternated wild ravings with confused mumblings.

Some script this was.

Penelope decided it was time for a little "Frazzle the frigglepumping" of her own.

As the Star Chamber continued apace at the opposite end of the village, well away from the gaiety of the Peasants' Rebellion, Sir Walter Raleigh was hastily organizing a search mission. The Queen had been gone entirely too long.

"Penelope should be back by now," he said, gathering what remained of the royal entourage.

"I knew we should have gone with her," Robin Hood lamented.

Little Ralph and Little Russell bristled.

"Is something amiss?" Sir Francis Drake asked.

"The Queen is missing."

Drake drew his cutlass. "We sail at the tide."

"I don't think she's in the lake," Raleigh pointed out, rather mildly, he thought, under the circumstances.

"It's just an expression," Drake said. "We'll find her."

As soon as Lola saw the little circle of men around Andy, she joined it. "What's up," she asked.

"Some varlet has taken the Queen."

"We don't know that," Andy said, "but . . ."

Lola pulled a compact cellular phone from her purse and quickly punched in a number. "It's going down." Replacing the telephone, she said, "Let's go find her."

As the search and rescue party was organized, the Empty Creek chief of police, his homicide detectives, and several uniformed officers, acting on an anonymous telephone tip, were surrounding a rundown little house not too far out in the desert.

Although the lights of the house were on, the curtains were drawn and it was impossible to see what was going on inside.

Tweedledee and Tweedledum, standing on opposite sides of the front door, listened intently, but all was quiet within. They looked to Dutch, who nodded.

Tweedledee moved to the door, measured his distance

carefully, and gave a mighty kick. He had always wanted to do that.

The door crashed open.

Police officers surged through the opening, all shouting conflicting instructions.

"Police! Nobody move!"

"Hands up!"

"Everybody on the floor! Now!"

Their abrupt entrance so shocked the young bearded artist that his brush flew unerringly in one direction and his oil-laden palette in another. The brush struck Dutch a glancing blow, leaving a nice streak of magenta across his cheek. Tweedledee was not so fortunate. The palette struck him full in the face, leaving him covered with all the primary colors and a few others for good measure.

The nude model—who was the artist's wife—shrieked, grabbed for her robe, dropped it, grabbed again, missed, and, still shrieking, opted to run for the bathroom, where she locked herself in and refused to come out until the lawsuit was settled in her favor.

Meanwhile, back at the Star Chamber . . .

The Queen was sentenced to death.

The actress was sentenced to death.

The witch was sentenced to death.

The headsman's ax waited for the Queen; the stake for the actress and the witch.

"To the Tower," Marlowe cried.

He was absolutely, unequivocally bonkers. That's what comes of embracing atheism at such a tender age, Penelope thought. Or espionage. Or both.

"Oh, what fun," Helen of Troy cried.

Easy for you to say. The ironmonger's heavy manacles were tight upon the Queen's wrists. She shook the chains angrily.

The frail young actress looked helplessly at her Queen. With the pronouncement of the death sentence, the actress no longer wished to remain in character. "Waragonthumphdado?" Sharon asked.

Penelope translated easily. What are we going to do?

"Besame," replied Penelope. It was a most unroyal pronouncement. The Queen looked at Alyce. Another helpless shrug.

Where the hell was Stormy? Probably still wandering around trying to get out of the scold's bridle, but no one would remove it. They had heard her sentence pronounced with gaiety and laughter.

Where the hell was Kathy? No doubt, the lady-in-waiting was still serving her sentence in the stocks.

For that matter, where were Ralph and Russell? Off chasing their serving wenches? Some bodyguards they turned out to be, Penelope thought, although she knew full well it was her own damned fault for dismissing them from their duties.

But where in the hell was Mycroft? He had no excuse whatsoever for not being present in his Queen's hour of need.

A tumbrel drawn by a lazy horse creaked to a halt beside the condemned prisoners.

In *Amazon Princess and the Sword of Doom*, Stormy had burst her bonds when she was tied to the stake. Penelope tried to do the same, to no avail. Of course, as Princess Leogfrith, Stormy had a magic amulet to assist her.

Lacking an amulet—magic or otherwise—the Queen

grasped the slack in her chains, wound up, and whacked Christopher Marlowe a good crack upside the head. Wasn't that just like an Amazon princess or the Queen of England? Then, as Marlowe hit the ground like a felled timber, in another most unroyal pronouncement, Penelope screamed.

"Rumph!"

The Queen, the witch, and the actress all skedaddled, each to a different point of the compass. By the time Marlowe's little band of players had come to their senses and helped their leader regain his, Penelope was creeping along the bank of the lake, looking for a way back into the village proper without exposing herself by using the bridge.

On the other side, it seemed the peasants were still having a fine old time waving their torches, pelting tax collectors, and wenching to a fare-thee-well.

Penelope was about to give it up and just make a run across the bridge, when the unmistakable figures of the Royal Bodyguard led by Sir Walter came out of Soothsayer's Row and stopped for a conference at the foot of the bridge.

Feeling a little like Moses in his little ark of bulrushes, Penelope crept forward and called out softly, "Oobtere."

"Penelope, what happened?" Sir Walter cried. "Where have you been? I've been so worried."

"Urgletemumphry," Penelope replied.

"I can see that, dearest."

"Who did this to you?" Ralph—or Russell—asked. "We'll get him."

"Mulew!"

"I can't understand a word you're saying, Penelope."

"I have a solution," Robin Hood said. "Let's get her out of that stuff."

Good idea, Beamish, Penelope thought, nodding enthusiastically. A very good idea.

The little party hurried across the bridge, breaking tradition by not stopping for the usual lover's kiss. It would have been too difficult to find the Queen's lips anyway, what with all that leather.

Penelope was quite mistaken about her peasants. Worried about their Queen, the rebellion had ended early and plans were being made to find and rescue the Queen.

There was Captain Sneddon's Companye of Foote drawn up in battle order. To their right, Drake's boarding party brandished swords menacingly. The Black Knight and the White Knight were mounted, lances held to the ready. The guns of the Royal Artillery were manned. Stormy was at the head of the Picts. The peasants were bunched together, holding their rakes and pitchforks aloft.

The Queen and her party emerged from the shadows.

The army and the navy of England greeted her with a resounding, if somewhat puzzled, "Huzzah!" What dastardly peasant had dared put the Queen in chains, treating her like some brazen fishwife?

The Queen replied, "Gesetchofsem!"

The Lord High Sheriff quickly produced a master key and, in a matter of moments, the Queen was freed of the brank and her fetters. Standing before her troops, she was now in a rather fine fettle and decided to deliver a brief version of Elizabeth Regina's speech to her troops at Tilbury on the approach of the Spanish Armada.

Grabbing a torch from a handy peasant and a cutlass from one of Drake's sea dogs, Penelope raised them high and cried, " 'I know I have the body of a weak and feeble woman

[Hah!], but I have the heart and stomach of a king, and of a king of England too; and think foul scorn that Parma or Spain, or any prince of Europe should dare to invade the borders of my realm.' "

"Huzzah!"

Penelope was ready to launch into Henry's speech on the eve of Agincourt, when there was a shrill cry in a lilting Irish accent from the rebel encampment, "Gemphoureboodyand-soophem."

This was followed by a muffled cry of pain and a not so muffled string of oaths. Obviously, the actress had been recaptured, but not without a struggle.

Alyce, too, had apparently been run to ground, for she shouted, "Dunsemdarde."

Henry's speech would have to wait, Penelope decided. It would have been far more dramatic had the rebels slowly emerged from night's shroud, but alas, it was not to be. Lola's camera crew lit the scene with their lights.

The ragtag band was drawn up in battle formation. Behind them, Alyce and Sharon were bound to stakes, faggots piled high about their legs.

"Look, yon, revealed by dawn's lovely frail rays," the Black Knight cried, quite ignoring the fact that dawn was hours away. "Fair damsels in distress. Methinks I shall rescue them and be rewarded by their soft lips."

"Methinks I saw them first, varlet," the White Knight said. "They are *my* grail."

But there were a great many among Elizabeth Regina's loyal subjects who wanted to rescue a fair damsel or two and vie for the reward of a sweet kiss.

Sir Robert Dudley quickly shed his foliage and drew his rapier.

Lothario produced a quite unelizabethan nine-mm semiautomatic Beretta from beneath his doublet.

Little Ralph and Little Russell kissed their wenches before hefting their staffs.

Robin Hood did likewise before notching an arrow into a good English longbow that was twice his size.

"Aren't they brave?" the wenches cooed.

Elizabeth Regina was about to give the command to advance, when the Royal Cat hurtled from the shadows, launching himself at Marlowe. Twist my tail.

Big Mike landed on Marlowe's back and dug in.

Marlowe's shrieks filled the night as he flailed and danced about, wildly trying to dislodge the Royal Cat.

Ha!

Big Mike rode him like a cowboy on a bucking bronco.

It was as good a time to charge as any. So . . .

"Charge!" Elizabeth Regina cried.

As she raced across the village green at the head of her troops, Penelope turned toward Lothario and shouted, "By the way, it's Marlowe. He's the killer." It was a detail that Penelope couldn't understand how she had failed to mention earlier.

The ensuing melee was brief. Marlowe's band quickly lost heart and broke ranks, attempting flight, but they were swiftly surrounded by peasants, soldiers, sailors, and sundry others—all poking and prodding them with sharply pointed instruments.

Lothario, torn between duty and rescuing Alyce from the

stake, finally opted for duty and approached Marlowe warily, not because he was afraid, but because he could not quite figure out how to get a snarling Mycroft off the culprit. He had no desire to be maimed for life at the paws of a cat.

Marlowe solved that problem when he fell to the ground and rolled over on Big Mike. That was apparently a grave mistake on his part, as he quickly leapt up again, screaming. Big Mike had solved *his* problem by biting Marlowe on the butt.

In turn, Lothario solved his problem by sticking the barrel of his pistol in Marlowe's ear. "Hit the ground," he shouted.

It had certainly been an up-and-down night for England's second leading playwright.

Preoccupied as he was, Lothario missed the rescue of his beloved Alyce from the stake. It was just as well, because once Sir Walter had released Alyce from her bonds, caught up in the emotion of the moment, she threw her arms around him and gave him a big fat hero's reward as well as a lifetime coupon for astrological consultation.

Sir Robert Dudley's midlife crisis had apparently run its course, because while he untied Sharon from her stake he cried, "I love you. Will you marry me?"

"Oose," Sharon cried right back, "ohoose." Now, there was another proposal worthy of recounting on *The Newlywed Game*.

The mounted knights had reached the fair damsels first, but encumbered as they were with heavy armor, they were unable to dismount without the help of their squires, who had been left far behind during the gallant charge. So they could only watch helplessly as the rewards were distributed.

"Sheeit," the Black Knight said.

"Quite right," the White Knight replied.

Sirens penetrated the night, and black-and-whites screamed through the green fields of Elizabethan England, only a little late, but it wasn't really their fault.

As the battle drew to a close, the Queen was on her hands and knees, slowly crawling toward the Royal Cat, whispering reassuringly. "Hey, Mikey, it's only me. Everything's okay now. It's all over."

Big Mike looked disappointed. Oh, well, maybe the Spanish Armada would show up again.

As Marlowe was hustled away by the Lord High Sheriff's men, he babbled the eloquent anguish penned by his namesake, " 'Ah, Faustus, Now hast thou but one bare hour to live, And then thou must be damn'd perpetually! Stand still, you ever-moving spheres of Heaven, That time may cease and midnight never come. . . .' "

Marlowe struggled briefly at the door of the police car. " 'O soul, be change'd into little water drops, And fall back into the ocean—ne'er be found! My God, my God, look not so fierce on me!' "

Tweedledee, however, was looking most fiercely on Marlowe.

" 'Adders and serpents, let me breathe awhile! Ugly hell, gape not!' "

Tweedledee pushed Marlowe roughly through the gaping door of the police car, but before he could slam it shut, Marlowe's head emerged. " 'Come not, Lucifer!' " he cried. " 'I'll burn my books!—Ah, Mephistopheles!' "

The door finally slammed shut on the last words of Faustus.

You had to give him credit for that, at least, Penelope thought. He had a wonderful sense of timing.

CHAPTER
TWENTY

Finally, with a great deal of relief, the Elizabethans partied like it was 1599. The pall cast by the deaths of Carolyn Lewis and Richard Burbage cleared swiftly in the aftermath of the Great Charge and the realization that the murderer had been taken from their midst.

Everywhere they went, Penelope and Big Mike were greeted with praise and loud cheers. "One hell of a Queen," was the consensus. "One hell of a cat too."

And because of their brave charge that routed Marlowe's band, everyone felt they had a hand—or four paws—in the apprehension of the murderer.

Master Will Shakespeare, now cleared of suspicion and complicity in murder, recited Henry's speech before the battle of Agincourt, growing more enthusiastic and boisterous with each pint of ale he downed.

> "We few, we happy few, we band of brothers;
> For he to-day that sheds his blood with me

Shall be my brother; be he ne'er so vile
This day shall gentle his condition;
And gentlemen in England now a-bed
Shall think themselves accursed they were not here,
And hold their manhoods cheap whiles any speaks
That fought with us upon Saint Crispin's day."

Penelope thought Master Will's first few recitations quite good but, as the evening wore on, she began to wish she had delivered the speech herself, paraphrasing with the proper feminine references and inserting "the Ides of March" at the conclusion.

Even some of those who had been party to Marlowe's Star Chamber now denounced him and felt instrumental in his demise, taking a great deal more credit than was deserved.

"I knew something funny was going on," a preening Master Edwards told anyone who would listen, "that's why I went along with his plot. The Queen and the ladies were in no danger whatsoever."

Yeah, right.

"He couldn't wait to tie me to the stake," Alyce whispered. "He was having a great time."

"Definitely kinky," Sharon concurred, "and rather free with his hands too." Her newly acquired fiancé bristled at the thought of another touching his cherished intended, but Sharon calmed him by saying, "Never mind, darling, it was worth every moment to have you rescue me like that. I was so proud of you. You can untie me anytime."

Ever the entrepreneur, Ralph—or Russell—quickly offered a catalogue to Sharon. "You might be interested in this, and there's a discount for couples."

The Queen let the ironmonger's transgressions slide—for the moment. With one day remaining in her reign, there was yet time enough to send a braggart or two or three to the pillory and the dunking tank. Penelope thought it might be high time that Master Blaine Edwards, Ironmonger by Appointment to Her Royal Majesty, sampled the bite of some of his own wares. Many a wench and fair maiden would happily applaud.

Helen of Troy, however, was distraught. "I can't believe it," she wailed. "I just can't believe it. He seemed so nice."

Penelope took pity on her because she did seem to think it was all make-believe. "Kathy, do you know any Renaissance men who aren't spoken for?"

"Well, there is one of Timmy's friends. He just got dumped by a milkmaid. She ran off with a strolling troubadour."

"This friend . . . he doesn't happen to write poetry, does he?"

"Oh, yes, but not at all like Timmy. He's more the ode-to-a-stately-saguaro type."

"Perfect. Introduce him to Helen of Troy for me, would you, please?"

As for the rest of Marlowe's players, even the devils and the seven deadly sins, who had been so enthusiastic in their support of Marlowe at the Star Chamber, Penelope was willing to forgive them. Marlowe had duped them all, enlisting them into his conspiracy on the pretext of ending the Faire on a spectacular, if treasonous, note.

All this and more had come out as each was questioned by teams of police officers—"Overtime's going through the roof," Dutch complained—cleared of complicity, and ultimately released to join the party, sheepish unindicted coconspirators that they were.

Still, Penelope shuddered. She had tested the headsman's ax and found the blade extremely sharp, making the soft hair on the nape of her neck stand out in stark terror. She wondered how far Marlowe would have gotten before anyone realized he wasn't playing.

Even Gluttony, an overweight and frightened young computer programmer who tearfully confessed to trashing Amanda at Marlowe's behest, was released pending charges being filed by Quentin Parnelle. "But I didn't know he was killing people."

"Why Amanda?" Penelope had asked.

"Marlowe wanted to bring some friends without being noticed, but they got caught robbing a bank."

That would explain Marty and Carl, the Keystone Kops of the bank robbery set.

Laney, Wally, and Alex quickly arrived for the postarrest festivities. One or another of her network of informants had obviously called to tell Laney of the police-car parade heading for the Faire.

"You should have told me," Laney said.

"I didn't know."

"I always miss the fun."

Some fun, Penelope thought, being paraded around in irons and a scold's bridle, sentenced to death, practically on the way to the Tower and the headsman's block, creeping around in the night, and worried sick over Mikey. "Next time I'll let you do it."

"Oh, can I, really?"

Lola scooped everyone with her exclusive footage of Marlowe's arrest and interviews with Penelope and Big Mike.

Penelope gave full credit to Mycroft for discovering the cache of incriminating materials.

"When did you first suspect Marlowe?"

Too late, Penelope thought, much too late. "It was a combination of his taste in music and a chance remark that he often suffered bouts of depression. As you know, curare has a number of medical uses, and it is sometimes used in the treatment of mental disorders like schizophrenia. . . . ."

Penelope wondered if Lola's tape of Marlowe's grand exit would be used as defense evidence of insanity.

"And there you have it, directly from the scene of two brutal murders, now solved because of the formidable detecting team of Penelope Warren and her partner, known with more than a little justification simply as Big Mike."

The closing shot was of Lola reaching out to give Mycroft a fond scratch or two. "Isn't he brave?" Apparently born for the camera, Mycroft purred right on cue.

After filming her cutaways, Lola raced off to the studio just in time to make the late news. "Don't end the party without me," she called back over her shoulder.

Little chance of that. The lusty Elizabethans were ready to get into their cups.

Feeling the chill of the night, Penelope slipped back to the campground to change into something warmer. There were definitely goose bumps popping out on the royal melons and more than one tipsy Elizabethan had volunteered to warm her up a little. She fended them off politely, opting for a good heavy sweater instead.

It was pleasant strolling through the night without having to look over her shoulder all the time. It was equally pleasant to arrive and find that the door had not been used as a bulletin board for another sinister note.

Penelope had just finished changing in front of the heater and gone to the refrigerator to cut a slice of cheese—with everything going on, she had forgotten dinner—when headlights flashed across the windows. An engine coughed and sputtered to a stop. Doors slammed. Knuckles rapped.

Now what?

Penelope opened the door to find Tweedledee and Tweedledum. "Well, hi," she said.

"Penelope," Tweedledee said. For him it was a formal greeting.

"Come on in. I was just getting a snack. Would you like some cheese and crackers? And a beer?"

"Well . . ."

"I promise not to tell Dutch."

The detectives grinned. "In that case . . ."

Penelope passed out beers and quickly arranged a small platter of cheese and crackers.

"You did good," Tweedledee said. "The cat too."

"Very good," Tweedledum echoed.

Penelope blushed. This was high and generous praise indeed, considering the sometime antagonistic relationship between Robbery/Homicide and Mycroft & Company.

"We just wanted you to know that."

"You'd make a good cop."

"Oh, I don't know . . ."

"It ain't too late, you know."

"Have another beer."

"Thanks, don't mind if we do."

"We'll need to ask some more questions, but they can wait till Monday. Tie up loose ends."

"Is there enough evidence to charge him?"

"Oh, he's confessed."

"Sort of. He's nuts."

"Keeps raving about his loyal service being rewarded by exile. You know what he's talking about?"

Penelope explained the Shakespeare-was-really-Marlowe theory.

"You mean this nut thinks he really is some writer from four hunnert years ago?"

Penelope nodded. "I think so."

"No wonder he wants to burn his books," Tweedledee said.

"Easier than dusting them off," Tweedledum said.

When the Queen returned to 1595 disguised as Penelope Warren, bookseller, she found Big Mike being fêted by a bevy of adoring maidens and wenches. If there was anything Mikey liked better than lima beans, it was being adored by a host of pretty young women. If they keep this up, Penelope thought, he's going to break his purring motor.

The Queen would have rescued the Royal Cat—at some risk of injury to her person because Big Mike neither wanted nor needed rescuing—but she was quickly surrounded again by her own admirers, all wanting to be seen with the heroine.

Aw, shucks, twarn't nothin', boys.

It seemed to be country-western night in Elizabethan En-

gland, and the Queen was asked to dance, in succession, by
Andy, Sir Francis Drake, the Spanish ambassador, Quentin
Parnelle, Andy again, and Sir Francis Bacon—all to the bal-
lads of George Strait and Garth Brooks.

Dutch joined the party, cutting in on Bacon, who looked as
though he wanted to tell the chief of police to buzz off, but
demurred when Penelope said he could have a second dance
later.

"Where's Stormy?" Dutch asked.

"I don't know. I haven't seen her for a while."

A roar went up next door.

"What's that?"

"The wet T-shirt contest," Penelope said. "They wanted
me to enter, but no way. The Queen must maintain a certain
standard."

"Too bad," Dutch said, managing to disguise his leer only
a little.

"That's what Andy said. You're all alike."

"You did good, Penelope, but you've got to be more careful. Between you and Stormy, I'm getting old and gray before
my time."

"Burke and Stoner complimented me too. I think they're
beginning to like me."

"Until the next time . . ."

"God, let's hope there isn't a next time."

Stormy rushed through the door, holding a trophy aloft.

Dutch groaned. His beloved was wearing an Empty Creek
Elizabethan Spring Faire T-shirt, a quite drenched and cling-
ing T-shirt that showed her ample bosom to advantage.

"My God, Stormy," Penelope cried, "you didn't?"

"I did," Stormy said, tossing her golden mane in triumph, "and I won."

A chagrined Debbie, followed by an equally chagrined Sam Connors, came in holding a much smaller trophy. "I can't believe it," Debbie said, "I've never lost before."

"It was all those Picts," Laney said as she came in. Her trophy was minuscule. "It was rigged."

"There, there, dear heart," Wally said, "you'll always be number one in my heart."

"Isn't he just the sweetest cowboy you ever met?"

Penelope saved the last dance for Andy, snuggling close, happy to be shuffling about (he wasn't the best dancer) in his arms. For his part in her rescue, although she knew in her heart that she could have rejoined her troops without aid, Penelope thought that Andy deserved a reward. It *was* rather nice getting rescued on occasion.

Penelope took Andy's hand and said, "Let's get out of here for a little bit."

"Where are we going?"

"Just out for a little air."

Penelope led him across Kissing Bridge for one last time, stopping to make up for the tradition they had broken earlier. Mmm. Oh, double mmm!

When they stood before the pillory, empty and looking eager to demonstrate its aphrodisiacal properties, Penelope said, "Go ahead, you little varlet, you. Do your worst." He would just have to play the dual roles of captor and rescuer.

As it turned out, Andy did his very best, considering how cramped their respective positions were.

———

Stretched out along a very nice branch in his favorite tree, the Royal Cat watched. It was hard to fathom the inscrutable feline expression, but he might have been wondering about the strange things Penelope and Andy got up to sometimes.

And so the Ides of March drew to a pleasant close.

AN EPILOGUE

In which, dear reader, our little tale set amid the imitation fields of Olde England, runs its merrye course to a happy conclusion for all save the atheist murderer, who was, in due course of justice, returned to a place from whence he came; to wit, an institution for the criminally insane, where he is allowed books, but no matches.

And a certain ironmonger got his, much to the delight of fair womanhood. Even the Queen took a turn at hurling a royal tomato with great accuracy, to the applause of all, including the Empty Creek High Gila Monsters, who had won their first baseball game of the season on the Ides of March.

Our players, good and true Elizabethans all, then retired archaic manner and custom for a twelve-month, until Aquarius should once more make its appearance, setting hearts, younge and olde alike, to twittering with the approach of the vernal equinox and the eternal joyes of springe.

And afore the cannon's first boom of 1596, there would be several marriages. The first—in June—saw an Irish actress exchange loving vows with her teacher and mentor, followed close upon by rites uniting Ben Jonson and his lovely Celia, otherwise known as Burton Maxwell and Our Leigh. In September a radiant Lola LaPola joined her life with that of the young bailiff.

Others pledged their troth, Alyce and Lothario and Robin Hood and Maid Marian among them.

Laney ordered quite a number of items from Ralph and Russell's catalogue.

Ralph and Russell quickly filled the order with the willing assistance of two former peasant wenches.

The ever-laconic Wally willingly helped open the package when once it arrived.

Sir Dog, his armor retired for the nonce, yipped and yapped when he wasn't sleeping, eating, or reliving old times with his buddy, Big Mike.

Until principal photography began on *Legs*, Stormy and Dutch were occupied with remodeling their kitchen, the completion of which necessitated a celebration enjoyed by all.

With the Empty Creek crime rate plummeting and little to keep their minds sharp, Tweedledee and Tweedledum gained ten pounds each from a surfeit of Mom's jelly doughnuts.

The Lady Kathleen studied, worked, and provided continuing inspiration for her juggler's poetic flights.

Harold, the royal mouse, and a lady friend—soon christened Harriet—moved into the garage, where they were sometimes visited by the Royal Cat.

Master Will Shakespeare took to composing sonnets during the hot summer months when the snowbirds all went back to

Iowa and Minnesota or wherever they came from to escape the searing temperatures, taking their desire to rent recreational vehicles with them.

As for the Queen and her loyal consort, life settled back into the comfortable—and thankfully uneventful—routine they rather enjoyed. The former Sir Walter Raleigh (for he had abdicated his position at the same time as the Queen) took to browsing through Laney's many exotic catalogues. As a result, he was constantly surprising his sweetie (who didn't mind in the slightest) with one erotic doodad or another. It certainly made for the most interesting of evenings.

There *was* the little matter of the Empty Creek Arabian Horse Show (and a few other trifles hardly worth mentioning), but beyond that life was sweet and good.

Big Mike agreed, although he did take a little time off to wander his desert domain, letting its denizens know who was in charge, just in case there had been any memory lapses during his reign at the Faire.

He also renewed his acquaintance with Murphy Brown, who promptly produced another litter of snarling, hissing, cuddly Mycrofts—much to the dismay of Josephine Brooks, Murphy's owner, who thought the sleek calico should hie herself to a nunnery.

But as Penelope pointed out to a distraught Jo, royal lines deserved sturdy heirs.

Big Mike agreed with that too.

WESTFIELD PUBLIC LIBRARY

7 8292 000112162

112162 Allen,
Garrison

WESTFIELD PUBLIC LIBRARY
333 West Hoover Street
Westfield, IN 46074

WESTFIELD PUBLIC LIBRARY
333 West Hoover Street
Westfield, IN 46074

$1.00 Fine for Removing
the Bar Code Label!!

DEMCO